RIGHT UP
YOUR ALLEY

Right Up Your Alley

Sharolett Koenig

Library of Congress control number: 2001116570

Koenisha Publications
3196 – 53rd Street
Hamilton, MI 49419
Phone or Fax: 616-751-4100
Email: koenisha@macatawa.org
Web site: www.koenisha.com

For my husband, Bud, and my children, Rachel, Jared, Josiah, Rebekah, and Hannah. Our God is an awesome God.

I would like to thank the following for sharing their knowledge and expertise:

Lucy Zahray, the poison guru

Connie Geiger Allred and C.J. Allred, private investigators at Lady Eyes

Pro Guns, gun shop in Muskegon, MI

Prologue: Monday, Monday

It was 5:00 Monday morning, the thirteenth of July, when Mary Harris drove her black Toyota into the parking lot of Clayton's Investment and Finance Corporation. The lot was empty except for the two cars belonging to the overnight maintenance crew—the janitor and the security guard. The changing of the guard would take place in a couple of hours, and the daytime work force, a brisk, honest money-handling business, would begin to arrive. She knew they were honest, she'd checked them out before signing on as the company's temporary computer systems consultant.

Mary opened her car door and eased out, holding onto her oversized square canvas bag, which sported the slogan "I Love a Good Mystery." She walked the short distance to the glass double doors, ran her access card through the security lock, and let herself in.

Taking out an ad in the yellow pages had been the smartest thing she'd ever done. She had clients waiting in line for her computer consulting service.

The information age of computers was booming. And while the self-made entrepreneurs of her generation had been seeking degrees in corporate management and financing, she'd pursued courses in secretarial and office machine duties. She was a quick learner, always had been, and computers had come of age during her college stint.

She walked down the well-lit hallway to the elevator, which took her to the basement of the building where Mr. Clayton had decided to install the new computers. Her job was to make sure the old filing system was smoothly assimilated into the new program.

Mary was an expert in custom designing and setting up state-of-the-art systems that brought businesses up to the present and ready to take on the future with a vengeance. She offered seminars, which enabled employees to man the cutting-edge computer systems she installed. All she had to do was advertise. Once a client called and set up an appointment, she had them in the palm of her hand. She relished the feeling of having prosperous, well-adjusted businessmen needing her assistance. She had power, and she'd acquired money—enough money to enjoy life to the fullest.

But now was not the time to enjoy. She realized her window of opportunity was limited. Colleges and universities, as well as every other conceivable institute of higher learning, were cranking out computer experts from a generation nursed on Nintendo and Sega. She had enough money socked away for that inevitable day when job competition would put a cramp in her style. That was when she planned to enjoy life.

Until then, she was working hard and planning carefully. Her future was safe and secure. She was in control. She would never have to depend on anyone for anything.

Mary stepped out of the elevator and shivered involuntarily. The rest of the air-conditioned building was cold, but the basement was unbearable. She wore a long-sleeved silk blouse under a dark blue cotton sweater, which picked up the shade of blue in her plaid, mid-calf-length, pleated wool skirt. She walked silently and purposefully in her black, rubber-soled orthopedic oxfords.

By the time she reached her desk in the center of the large office, her nose had picked up on the irritating odor. It was an irritant contained in so many modern-day products that, at first, the doctors had diagnosed her condition as a psychological illness which manifested in symptoms of debilitating allergic reactions. Now, however, some doctors had given it an acronym, MCS, short for Multiple Chemical Sensitivity.

Mary's particular nemesis was formaldehyde, chemically known as the aldehyde HCHO—recognized by most people as the pungent preservative dealt with in high school biology class while dissecting frogs; but NOT recognized by most people as the toxic component in many common household products, such as, disinfectants, furniture polish, detergents, clothing, paper, cosmetics, and food.

Considered a "super-sensitive" by her clinical ecologist doctor, Mary was just plain weird to everyone else. Her regular doctor had written off her MCS symptoms as the usual signs of being over 40 years old. But how many people, she wondered bitterly, tolerated bone and joint pain, headaches, vertigo, and fatigue under the guise of the "normal" aging process?

She set her canvas bag on the desk and withdrew her lunch. She refused to eat in the cafeteria on the main floor and had convinced Mr. Clayton, the C.E.O. of the company, to install a countertop refrigerator near the bathroom in the corner of the office. Fearing that further concessions would encourage too many unauthorized breaks in the workday, Mr. Clayton had refused subsequent requests from the other employees for a microwave and a coffeemaker.

Not having a coffeemaker and prompting the move of the records department to the basement made Mary the scorn of some of the regular employees. But, if exercising a little control over her work environment made her unpopular, she decided it was no big loss.

This was her last week at Clayton's Investment and Finance Corporation. They could make any changes they deemed necessary, once she was gone.

Mary opened the refrigerator door to set her lunch inside. The chill air took her breath away as she leaned in, and her lunch dropped on the floor. Her hands automatically went to her throat to fight off the invisible constriction. She slammed the refrigerator shut and made her way across the room. She climbed on a chair to manipulate the latch on the ground-level window.

The polluted air from the paved parking lot wafted in slowly. It was heavy with the humidity of a New York summer morning, not as fresh as it had seemed when she parked there moments earlier. But the pain in her chest was beginning to lose its edge.

It was quickly replaced by a wave of dizziness and nausea, so she closed the window and slowly eased herself to the floor. This called for a formal written complaint, Mary decided, complete with a threat to file suit for endangering her health, as soon as she felt better. She trembled with anger.

Apparently, Mr. Clayton had hired the cheapest janitorial service he could find, to fill in for Trisha while she was on vacation. And the idiot replacement had decided to fumigate for microorganisms and disinfect with a cheap all-purpose cleaning solution containing lots of formaldehyde, no less. Mr. Clayton would hear about this, and pay dearly! Her insurance didn't cover what was considered a controversial diagnosis and treatment for MCS.

With her head and lungs congested from the sudden allergic onslaught, Mary searched her bag for the inhaler she carried for just such emergencies. She couldn't find it. But luckily, as always she had her own tissue paper. She carried a roll into the bathroom where, no doubt, the inept janitor would've replaced the empty roll with a cheap irritating brand. She glanced in the mirror and saw her tearing, blood-shot eyes and her red, runny nose, and confirmed that her face looked as puffy and red as it felt.

She removed her glasses that presently weren't doing much to improve her blurred vision, and began running cold water in the sink and splashing it on her face. Nevertheless, she broke out in a sweat and moved her face the short distance just in time to heave in the toilet. It certainly was her lucky day, she thought. She hadn't eaten any breakfast.

Mary knew she should go home right then, but this was the first day of training the new records department manager. And, at the end of the week, she would collect the final installment of the fee she'd negotiated for this job. She didn't want to give Mr. Clayton cause to nit-pick about services rendered. She was a professional and deserved to be treated like a businesswoman of equal stature. Men tended to view her with disfavor, just because she was middle-aged and unattractive. But she refused to compromise her health for the sake of flattering her minimal features with toxic cosmetics and dye to cover her graying hair.

She repositioned her thick-lensed glasses and shuffled back out to her desk. The effort made her wheeze, and her chest felt tight as she slumped into her chair. Perhaps she should go home after all, but she didn't feel strong enough now to do that. She stared at the clock on the wall. People would begin showing up for work in less than an hour. Maybe then someone could take her home.

She turned to the computer and listened for the familiar melodious blips and bleeps as she clicked into the program. The monitor looked cloudy. Probably the temporary janitor had overzealously cleaned and left behind a trail of soap film.

Mary gasped a sigh and reached for the bottle of hand lotion on her desk. She deposited a good amount on the top of her left hand, and then removed half of it with the top of her right hand. She could never quite understand why people started the process of rubbing in hand lotion with the palms of their hands. She always put it on top, right where her hands were dry and irritated. She had yet to discover the environmental culprit that was reeking so much havoc on her hands. She rubbed it in meticulously, making sure to coat her knuckles and the skin between her fingers and up on her wrists.

Her labored breathing was making her feel tired and feeble. She reached for her white cotton gloves. Today she would be printing out a lot of hard copy for the trainee. And she suspected that the small amount of formaldehyde used to give the shiny finish to most computer paper was at the heart of her hand irritation. She'd written letters of complaint to all the prominent paper manufacturers. But, to date, she'd received no response.

Mary felt light-headed from lack of oxygen. She forced herself to remain calm, despite the fact that her breathing was growing increasingly difficult and painful. She knew she had to maintain control over the situation, because if she panicked it would be all over for her. The thought that someone might not come in time to help her, began to force its way against her strong self-will. She was aware that her heart was palpitating, and she focused even harder on relaxing her muscles.

Then the crushing pain seized around her chest. Slowly she moved her hand toward the phone. She watched her hand tremble while it hovered momentarily over the receiver. But her eyes fastened on the business card next to it. The boldface type, **LEELAND FAMILY PLANNING CLINIC**, stood out against the blurred background. Mary dropped her hand on the card and frowned—her last gesture in life—as she fell forward and lost consciousness.

Chapter 1: Home is a Wounded Heart

Tim was later than usual, and Brent and Patty were already working when he walked in the door. Working was what Brent called it when he leaned back in his upholstered office chair on wheels, propped his loafer-clad feet on his cluttered desk, and sipped strong black coffee from his favorite stained mug. And, as usual, Brent Weaver was wearing his green T-shirt with the words **when Irish eyes are smiling (they're up to something)** scrawled across the front in big white and yellow letters.

Tim had discovered he didn't have a drop of Irish blood in him when he located his birth parents, the Smiths. Nevertheless, he'd retained his adoptive parents' moniker, MacCulfsky, after their death—a decision which had prompted Brent to suggest naming their fledgling private investigative service IRISH EYES. The clincher was their secretary, whose name put them both to shame. Nothing in the *Name Your Irish Baby Dictionary* could top Patty O'Malley's name.

Tim wiped the sweat from his face with the towel draped around his neck. Every morning he ran a few laps at the nearby Cleermantown High School field track in preparation for his day, which consisted of classes at the local community college and working as Brent's trainee to get his own P.I. license.

"You wouldn't sweat so much if you'd cut that hair," Brent commented. He sat up and his chair landed on all five wheels. Tipping back in it without tipping over was a nervy feat that made Tim wonder if the retired police detective possessed supernatural abilities or if the chair had faulty wheels.

Actually, Tim was a full partner in IRISH EYES. He owned the building and lived upstairs in the converted attic apartment. But that only made it harder to tell Brent and Patty he now wanted out of the P.I. business. He'd have to kick them out of the main floor office, or charge them rent.

Patty was admiring his legs when Tim looked in her direction. She was Brent's significant other and old enough to be Tim's mother. And, like his mother, she approved of everything he did, including wearing his hair long.

Tim started up the stairs.

"Get some pants on, Kid, and get back down here," Brent called after him. "I got a case here that's right up your alley!"

Tim stood in the shower and mentally rehearsed how to tell Brent and Patty his decision. He'd thought the P.I. business was right up his alley, utilizing his natural talent for perseverant research. But that was before he'd discovered criminal minds don't stop to consider the consequences of their behavior. That hole in his thought process had resulted in a fatal error he would never forget. And it was difficult to live with the constant fear that he might make the same mistake again.

Only a month ago, missing persons had been his chosen specialty. Computers was something he'd come by naturally and retrieving a twelve-year-old kid who'd been lured away from his home by a cyber nut was a cinch—until it had gone down all wrong. The culprit was a known child molester. And in an insane fit of desperation, when Tim was closing in on him, the creep had murdered the kid.

Now Tim knew he wasn't capable of performing detective work in the field. He wanted nothing more to do with death. Life was too short to take chances, or to watch people being blown away, especially children who were supposed to have their whole lives ahead of them.

And Brent had been real consoling when he said, "Just do the best you can, and the rest will have to work itself out."

The parents had forgiven him, even thanked him for his courageous attempt to rescue their child, but Tim couldn't forgive himself. He couldn't get beyond believing that maybe there was something more he could've done. Something else he should've thought of to prevent what had happened.

He was going to spend months waiting to give his testimony in court, reliving every detail over and over until they were burned into his memory. Just like the memory of a shoot-out a year ago that nearly cost him his own life.

He touched the scar under his left collarbone where the bullet had left its mark. Fresh out of high school, he'd gotten in over his head while searching for his birth parents. Fortunately, Brent had enough clout to pull some strings and get him out of that mess. Tim already had enough close calls to last him a lifetime. It was time to leave the P.I. business to those who could handle it.

"I've decided I want to be a lawyer instead of a P.I.," Tim announced when he reached the bottom stair.

Patty looked up, but Brent was tipped back in his chair with his eyes closed, listening, Tim decided, because he wasn't snoring...yet.

"Actually, being a lawyer is a lot like being a P.I.," Tim continued. "The only difference is no fieldwork, no personal involvement." Tim pinched his knuckles, his odd nervous habit that drove him crazy. "And the college courses I'm taking now would transfer to a legal degree."

Brent opened his eyes and sat up, causing his chair to land on its wheels with a loud bang. "Fine. Get a haircut tomorrow, Mr. Ivy League." Without getting to his feet, he shoved off and rolled to his favorite spot behind Patty's desk. He put his left arm around her and reached for a folder on her desk with his right hand. "But right now take a look at this." He tossed it in the middle of Tim's desk.

"What part didn't you hear?" Tim said looking at Patty for confirmation. "I said I want to be a lawyer INSTEAD of a P.I."

Patty's eyes grew wide with concern when Brent continued to ignore Tim.

The three of them had separate desks in the corners of the small office. Tim's desk was closest to the stairway facing toward the center of the room. Brent's desk and Patty's were on the opposite side of the room facing Tim's. His desk had the commanding position, but Brent was the one who called all the shots.

And Patty was the one in charge of office décor. Naturally, everything was green—the vertical blinds and valance on the windows, the chairs, the cups they drank from, the pens, their letterhead stationery, the mat in front of the door. Everything in the office was the color of money—except Brent's chair, which he'd brought from his former office at the Cleermantown police station. And when the sun shined just right through the windows in the evening, the place glowed like an emerald.

The folder Brent had tossed in the middle of Tim's desk, which Tim was reluctant to pick up, wasn't a manila folder either. Patty had managed to find an office supply store that specialized in adding color to any office. They added green folders to theirs.

Brent planted a kiss on Patty's cheek, which she coolly accepted while trying to be professional.

Tim stared at the folder a while realizing Brent had the audacity to believe he would open it. Tim looked around for something else to do, but there was nothing. He hesitated, then finally reached for the folder and opened it just to see what kind of case Brent figured was "right up his alley."

The paper on top was a copy of a letter to a Ms. Bernadette Higgins. It began: It is my extreme pleasure to inform you that you are the grand prize winner of our recent promotional sweepstakes entitling you to a cash award of **one million dollars.**

Tim skimmed through the remainder of the body of the letter, which contained details of the rules and qualifications and how the winner was to go about collecting the prize. He looked at the rest of the contents of the folder—notices of further attempts to contact Ms. Higgins. The last page was a letter to IRISH EYES enlisting their service to find her.

He hated to admit it...but it was intriguing, and it sounded easy enough. Just find the lucky woman and tell her the good news. Easy... right? "So why don't they just give the million to another lucky draw?" He tried to sound uninterested as he closed the folder and casually tossed it back on his desk.

"The rules state that they must make every reasonable attempt for 90 days after the drawing," Brent said. "And there are exactly 30 days remaining, as of today."

"Yeah, I read that part," Tim said. "But who else reads the fine print? And who would know?"

Brent shoved over to his own desk and tipped back again with his eyes closed and his feet propped up. "A sweepstakes with ethics, run by the rules, DOES seem a bit rare," he mused. Then added, "I Wonder how many times I've won something and didn't receive the notification?"

"The whole thing smells fishy," Tim said.

"Not really," Patty said. It wasn't usual for her to join in when they discussed cases, unless it involved the financial aspect of the deal. "A lot of the big sweepstakes employ outside help to find the winners.

They don't want to be bothered with it. But they don't want to be in court over a forfeiture clause." She continued when she knew she had their attention. "This one's sponsored by a well-known travel agency. Their financial statement is as solid as a rock. The sweepstakes is legit."

"I didn't know you did background on our cases," Brent remarked without opening his eyes.

"I read it in *The Wall Street Journal*," Patty replied.

"So you don't think the part about the finder's fee being a variable percentage of the prize money is a problem?" Tim asked.

"It boils down to this," Patty continued. "The sooner you find the winner, the more you get paid. If you don't find her within 30 days, you don't get paid at all." She put some paper in her printer. "It's an incentive pay scale, but it's substantial. Even if you find her on the last day, it will cover your expenses plus a little for your effort."

Tim leaned back in his chair and began pinching his knuckles. He was planning to take on a heavy load of classes next semester. It didn't make sense to bother with a case now when he was planning to quit the business and change his course of study. Still...it had a built-in time limit of only one month. And...the fee... He opened the folder to the last page and stared at it.

"No dead bodies in this one, Kid," Brent added quietly from his corner, "unless you break the news to Ms. Bernadette Higgins too suddenly and she keels over dead from a heart attack." He smiled his crooked smile that looked more like a smirk. "You can't lose on this one, Kid. I promise!"

Tim's mind was already working out a plan for finding the missing sweepstakes winner. This case WAS right up his alley, and it was too late to say no. He'd allowed his mind to think about it too long. He picked up a pen and signed his name.

"I'll fax a copy back to them," Patty said as she rose from her desk and walked over to his. She took the letter and left the folder so he could study it.

He looked at Brent seemingly asleep with his eyes closed, tipped back in his chair, feet propped on his desk. *Someday,* Tim thought, *he's gonna tip too far.*

Chapter 2: Do It

In a criminal investigation, you have enough
evidence when you can reconstruct the crime. In a
missing person investigation, the crime is
disappearing. You have enough when you can
reconstruct the disappearance. In a criminal
investigation, you find out whodunit by reconstructing
the howdunit. In a missing person investigation, you
know whodunit, so you have to reconstruct the
howdunit to figure out where they've disappeared to.
Tim knew that, and he lived by it when conducting an
unofficial missing person investigation.

However, the first thing he decided to do now was
figure out his fee. Maybe that seemed selfish to
someone else. But, at this point, he needed incentive
to keep going.

The contract was fairly simple and straightforward.
Tim got out his calculator. The pay scale began at
three percent of the million-dollar grand prize total,
and decreased by increments of one-tenth of a percent
each day. Meaning that if he located and escorted Ms.
Bernadette Higgins to the main office today, where
they would verify her identity, he'd collect thirty

thousand dollars, for one day's work. Tomorrow would net him twenty-nine thousand dollars. The next day it would drop down to twenty-eight thousand (still not bad), and so on. Until thirty days from today, when his fee would turn into a big goose egg and the contract automatically terminated. A contingency fee with a twist and a deadline. He hoped he wouldn't regret this whole thing.

The contract also contained some small-print warnings and waiver-type jargon, and included a clause about forfeiting the entire fee if he tried to sneak in a counterfeit for the real Ms. Bernadette Higgins. No problem there, he was chronically honest. The sound of snoring interrupted Tim's thoughts.

Brent's appearance in the office during the day was only for show and to spend time with Patty. He pulled the nightshift surveillance jobs, which were the bread and butter of IRISH EYES. Tim worked all the easy day jobs, so he could maintain his grade point average. This case, his last, would lift the burden from his partner and make it easier for Tim to quit with dignity, if he could pull it off within a few days. And he had no doubt that he could—after all, it was right up his alley.

There was just one last thing he needed to do before he settled into solving this case as a typical missing person investigation. He needed to eliminate the dead body possibility. If Bernadette Higgins was dead, case closed! He would collect a handsome fee for almost no effort.

Visiting the morgue was normally Tim's last option when searching for a missing person. Following all other leads first, allowed loved ones, as well as the authorities to know the person's whereabouts leading up to the death. It gave closure to a case.

Twice before his investigations had ended in the morgue. One case was a dead-beat father who'd drunk himself to death. The other was a runaway wife with a heart condition who'd died of a massive coronary. In both cases it had been important to provide the circumstances surrounding the death.

But the primary reason Tim didn't usually start at the morgue was simply because it gave him a bad, lingering case of the heebie-jeebies, complete with goose bumps, hair standing on end, and stomach churning. It just didn't feel normal being around dead people, and he knew he'd never get over feeling squeamish about it.

Everything about this case was backwards. And Tim decided to get the heebie-jeebies out of the way first. The fact that the county morgue was in the basement of the Cleermantown hospital didn't help matters any.

Tim took the stairs, instead of the elevator, so his stomach wouldn't get a head start. The cold, steel-gray-painted stairs echoed every footstep. When he reached the landing, where the staircase took a ninety-degree turn, he hugged the wall to steady himself. But it felt icy cold, and he continued his decline.

The smell grew stronger and, at the bottom of the stairs, Tim stood and forced himself to take several deep breaths. Brent had told him it was better to breathe it in and get over the urge to puke, instead of getting dizzy and light-headed from trying to avoid breathing the smells. Tim tried it.

Brent's record for bad advice still stood. Not only was the horrible smell offending his nose, but Tim also felt dizzy and nauseated. And he hadn't even opened the door yet. He entered the large open area, one side of which was an office, of sorts.

"Hello, Timothy." Dr. Morgan exuded warmth and friendliness despite her occupation. Her pathology students had shortened her apt name to the unimaginative, Dr. Morgue. She pushed away from the old metal desk and stood. "Let me guess. You're looking for a Jane Doe that matches the photo you're holding in your hand."

Tim looked down on the wide center part in Dr. Morgan's thinning brown hair as she drew close. "Yes, ma'am," he answered holding out the photograph.

Dr. Morgan quickly slipped on her reading glasses, which she wore on a chain around her neck. She took the picture and examined it and then gave it back to Tim. "I had a Jane Doe until this morning."

Tim slid the three by five of Bernadette Higgins back into his pocket and unintentionally glanced down at the large glossy lying on the desk. The post mortum complexion and stiff pose made him turn away. He was sure his complexion had paled to a matching hue.

"As you can see," Dr. Morgan said removing her glasses and letting them drop to her ample chest, "she wasn't the woman you're looking for."

Tim nodded and tried to take shallow breaths. He caught himself pinching his knuckles.

"Tell me, Timothy," Dr. Morgan said holding his attention. "When are you planning to attend my lectures?"

Tim smiled feebly and took a step backward. "I wasn't planning to, at all."

"You know it's a requirement for anyone pursuing forensics." She stepped closer.

"I'm leaning more toward civil litigation," Tim said with new resolve. "It's...It's more interesting."

"Nonsense," Dr. Morgan said slipping her hand under the bend of his elbow. "More interesting than criminal investigation? I peeked at your transcript. You're getting straight A's. You'd be crazy to change your field."

The way she said the word crazy sounded spooky to Tim, and he suddenly became aware that she'd maneuvered him a few steps toward the dreaded double doors.

He stopped and pulled his arm away from her. "I don't think you really understand how I feel about..."

Dr. Morgan chuckled. "A strong, handsome young man like you?" She held out a sickly green hospital-type overcoat. "You'll get used to it."

"I'm not prepared," Tim protested and took another step backward, in the wrong direction. "Some other time, maybe."

"No time like the present." Dr. Morgan persisted and managed to slip the lab coat onto Tim's right arm and around his shoulders. "What did you eat for breakfast?"

"Nothing." He preferred to save his appetite for a big lunch, but he realized his routine was about to be upset.

"There you go." Dr. Morgan pulled her dumbfounded pupil through the doors before Tim knew what was happening. "You're as ready as you'll ever be." She stood on her tiptoes to whisper in his ear. "And no one but me will see you get sick."

Tim shoved his hair behind his ears and clasped the coat around him. He'd visited the morgue before to collect autopsy reports, but he'd never gone beyond the office. The room they entered resembled a very big operating room, with one big difference—autopsies, not operations, were performed here. Cause of death was the only determination in this room. People were beyond saving when they entered these doors, and Tim found it difficult not to feel like one of them.

"What are you doing your research paper on?" Dr. Morgan asked Tim as he reluctantly followed her toward a large stainless steel table in the middle of the room. A form, completely covered with a white sheet, lay on top.

Tim's eyes began to water and he stared up at the ceiling. "I thought I'd..." His throat felt tight. "...do something on poisoning as a means of homicide," he answered weakly.

"Ah." Dr. Morgan nodded her approval. "Nonviolent murder is one of my favorite topics. Poisoning can be very tricky and it takes a devious mind to do it well." She slipped on surgical gloves and handed a pair to Tim. "You'll need these."

"No, I won't," Tim protested and backed away. But he took them from her anyway. He wasn't planning to even look. She pulled back the shroud and revealed the head of a man and his nude torso. Tim quickly turned away, but the sight remained visible behind his tightly closed eyelids.

"I don't have a poisoning victim at the moment," Dr. Morgan continued, "but I can give you some hands-on insight into the effects of ingesting a poison. And the effects lead to detection."

Even with his eyes closed, Tim's imagination conjured up mental images of the appalling procedure as Doctor Morgan opened the cadaver. He discovered he couldn't pinch his knuckles with the gloves on, so he steadied his nerves with listening to Dr. Morgan expound her expertise.

"Poison isn't always detected unless there is reason to suspect poisoning was the causative factor in a death. And then there is the job of proving whether the poisoning was accidental or homicidal. If accidental, who's to blame? If homicidal, there must be proof of malicious intent and forethought."

Tim managed to keep his eyes open by turning his side toward Dr. Morgan while she performed her job. But he had to plug his ears when she stopped talking to use a small precision electric saw to cut through the sternum. Then she tapped him on the shoulder so he'd listen to her, and he nearly jumped out of his skin.

"Fifty-eight percent of all murders are committed with a firearm of some sort. Of the remaining forty-two percent, knives are the most common weapons. Direct violence using hands, fist, or feet falls into that small category, along with fire and blunt objects. So you can see, poison as a means of homicide has fallen out of favor since the middle ages when it was more common."

By pretending that it had nothing to do with a recognizable human body, Tim mustered the courage to glance at the internal organs lying exposed.

"Poison is not a common method for many reasons." Dr. Morgan's monologue captivated his interest, despite the morbidity of the subject. "One reason being, the many variables that make the effects of poison unpredictable and unreliable—the size of the victim, the tolerance of the victim to a particular toxin, the reaction of the victim, and whether he seeks emergency treatment.

"Nowadays, with the F.D.A. controlling what's on the market, people believe that poison is unavailable. The truth of the matter is, there are so many hazardous ingredients in common household products, it's a wonder anyone survives beyond childhood."

Tim leaned closer and watched as she visually explained some the effects of poisons on the internal organs. Gradually, she not only induced him to touch some of the organs, but he found himself shockingly absorbed in fondling the liver to acquire a feel for its normal texture. He withdrew and looked at the blood on his gloves in horror.

Dr. Morgan quickly continued. "Another reason poisoning is not so common, its saving grace, you might say, is its taste. Most poisons taste bitter. Some have a repulsive odor. But not all have such telltale warnings, and most can be disguised in spicy foods or drinks. Dr. Kavorkian and his death-with-dignity heresy aside, one should wonder how many natural-cause and age-related deaths are actually poison induced.

"Poisons can supply death in any form—lingering, quick, painful, or gentle as sleep. And homicidal poisoning can easily be disguised as accidental or suicidal poisoning."

"So you're saying, the perfect murder is by poison," Tim concluded, warming to the subject.

"It helps to have a good lawyer too." Dr. Morgan chuckled. "In my opinion, women commit murder by poisoning far more often than men, because it requires premeditation. And women are more likely to plan an act of revenge than to react violently. They get the timing right, so they have an alibi. They set it up so it works. They factor in every detail and wait patiently to spring a death trap."

"What you're saying is..." Tim couldn't help smiling. "Women are more likely to get away with murder."

"You may quote me in your research paper, if you'd like." Dr. Morgan removed her gloves, and Tim followed suit. "I'll send you a copy of your first autopsy." She pointed at the little camera focused on them from a high shelf. "I always record it, and then review it for my reports."

Tim had learned more in the last hour than he ever could, poring over textbooks. But he blushed. "Just be sure to address it to me. I'd hate for Brent to get his hands on it. I'd never live it down."

"You did great, darling, for your first time." Dr. Morgan helped him remove the lab coat and tossed it, with hers, into a receptacle as they walked through the doors again.

Tim made a beeline toward the exit before she could detain him any longer. "Thanks for all your help and information."

"See you next semester?" she called after him.

Tim bounded up the stairs two at a time. He rushed outside into the bright sunshine and filled his lungs with fresh air, even New York City air seemed fresh. He had just enough time to shower again, taking extra care to scrub the loathsome smell from his hair, and change clothes before meeting his old friend, Clarence Drib, for lunch.

Chapter 3: Someday Baby

Tim took one look at the soup-of-the-day he'd ordered and pushed it aside. Tomato soup would never have the same appeal, after today's visit to the morgue. He was seated at their usual table in downtown Cleermantown's main claim to fame, the Sidewalk Café. It was their meeting place, and Tim had only to wait a few minutes until he pinpointed the little, shiny round head of Clarence Drib bobbing along in the glare of the noonday sun.

"Praise the Lord," the old retired journalist greeted him as he sat down. "I was beginning to think you had died and everyone forgot to let me know about it."

It had been a while since they met for lunch. "You called enough times to find out," Tim said quietly. "Thanks."

Waldo scratched at his shoe, his typical doggie greeting, until Tim reached down and rubbed the Pekingese behind the ears. Waldo was the reason they met at the Sidewalk Café. The owner treated the dog as one of the customers. And Waldo regarded the privilege by lying under the table out of view where he quietly lapped the water the waiter brought him in a Styrofoam bowl.

"Did you go away, or just not answer your phone for two weeks?"

"I visited my family in Illinois?"

"How are they?"

"Fine." The waiter delivered their food. "The kids are all growing up. Kathy has a new job at some hotshot lawyer's office." Tim hadn't always had brothers and sisters, and after only a year, it still seemed strange to talk about them as part of his life.

"Good for her," Clarence said enthusiastically.

"Good pay," Tim commented.

They enjoyed the good food for a while in silence.

"You'll be called on to testify." Clarence broached the subject first.

"I've already been served notice."

"When will the trial begin?"

"Soon, I hope," Tim said unsure. "I want it over with quickly." He knew Clarence was aware of the details enough to know that a date hadn't been set yet. The old man was simply making conversation so he'd talk about it.

"You'll be there, won't you?" Tim asked.

"Right behind you all the way."

He'd been there as his friend, and as a reporter, he'd championed Tim's cause.

"I'm working on a new case," Tim said changing the subject.

Clarence nodded. "I'm glad to hear you're back in the thick of things."

"It's my last case," Tim said. "I'm quitting after this one."

Clarence leaned back, and the alert waiter cleared away their dishes. "Tell me about this last case."

Tim leaned forward placing his elbows on the table. "It's pretty cut and dry actually—a missing person, a sweepstakes winner who skipped town without leaving a forwarding address. I should be able to locate her in a day or two by computer, three days max. And a million-dollar bait hook will bring her running."

"Sounds easy enough," Clarence agreed.

"At least she's not dead. I've already checked the morgue."

"Every missing person leaves a trace. It's just a matter of time till they surface again."

"That's the catch," Tim said. "Time."

"There's always a catch." A gradual smile spread over Clarence's broad face. "Throw in a time limit, and the simplest case becomes the hardest to solve."

"It's not like that," Tim assured him. "Time is not a problem. It's just that my fee is determined by how quick I find her. I get a percentage of her prize money, but it decreases with each day that goes by. After thirty days, I get zip."

"At the risk of sounding cliché-istic, 'Time is money, young man!' What are you doing hanging around and shootin' the breeze with an old geezer?"

Waldo peeked out from under the table at the word "geezer" as if he were the one being referred to.

"I guess it's time to head back home," Clarence said as he stood, "before it gets too hot."

Tim stood and stretched. They parted and walked in opposite directions—Clarence and Waldo toward their apartment building, and Tim toward his car in the city parking lot.

Clarence turned and added, "Don't let the money become a problem, Son."

"Don't worry," Tim responded. By the time he reached the parking lot he was pondering the old man's unusual warning. It was unnecessary. The conditions of the contract had already spelled out the obvious implications of time and money, and he refused to let it become a problem.

In fact, the money was so NOT a problem, that Tim spent the afternoon at the library taking care of a more pressing matter—the research paper for his Forensic Science class. He spent the afternoon writing out the gist of what Dr. Morgan had taught him during his morning visit. He would wait for the videotape to add details and then research any points that needed filling in.

It was after five when Tim returned to the office. Brent and Patty had already left and locked up. He knew they had, because he wore a pager and there had been no activity all day. He turned the light on over his desk. No messages on his answering machine meant he could spend a nice, quiet Friday evening watching TV.

Then he saw the Post-it note stuck on the screen of his computer monitor. It was Patty's handwriting, *check your email*. She'd left the message discreetly, because if Brent got wind of any more love letters he'd never let Tim hear the end of it. Brent was merciless when it came to teasing him about Rhonda Ghent.

Tim sat down at his desk and turned on the computer. Rhonda Ghent was the little fifteen-year-old girl he'd managed to return home safely last summer. But not before a one-sided romance had developed.

She was head-over-heels in love with him. And she began expressing the intimate details of her feelings, and her life, by emailing him at IRISH EYES.

Patty had been very understanding and sympathetic about the situation. But Brent regaled him with gushy poetry in a falsetto voice, and took every opportunity to remind Tim of his platonic affair. It had gone on for weeks with just the first letter. From then on, Patty forwarded the emails to Tim's personal separate line on his computer and deleted them from the IRISH EYES computer line, so there would be no chance of Brent finding out about them.

Actually, Tim enjoyed reading Rhonda's emails. They were full of normal everyday events taking place in an average Midwest, small-town high school. It reminded him of his own life before so much had happened to change it. And, he had to admit he found her puppy-love attraction to him uplifting at times, especially when he was feeling a little depressed. Her expressions of love were so open and frank.

He smiled as he waited for the printer to print out her latest terms of endearment, so he could take the letter upstairs and read it in leisure while he ate supper.

Tim hadn't expected another letter after that first one almost a year ago. But, to his bewilderment, Rhonda continued to write. He believed that if he didn't encourage her by answering her letters, she would go on with her life as if she'd never been with him.

They'd been chased by an underworld crime figure determined to eliminate all the loose ends of his sinister past. Consequently, it had taken Tim more than a month to return Rhonda to her home and family. And, apparently that had been long enough for her to forge a romantic bond with him.

He wondered at her persistence until one day when his curiosity got the best of him, he broke into Patty's private files on the IRISH EYES computer. It was a breach of Patty's trust—the wrong thing to do, he knew. So he never told Patty about it.

The end did not justify the means, but the end revealed what he needed to know—why Rhonda kept writing. Patty was communicating with her. Telling her that she was forwarding her emails to Tim. That he was reading them, even that he enjoyed them.

As Tim contemplated how his life had gotten to the point where his entertainment included love letters from an underage groupie, a strange feeling rose in the pit of his stomach. Rhonda, in this most recent romantic chapter, had included a school picture. His printer was sounding off the full glorious color of her big beautiful blue eyes as the ink cartridge zipped back and forth across the page.

Tim turned off the computer when it finished printing and stared at Rhonda's image while he went up the stairs to his apartment. He shoved a frozen dinner in the microwave, and unexpectedly recalled what an excellent cook she'd become during their cross-country adventure together. He could honestly say he taught her everything he knew, but she definitely had culinary talent.

He learned, as he continued reading the letter, that Rhonda had just turned sweet sixteen. Her birthday wish for cooking equipment and paraphernalia had come true. Always devoted to her love of learning to prepare food, her letters proved that he'd done the right thing by returning her to the safety of her home and family last summer. She was growing up into the young woman he knew she could become. Rhonda would never let him down.

Her successful reunion with her family, as well as his own, had been a major influence in his decision to become a private investigator specializing in missing persons and adoptee searches. But that was a year ago, before his last case that ended in the death of a young boy, before he'd discovered just how wrong he could be about some people.

Tim read the remainder of Rhonda's letter, recounting her drivers' education classes. *Look out world! Rhonda's behind the wheel.* Just the thought of it made him shutter inwardly. It reminded him that he needed to do more praying. He looked at the picture and studied her breathtaking beauty that even his computer printer had captured. *Look out men! Ready or not, here comes Rhonda!*

Chapter 4: If You Know What I Mean

Tim spent the weekend letting his fingers do the walking, the first step in any missing person investigation. He traveled the highways and byways of sophisticated computer tracking directories, which he regularly updated. In most cases, the expense and effort paid off. Usually he at least came close to a missing person's whereabouts before he resorted to actual fieldwork.

However, on Sunday morning in church, Tim decided to raise his hand when the pastor asked if anyone in the congregation needed a miracle. Not that he thought it would take a miracle to find Ms. Bernadette Higgins (the soon-to-be millionaire—minus his finder's fee, which he hoped would remain a five-figure sum), but he thought it couldn't hurt to enlist God's help in the endeavor. After all, finding people was right up God's alley too.

On Monday morning Tim shifted into phase two of his missing person search plan. He'd exhausted all the computer leads. Ms. Bernadette Higgins' dossier was sparse and led to only one place, an apartment complex in a very nice neighborhood of Cleermantown.

Tim parked his blue Tracker in the parking lot and located the all-purpose superintendent mowing the grass in front of the building. He walked over to gain his attention.

The superintendent shut off the loud engine and wiped the sweat from his forehead with his arm. "What can I do for you?"

"My name's Tim MacCulfsky." He stuck out his hand, but the man knew how to get rid of annoying solicitors. "I'm looking for someone," Tim quickly added, "and I hope you can help me."

The man wiped his hands on his jeans before accepting Tim's hand. "Name's Bill Garcia." His handshake was robust and Tim was hard pressed to return the same amount of energy. "Tell me who you're looking for and I'll point you in the right direction."

"Bernadette Higgins."

True to his words, the superintendent turned and pointed to a door.

"Do you know if she's home right now?"

"Should be," Bill said looking toward the parking lot. "You parked next to her car."

Tim followed the superintendent's gaze to the red Corvette parked next to his own economical version of a sport utility vehicle. Tim let go an involuntary whistle.

"She's flashy, that one," the superintendent remarked.

Tim headed toward the apartment door. "Thanks, Bill."

"No problem." The superintendent returned to his lawn mower where he took a long swig from the water bottle dangling from the handle while he watched Tim.

Tim rang the doorbell and waited. He rang again without raising a response. Then he knocked. Still nothing.

Bill watched and approached slowly, then added his more urgent pounding on the door. "You don't suppose anything happened to her, do you?" His voice betrayed a hint of panic. "That would be just terrible after what happened to Mary."

"Who's Mary?"

"Mary and Bernie—excuse me, Ms. Higgins—share the apartment. At least, they used to. Before Mary was found dead last week."

A dead body! Brent had promised there'd be no dead bodies. Tim got his first feeling of foreboding about the case. He should've known! Brent didn't exactly have a perfect track record for being right.

Tim watched Bill trying to look inside through one of the windows. Maybe the superintendent was agitated enough to do what he was about to suggest. "You have a key to the apartment, don't you?"

Bill hesitated only a moment before rushing away. "I don't keep the keys on me," he called over his shoulder.

Tim felt the sun warming his back while he waited the few minutes it took for the superintendent to return. The man's hands shook, so Tim took the keys and unlocked the deadbolt and let the door swing open. "Wait here," he said, "just in case."

Bill's expression revealed that he wasn't any more eager to discover a dead body than Tim was.

"Ms. Higgins," Tim called loudly as he made his way inside. "Bernadette Higgins." He was careful not to touch anything while he inspected each of the four rooms. No one was home. And better still, no dead bodies lying around. Using his shirttail he slid open the closet door in the bedroom and peered inside.

Bill waited anxiously until Tim signaled him the all clear. Then he stepped inside and shut the door.

"Any idea where she might be?"

The superintendent shook his head. "I haven't seen her for several days. In fact, if it weren't for her car being in the parking lot, I would think she was on one of her trips. She usually leaves it at the airport."

Tim frowned. "Wouldn't it be safer to leave it here with her roommate?"

Bill nodded and glanced around uneasily.

Tim picked up a couple of unopened envelopes from the coffee table. Both were addressed to Bernadette Higgins. One was from the travel agency sponsoring the sweepstakes, probably another notice about her good fortune. Her dossier contained several similar examples of previous registered mail notices. All were marked UNDELIVERABLE. RETURN TO SENDER. "One of her trips?" Tim asked.

"Yeah," Bill said. "She travels a lot. I think it has something to do with her...her occupation. I think she works nights. That's when I see her leaving all dressed up."

"Where does she go on these job-related trips?" Tim asked.

"All over the world. Exotic places. She sends Mary so many postcards when she's gone, their mailbox overflows." Bill looked around the room and his eyes settled on a porcelain hummingbird figurine suspended by a thin gold wire above a delicate flower. The fragile arrangement was positioned on a doily so exquisite it could only have been made by hand.

"Doesn't Mary check the mail?" Tim asked absently. He discovered a bookshelf with a fold-down desk. It contained the usual letter-writing supplies. And Tim started writing down the names, addresses, and phone numbers of the businesses advertised on the barrels of the pens.

"Mary visits her folks when Bernie's away. Between you and me," Bill confided, "I think she doesn't... didn't...like being alone."

Tim made his way back around the living room and opened the door. The mailbox was right outside, so he opened it and checked the contents, hoping Bill wouldn't remember that it was a federal offense to tamper with another person's mail. He was sure Bernie would forgive him once she found out he was her lifeline to an instant million. It would make his job easy if the mailbox contained a wish-you-were-here postcard disclosing Bernadette Higgins' present whereabouts.

But it was not to be. The mailbox contained only bills, all addressed to Mary. The absence of a phone bill disappointed Tim, but it saved him from the hassle of having to open it in front of the superintendent to see if Bernadette left her calling card on the itemized invoice.

"How did Mary die?"

"Just keeled over at her desk...for no apparent reason." Bill followed as Tim circled around the living room and entered the bedroom. "Happened at her workplace last Monday morning. Something to do with her illness."

The double bed was neatly made and everything seemed to be in its place. The blinds were open and the curtains pulled back to let in sunshine.

"Her illness?" Tim looked at the beautiful figurines arranged on doilies atop the glass shelves of a five-foot high knick-knack stand. In the light from the window he could tell that none of them had been disturbed or removed since the last thorough housecleaning.

"She had real bad allergies," Bill said joining him in front of the knick-knack stand.

"Did Bernie know about Mary's death?"

"You're not here to break the news to Bernie, are you?" he asked. "So why are you looking for Bernie?"

"I have news of a different sort," Tim answered. Wasn't it Brent who'd warned him not to break the good news to her too suddenly so she wouldn't keel over from a heart attack? Would Bernadette Higgins be able to withstand the double shocker, Tim wondered. He pictured himself meeting Bernadette Higgins for the first time, shaking her hand, and delivering the punch line to a "good news/bad news" joke. *The good news is: You're a millionaire! The bad news is: You're roommate's dead!*

"Is she in trouble or something?" Bill was starting to show the first signs of suspicion and guilt at having allowed a stranger inside the apartment.

"No, nothing like that," Tim answered quickly. "I have some good news for her. But I'm not at liberty to disclose the exact nature of it." Some legal jargon might help to dispel the superintendent's worry. "But, let it suffice to say, she will be glad to hear it."

He resumed his search with Bill following his every move. Walking through a place gave Tim a feel for the personalities of its occupants when he didn't know what to look for. Especially if the occupants manifested odd quirks. He was already aware of one possibility that could narrow his search significantly—

one bedroom, one double bed might mean a gay relationship. The absence of computer information about Bernadette meant that Mary was the paying partner in this feminine duo. She had an income and apparently wrote all the checks. Bernadette's means of support were invisible.

Tim got down on his hands and knees and peered under the bed, always a convenient place for hiding things. Nothing. One of them was a fastidious housekeeper. He carefully smoothed the silky brown bedspread, overlaid with a delicate white crocheted coverlet, to its original position with the scalloped edges reaching to the thick-pile, chocolate brown carpet.

He stood up and looked around. He was convinced that Mary was in charge of decorating and cleaning the apartment. Something Bill had said—that Bernadette was flashy, and he sees her leaving all dressed up— maybe flashy compared to Mary. The apartment was done entirely in bland colors, mostly brown or beige. But the overall effect was a stunning understated backdrop for the intricate handcrafts and colorful figurines displayed throughout the apartment.

Tim stuck his head inside the bathroom before leaving the bedroom. "Did Mary wear makeup?"

"I don't think so," Bill answered. "She was sort of a plain Jane, if you know what I mean."

Tim knew what he meant, and he quickly pocketed a makeup compact sitting on the vanity sink. There was only one toothbrush visible in the holder on the wall.

"Bernadette wore enough for the both of them, though." Bill left the room and seemed anxious to leave the apartment.

Tim wandered into the kitchen area to have a quick look around. "How old was Mary?"

"I would guess around forty or so. I don't really know."

Bernadette was thirty-four, if the information she'd given the travel agency was correct. Tim could tell the superintendent was growing uneasy at being in the apartment uninvited. But something on the counter top caught Tim's eye—an unusual gadget, next to the electric stove and surrounded by a juicer, a toaster, and a bread-maker. He walked over and leaned down to examine it. "You ever see one of these before?"

Bill reluctantly joined him by the counter to stare at the oddity. "Formaldehyde monitor." He read the label out loud. "That's what Mary was allergic to—formaldehyde."

Tim noticed that the uppermost contents of the trash can lacked junk food wrappers, but instead had an abundance of plain paper wrappers, like the ones found in health food stores.

"We should leave," the superintendent finally said.

"Probably a good idea." Tim realized he'd worn out his welcome as he led the way to the door. Once outside, he handed Bill his business card. "If you hear from Ms. Bernadette Higgins, or if she returns, please give me a call immediately. It's important that I get in touch with her."

"Will do," Bill said reading the card. "You look too young to be a private eye."

That's what everybody says, Tim thought as he drove away. Which was another reason he wanted to get out of this line of work.

Chapter 5: I Got the Feelin' (Oh No No)

Tim could definitely sympathize with someone who was allergic to formaldehyde. He wasn't too fond of it either. It reminded him of his not so long ago days in high school biology class and his aversion to dissecting dead animals. He'd feigned a few sick days only to find out the event had been fortuitously postponed until his return to school. It was hard to maintain his macho image in front of his female lab partners, who became engrossed in the procedure while he became just plain grossed out. And the visit to the morgue three days ago had served as a flashback as well as a preview of what was to come.

It was only natural that he pursued the search for Bernadette Higgins from this new angle—her connection with Mary Harris, her roommate and his only lead. First thing tomorrow he would pay a visit to Clayton's Investment and Finance Corporation, the name of the company he'd spotted on Mary's paycheck stub while looking through the desk in their apartment.

He met Clarence Drib for lunch, and they discussed the facts of the missing person case, which Tim was no closer to solving now than he was three days ago when he first opened the folder and read the strange contract.

"I must be overlooking something."

"Don't lose sleep over it," Clarence advised. "It'll come to you, probably when you least expect it."

"It's probably something really simple and stupid. But what?" Tim scoffed down his food, another nervous habit to which he succumbed when he couldn't pinch his knuckles. "She listed her roommate as her emergency contact. But how many times does an emergency contact die right when a person has an emergency?"

Clarence shrugged and continued eating. Waldo looked at Tim from under the table and cocked his head, sensing his agitation.

"A cool million just waiting to be claimed, and Ms. Bernadette Higgins is playing hide-and-seek on an international scale." The thought that he might have to board a jet to retrieve her, suddenly occurred to Tim and his fear of heights gave his stomach a jolt. That, and his pager going off at the same time, nearly caused a return visit from his lunch.

He pressed the button to stop the beeping and read the numbers. "I'll be back in a minute." He pushed his chair away from the table and stood. "Brent probably forgot where he stashed the cell phone." Brent had a habit of hiding it in odd places, so Patty wouldn't use it. The service was expensive and Brent reserved the use of the cell phone for fieldwork.

Patty disguised the real reason for paging him by reminding Tim of his weekly shooting range practice in half an hour. Then she casually slipped in, "You don't happen, by any chance, to know where the cell phone is, do you, Dearie?"

"Try under the car seat." Years of being on the police force had taught Brent to mindlessly stash things when he was in a hurry. The only problem was, he sometimes couldn't remember where he'd stashed them.

"I was right," Tim said when he returned.

"Detective Weaver staying busy these days?" Clarence had an unwavering respect for Brent and continued to use his official title even after his retirement from the police force a year ago.

"Mostly nights." Tim glanced at his watch. "Speaking of busy days, I have to put in a half hour at the shooting range before classes."

"Take care," Clarence said as they parted ways at the corner. Waldo eagerly headed home leading the way with his leash slack.

Tim, on the other hand, drove to one of his least favorite places. The fact that he had to wear soundproof earphones to keep from losing his hearing was a good indicator to him that gunpowder was not the noble invention it was originally intended to be. And shooting another person was something he was sure he could never do.

Nevertheless, Brent insisted that having a firearm was a requirement in the business. And learning to use it properly was mandatory. So every Monday after lunch Tim showed up at the shooting range where Brent's friend was paid to teach him the proper use of his Beretta. The rest of the week, Tim kept it locked away in the trunk of his car.

Somehow he'd progressed beyond getting used to aiming and firing the slightly more than two pounds, eight and one-half inches of dark steel. At first, he was classified as a hopelessly bad shot, until he explained that he could never shoot to kill. He purposely aimed to hit the knees of the life-size target, instead of the heart or the head.

Although he never reviewed the videotapes of himself on the range or practiced at home to improve his technique, Tim was now considered ready for "situational shooting—survival techniques when attacked."

"Anyone can stand on a firing line and shoot with reasonable accuracy," the instructor said. He glanced at Tim, and all the other trainees grinned. Tim's shoot to disable, not to kill, policy was an inside joke among them.

"Remember, you're most likely to be attacked when conditions are most advantageous to the criminal and least advantageous to you, such as when your hands are full. Attackers look for stooped shoulders or awkward movement. And then they catch you." The instructor came up unexpectedly behind Tim and jabbed him in the lower back with his finger.

Tim raised both hands over his head, which elicited sympathetic chuckles from his fellow trainees.

"That's a bad move," the instructor said, "because it takes your hands farther away from your own weapon. Bringing your hands down and knocking the gun out of your assailant's hand usually only works with a lot of luck, or in the movies where they choreograph every move perfectly."

In his mind's eye, some of Tim's favorite movie heroes just got shot down.

"Which is why we're going to practice the 'drop, draw, and shoot'."

They practiced. And Tim was hit in the side with a flying gym bag.

"The idea is to DROP what you're carrying," the instructor reprimanded, "not fling it at fellow victims and knock them off their feet. Keep your hand close to your weapon at all times. You want to survive an attack, don't you?"

They practiced more, until each trainee was able to look down and see the gym bag next to his foot after drawing and shooting. Tim was glad the session was finally over, and he returned his pistol, along with the waistband holster, to the trunk of his car and locked it.

Then He drove to the community college where he attended classes. Four hours later, he drove home, making plans for the rest of the evening. The paved parking area, which IRISH EYES shared with the neighboring real estate agency, was empty when he parked. But not for long. A van bearing the local TV station's logo pulled in next to him, and he was confronted with a camera and a woman carrying a microphone.

"Mr. MacCulfsky, is it true that you were with young Mark Lander when he was killed?"

Tim bumped into the microphone as he hurriedly walked toward the door. The cameraman blocked his path and Tim stopped and looked right into the camera perched atop the man's right shoulder. He didn't say a word. His mind reeled from the blunt question.

"Did you see Larry Howzinski stab the twelve-year-old youth, Mark Lander, to death?"

Tim lowered his head and pushed past the camera. His keys were in his right hand and his left hand was weighted with his briefcase full of heavy textbooks. He fumbled his keys trying to locate the one to unlock the door. The *drop, draw and shoot* technique popped into his head. He was caught with his hands full and unable to get away fast enough.

"May we have an interview with you, Mr. MacCulfsky?" the woman shouted in a last-ditch effort.

Tim managed to open the door and squeeze his briefcase, then himself, through the crack. He slammed the door shut and secured the deadbolt. Then he pulled the shades and closed all the blinds before turning on any lights.

He watched the van drive away with both the woman and the cameraman, but the incident left him feeling paranoid. Her questions had cut to the quick and left him in pain. He'd have to speak with the prosecuting attorney about pre-trial training, to prepare him for the kinds of questions he knew were going to be asked when he was put on the stand to testify.

After setting his briefcase next to his desk, his first order of business was to see if his day hadn't been a total loss. He carefully removed the plastic baggy he'd used to line the inside of his pants pocket, the kind with a handy zipper closure for sealing it shut. When done carefully he could seal enough air inside to protect the contents. And the contents of this baggy was the makeup compact he'd lifted from Bernadette Higgins' apartment this morning. It rested inside the pillow of air and, as Tim moved it under the desk lamp, he detected unmistakable fingerprints on the lid.

Fingerprints held a peculiar fascination for Tim. And the ability to lift them properly was a very useful skill in missing person searches. Not only for identification, but for following a trail and, if needed, as conclusive evidence. He'd purchased quite an extensive collection of fingerprinting equipment, some of which he hadn't had an opportunity to use yet. And right now, all he needed was a simple brush and powder.

He fluffed the soft bristles of the small brush by holding the handle between his palms and moving his hands back and forth a couple of times. He dipped the tip of the bristles in the container of dark magnetic powder and began working.

Handling the compact by its edges, he brushed lightly in the direction of the curved lines and gently blew his breath to remove stray grains of powder. The print was a clear one. He pressed tape onto the print, being careful not to make air pockets, which would spoil it. Then he pressed it hard, and lifted the print in one single motion. He applied the tape to the unlined side of an index card. "Yes!" he breathed triumphantly.

It was a perfect print of the four fingers from her right hand, a good indication that she might be right-handed. And from the underside of the compact he extracted a good thumbprint. All in all, a pretty unique set of digits.

Tim examined them closely with a magnifying glass. He could tell they were from a right hand because of the ulnar loops on three of the fingers. That meant the ridges tended to flow in the direction of the little finger. That was the most common occurrence in fingerprints. But the index finger flowed toward the thumb, very rare. And that thumb bore the very rare accidental whorl, with three deltas, no less. The complete set was a fingerprint expert's dream. He'd know them instantly if he found them anywhere else.

Tim spun around and looked at the large empty expanse of the bulletin board hanging on the wall behind his desk. The pictures and bits and pieces from the last case, were removed and in a file folder to be tucked away in his growing file drawer of memories.

As he stared at the bulletin board trying to decide how to arrange the sparse clues from his present case, he recalled the one and only time he and Patty O'Malley had ever disagreed on anything. It happened shortly after Patty had renovated the office area with her favorite color, forest green. And it had been a huge task for both himself and Brent to prevent her from encroaching on his upstairs bachelor apartment with her color scheme.

That was when he'd made the untimely decision to cover a major portion of the wall behind his desk with the bulletin board. In spite of its ugly tan color and aged pockmarked surface, it was what he used to brainstorm and solve his cases like giant jigsaw puzzles.

But Patty's desk faced the eyesore, and she had to look at it all day. She kept moving it to less conspicuous sites in the office, and Tim kept moving it back. Her Irish temper surfaced throughout the following days, and Brent exercised the good sense to keep his mouth shut, for a change. But the tension grew into a standoff between Tim and Patty. The crushing blow had been when he told her he didn't have to move it elsewhere, because he, after all, was the owner of the building.

Then one day he returned to the office, and the first thing Tim saw was Patty smiling at him, something he'd missed during the feud. When he turned toward his desk and looked on the wall, his bulletin board was covered with a smooth layer of forest green felt. It matched the rest of the office décor and concealed the marred surface, which he had to admit had been distracting, even to him. He chalked one up for the Irish.

Tim started with the photo of Bernadette Higgins' face. He positioned the dossier underneath. And then he tacked up the complete set of right-hand fingerprints. In the bottom left corner he stuck a small calendar on which he began a countdown to the resolution of the case—he marked off the days with the financial digression of his finder's fee. Today had been the $27,000 mark.

When he finished the bulletin board, he turned around and discovered a Bubble Wrap-lined mailing bag on his desk. He changed his plans for steak and potatoes to a lighter meal for supper. And afterwards, he'd watch the autopsy video.

Tim's attic apartment was comfortable and cozy, perfect for a nineteen-year-old college student living alone. Brent had helped him with the major work, roughing in the walls, flooring, drywalls, plumbing, windows, etc. But Tim had designed the floor plan and done all the little jobs himself. He had a small efficient kitchen, a bedroom and bathroom, and an open living room, which overlooked the downstairs office like a balcony.

The living room idea had been Brent's. He had convinced Tim that the arrangement would help him overcome his fear of heights in comfort. But it wasn't working, and Tim considered replacing the balustrade with a solid secure wall. It was the only room in which he didn't spend much time.

The apartment was what Tim considered finished. But he had yet to choose his color scheme and motif, as Patty called it. So far, he'd stuck close to shades of blue for the carpet and sofa, purposely avoiding green. And the kitchen appliances were white. If Patty had her way, he'd be sleeping in a veritable Irish glen and cooking with shamrock-shaped potholders. That was enough to prevent his going on long vacations in the near future.

His TV and VCR were arranged on an entertainment center in the living room. Tim popped in the video Dr. Morgan had sent of the autopsy she'd performed and recorded for him. He reclined on the carpeted floor to watch it, instead of sitting on the sofa, which he felt was much too close to the railing overlooking the downstairs. He took notes and fast-forwarded through several of the more nauseating views. At the end, he pressed the stop button and prepared to rewind it. But the sight that met his eyes stopped him short.

He was on the news. The image of him walking from his car to the door of his home and business, was captured as it had happened earlier. The only difference was that someone had dubbed in a voice to answer the woman's questions with, "No comment," and "Ask my lawyer!"

Tim sat with his mouth gaping in disbelief. "They can't do that!" he protested ineffectually.

Chapter 6: Thank the Lord for the Night Time

Tim was anxious to talk with Brent the next morning, but it was Patty who made a remark about the local news broadcast the moment they walked in the door. "You should consider part-time modeling," she suggested. "Maybe even TV commercials. You're great at dancing in front of a camera!"

"I didn't give them permission to videotape me. And I didn't say anything. The voice was dubbed. I would never tell them to ask my lawyer. They can't do that, can they?" Tim implored Brent.

"They don't need your permission," Brent answered. "You're a public figure."

"But I don't want to be a public figure."

"You don't have any choice in the matter."

"I can't afford to be a public figure." There was more meaning behind Tim's statement than he wanted Patty to discern. "Remember?"

"I remember." Brent was calm considering he DID know the implications of Tim's notoriety. "But you gotta keep it in perspective. It was only the LOCAL news."

Tim pinched his knuckles.

"Men," Patty said shaking her head. "They're always wanting attention. Then when they get it, they don't know what to do with it." She walked away and began setting up her work for the day.

"Just watch your back," Brent continued. "It'll pass unnoticed. It's been a year since you tangoed with Almighty, and the crime boss isn't about to blow his cover now." Brent spoke in a subdued voice, because Patty was not aware of Tim's past underworld connection. "You're not the hot item on his menu anymore. In fact, you're cold potatoes right now."

"Does that mean he'll eventually stick me in the microwave to warm up his vendetta against loose ends again?"

"That's a wait-and-see. Just go about your normal business." Brent's police connections had saved his butt once. "What's on your agenda for today?" Brent asked, his voice returning to its normal level of intimidation.

"That reminds me," Tim said. "You broke your promise!"

"And what promise was that?" Brent countered defensively.

"You said there would be no dead bodies on this case. You were wrong. My only lead to Bernadette Higgins is her dead roommate."

"So I lied. You can handle it, Kid. You're a big boy!"

Tim was upset, but the 'big boy' number made his temper flare. He walked out the door before he said anything.

Behind his back he heard Brent mimic Elvis Presley's signature signoff: "Ladies and Gentlemen, Timmy has left the building." It made Tim feel a little less endangered, knowing his partner could joke about his status as a local news celebrity.

The outer office of Clayton's Investment and Finance Corporation was much like any other office. The soft tapping of keyboards, the attentive feminine voices on telephones, the pleasant smile from the woman at the front desk when Tim quietly walked in and drew her attention; it was all preliminary to getting into the inner sanctum of a business that dealt exclusively in money, and lots of it. Getting in required the approval of Mr. Clayton himself.

The first step was getting past the woman in charge of the reception desk, who told Tim that Mr. Clayton was in a meeting. She would get back to him to set up an appointment, if he left his name and number.

Tim produced his IRISH EYES business card and said, "I need to see Mr. Clayton on a matter of extreme urgency concerning a former employee named Mary Harris." He walked over to a row of chairs against the wall and added, "I'll just wait here until he's free to see me."

The desired effect accomplished, Tim hardly had time to get nervous before he was buzzed past the security door at the far side of the room and escorted by a guard who opened the door to Mr. Clayton's office for him.

When it came to dealing with money, Tim always pictured a nervous little man wearing glasses and a visor. But the man sitting behind the gleaming cherry-wood desk had every reason to be self-assured. The man was tall, well built, and handsome. And rich, too—his hair was professionally styled, his suit tailor-made with a monogrammed handkerchief peeking out of the pocket. Tim noticed the gold cuff links when they shook hands. Tim was quick to sit down when the chair was offered, before the brand name on his jeans revealed where he shopped for his clothes.

Mr. Clayton leaned back in his executive chair and clasped his hands behind his head in a very relaxed manner. "What can I do for you, Mr. MacCulfsky?"

"I'm making a personal inquiry concerning one of your former employees, Mary Harris," Tim said. Beating around the bush with a pretext wouldn't serve any purpose and would only waste precious time, which was costing him a grand a day. He doubted if Mr. Clayton earned more than a thousand dollars a day. But the problem with that comparison was Tim was losing it, instead of earning it, with every day that passed.

"I'm afraid I can't be of much help to you. I didn't know Ms. Harris that well."

"What exactly was her job here at your firm?"

"I hired her as a computer consultant to bring our records department up to date.

"Did she make any friends while she was working here?"

"That is something I definitely don't know about her." Mr. Clayton brought his hands down slowly and rested his elbows on top of his desk. He began pressing his fingertips together in an exercise that had the humorous effect of reminding Tim of the childhood rhyme, *Here is the church. Here is the steeple...* "To tell you the truth, she had a tendency to make more enemies than friends."

"Would it be possible to talk with some of her coworkers?" Tim asked.

"The report said her death was accidental poisoning due to an allergic reaction. You're not trying to stir up anything, are you?" Mr. Clayton's fingertip exercise now reminded Tim of the punch line to a joke, *a spider doing push-ups on a mirror.* "I mean, you don't suspect foul play, do you?"

"No, nothing like that." Tim assured him. "I need to locate her roommate for a matter that has nothing to do with her death. I'm just exploring the possibility that Mary Harris might've spoken to someone about her roommate and where she might've gone on a trip. Just a long shot, actually."

"If that's all this is about, I can arrange for you to visit the records department."

"That would be very helpful," Tim said marveling at his unexpected good fortune.

Mr. Clayton made a phone call that Tim couldn't overhear, but he assumed the arrangements were being made to allow him access to Mary's former coworkers. Even as Mr. Clayton replaced the receiver, there was a knock on the office door.

"Please escort Mr. MacCulfsky down to the records department."

Tim hoped *down* referred to the kind of movement, as in *down the hall*, not down to a lower level, as in *elevator.*

"By the way, tell your associate, Detective Weaver, I said 'hello'."

"Will do," Tim said realizing his connection to the former police detective paid dividends at times like this.

In a world where six foot four was considered taller than average, Tim found himself dwarfed by men of impressive stature ever since walking into Clayton's

Investment and Finance Corporation. Before Tim could respond to his mention of Brent, the man in charge of overseeing his visit to the records department closed Mr. Clayton's office door and conveyed him down the hall and into an elevator.

His bodyguard escort waited while Tim exited the elevator first, then led him through a maze of office cubicles. In the middle of the room, they stopped in front of a desk. According to the nameplate, Dennis Lakey, records department manager, was the man who stood and offered Tim a chair facing his desk. They shook hands and sat down as Tim watched his escort withdraw and wait by the door.

"Mr. Clayton says you have some questions you want to ask about Mary Harris."

"Yes, if you don't mind, Mr. Lakey."

"Please, call me Dennis." He reached for the coffee cup on the corner of his desk. "Coffee?"

"No thanks," Tim said.

Dennis Lakey took the cup and filled it at the coffee machine on the counter across the room. Then he came back and sat down. He took a sip and set the cup back in its spot on the corner of his desk.

"How well did you know Mary Harris?" Tim began.

Dennis Lakey, amused by the question, smiled and shook his head. "I only knew of her from her personnel records. She went through a very stringent background check to receive a top-level clearance. That's because she was a temp and had access to all of our computer information."

Tim was confused. "You mean as head of the department, you never spoke to her?"

"Very few people actually spoke to her or even saw her. She preferred it that way."

Tim waited for the explanation.

"She worked alone at night when everyone else was gone. She had such a bad case of allergies, she didn't want to be around other people."

"How long did she work here?"

"About eight weeks. She spent all that time inputting information in the new computers, and integrating our old programs. She was supposed to spend her last week training me. But she died before she got around to it."

"Did she know anyone else here, or ever talk with anyone else?"

"Not that I'm aware of."

The cold air of the basement had been noticeable when Tim got off the elevator, but now, all of a sudden, he struggled to keep from sneezing and felt a chill.

"Next week we're supposed to have carpeting installed and some space heaters. That should help the working conditions a lot. Mary Harris is the one responsible for us being down here, which didn't exactly win her any friends."

Tim finally sneezed. "If she was such an oddball," he said with a sniff, "why was she hired?"

"To install the new computer system and program it," Dennis said matter-of-factly.

"No, I mean, why Mary Harris? There are other computer experts in Cleermantown, aren't there?"

"She was the best suited to our needs. She guaranteed a minimum downtime, because she was thorough and handled every phase of the operation herself. Her business presentation when she bid for the job impressed Mr. Clayton. And when he checked her references, he discovered her previous clients included some Fortune 500 companies."

"With qualifications like that, who needs a social life?" Tim said.

"Exactly," Dennis agreed. "The conditions of her contract didn't matter, as long as her prestigious clientele outshined the competition."

"Conditions?"

"Yeah, because of her allergies. One of the conditions was that she couldn't be around things that contained formaldehyde, which is why we're down here away from the new carpeting and wallpaper. And it's why we have these cold metal desks. Particleboard and adhesives used in most office furniture outgas formaldehyde fumes."

Tim nodded recalling the heavy expensive furniture he had seen in Mary Harris' apartment.

"I'm supposed to get a new desk next week," Dennis added. "It's hard to concentrate after finding her like that. I thought she was sleeping when I walked in and saw her facedown on my desk. I was about to touch her to wake her up, but then I saw her face all blue and bruised-looking. It was horrible. It took me forever to find Charlie and tell him to call 9-1-1." Dennis nodded in the direction of the bodyguard who'd escorted Tim and was still waiting by the door to show him the way out.

"Mary Harris even had her own clean-up crew," he continued. "Another condition of the contract was that when we hired her, we also hired her janitorial service. That way she could be sure her working environment wasn't cleaned with anything that would aggravate her allergies. A lot of disinfectants and cleaning products contain formaldehyde, you know."

"What's the name of this janitorial service?"

"I don't know." Dennis Lakey shrugged. "The cleaning woman worked at night most of the time also. But some of the ones who met her called her..." He cleared his throat. "They called her Trish-the-Dish. I have no idea why. I never met her either. But you can check at the front office and find out the name of our janitorial service."

With her peculiarities Mary Harris would've been an easier missing person to find than her roommate, Bernadette Higgins. And that was his last question for Dennis Lakey. "Ever hear the name Bernadette Higgins?"

Dennis thought as he sipped his coffee. "Doesn't ring a bell," he finally answered.

"She was Mary's roommate. She's the one I'm actually trying to locate." Tim stood up. "Thanks for taking the time to talk with me."

Dennis stood also and offered a parting handshake.

The man by the door came to attention.

"By the way," Dennis added, "Mr. Clayton told me to give you these things. He said you'd know what to do with them."

Tim took the large flat covered box.

And before he could ask what it was, Dennis explained. "The police came for Mary's car, but they didn't bother to get her personal things. This is the stuff she left here in the office and on my desk."

"Oh." Tim nodded. He didn't want Mary's stuff either. He didn't have any idea what to do with it, since she hadn't listed any living next-of-kin on any official documents. "I'll turn it over to her roommate," he said adding a note of optimism, "when I find her."

"Good luck!"

"Thanks," Tim said maneuvering the box so he could reach one of his business cards. "Please, call me," he said handing it to Dennis, "if you find out anything that might be helpful."

"Sure thing," Dennis said placing it on his desk.

Tim realized his business card would go the way of all business cards, because they were so common and taken for granted. However, when he asked at the front desk about the janitorial service, the woman gave him a business card advertising **Clean & Safe Janitorial Service** and listing Trisha Garing as the manager, along with her phone number.

Tim had once heard that everyone is only five contact people away from anyone else, which had the potential of making a missing person easy to find. But they had to be the right five people. And he was about to meet his third link in the Bernadette Higgins chain of contacts.

Chapter 7: Don't Think...Feel

It wasn't until late the next morning, day $25,000 in his calendar countdown to find Bernadette Higgins, that Tim finally spoke with Trisha Garing on the telephone. He had tried the whole previous evening, but kept hanging up on her answering machine.

He was about to hang up again when he heard a click and a sleepy voice mumbled, "Umm...yeah...good morning."

"Is this Ms. Garing of the Clean & Safe Janitorial Service?"

"Yes, it is," the voice answered in a more business-like tone. Tim pictured in his mind the owner of that voice pushing herself from a sprawled sleeping position to a semi-upright posture in the middle of a bed somewhere. "How can I help you?"

"I want to hire a janitorial service." It was a pretext, but it wasn't such a bad idea in light of the fact that Patty kept reminding him her job description didn't include cleaning.

"Business or residential?"

"Small business office," Tim answered.

"One time, occasional, or do you want cleaning service on a regular basis?"

"Umm...I'm not sure."

"Why don't you tell me where your business is located, and I could come and take a look. There are some forms to fill out and terms to discuss before I can figure out if I can fit you into my schedule."

Tim looked around at the empty office. Brent and Patty were out on a job, but they could return at any moment. And he didn't usually arrange to meet clients or interviewees at the office. "Could we discuss it at your office?"

Tim heard a grunt and figured Ms. Clean & Safe had gotten out of bed. "Tell you what—why don't we continue our discussion over...lunch?" And had looked at a clock.

Tim quickly glanced at his watch. It didn't leave him much time to study for his two o'clock test. He'd planned to skip lunch today and catch an early dinner afterwards. "Where?"

"Are you familiar with a restaurant called The Porthole on Twenty-third Street?"

"No, but I'll find it," Tim answered.

"Fine," she said. "What did you say your name was?"

"Tim MacCulfsky."

"I'll see you at noon, Mr. MacCulfsky."

"Right," Tim said and hung up. *Wrong.* How would he pick her out in a lunch crowd? Look for the woman with the worst case of dishpan hands?

Taking summer classes at the local community college had benefits. For one thing, he would have his degree in three years, instead of four, when he qualified for his New York State Private Investigator license. But there was a downside too. The teachers who taught summer semester classes felt a need to cram into less than two months, everything they normally spent three months teaching during the fall and spring semesters. Consequently, the tests were fewer, but covered much more material.

Tim spent the hour he had left reviewing the notes from his Criminal Behavior class and skimming the textbook. He hoped that meeting Trish-the-Dish for lunch would have a positive effect on his brain.

He arrived at The Porthole early and sat in a booth. He browsed the menu, but kept an eye on the door in order to have the advantage of assessing Trisha Garing before he actually spoke to her. People came and went. It was the lunch rush hour. He noticed several groups of office women, numerous couples, but no lone woman coming through the door, who looked as if she were meeting an appointment.

Minutes later, Tim glanced impatiently at his watch and then at the door. *Just like a woman—always late!* No sooner had he thought it, than he saw the attractive, dark-haired young woman who had been sitting in the booth across the aisle get up and walk over.

"You look as if you're waiting for someone," she said standing over him.

"Are you Clean & Safe...?" He felt his face flush. "Trisha Garing?" He quickly shoved out of the booth and stood next to her.

"Live and in your face," the young woman said smiling.

He took her hand and offered her the seat across from him. She was tall, he realized, as the top of her head came into view when she sat down. "I'm sorry I didn't notice you sitting there. You're not what...I mean...actually, I expected a much older woman, for some reason."

She laughed. "That's okay. You're not what I expected either." He felt her brown eyes examining him. "Your voice sounded so serious on the phone. I expected a Tommy Lee Jones-type."

"That would be my partner," Tim said with a smile. He never knew how to describe Brent and his behavior, until now.

The waitress came and took their orders. As Trisha Garing talked, Tim was amazed at how wrong his impression of her on the phone had been. He hadn't expected her nickname, Trish-the-Dish, to ring true. He'd thought it was probably a sarcastic reference to the stereotypical image of a cleaning lady with ragged clothes, stringy hair, and a bedraggled face.

"So..." Tim said losing track of his real purpose for meeting with Trisha Garing. "How did you get into the business of cleaning?"

"You want the long story, or the short version?"

"Why not begin with the short version?" Tim said amused.

"I saw a need, and decided to fill it."

"Good business strategy."

"What kind of business are you in?"

Tim cleared his throat. "I'm a private investigator."

"Oh." Trisha rolled her eyes and sighed in seeming disappointment. "Like we really need more cop-types in Cleermantown."

The sudden chill in her voice made him mindful of his business. The waitress brought their food and gave Tim a chance to collect his thoughts.

"We might as well get down to business," Trisha said. She took a sheet of paper and a pen from her purse and laid them next to her plate on the table. "How many square feet does your office include? And is it upstairs or a ground floor?" She took a bite and waited for his answer while she chewed.

"Three thousand square feet, and it's a ground floor office," Tim said. He began eating also. "Do you like janitorial work?"

Trisha quickly took up her pen and wrote down his answers. "It's a living." She said keeping her eyes on her paper while she talked and ate.

"Seriously," Tim pursued, "what made you choose this line of work?"

Trisha shrugged and met his eyes with hers. "What made you decide to be a private investigator?"

Tim smiled as he recalled the original fascination of finding his own birth parents. "I guess I thought it would be my chance to make a difference in this world. You know, find missing people, solve cases."

Trisha's brown eyes were attentive when he looked at her. "You don't sound so sure anymore." She continued eating, but kept her eyes on him.

"I've decided to be a civil lawyer instead."

"More money in that field," Trisha agreed.

"It's not the money," Tim said. "It's less direct involvement with people."

"You don't like people?"

"I don't like being involved in other people's personal lives," he said.

"Oh, I see." Trisha's short brown hair curved around her ears and Tim found himself admiring them. "You don't like personal involvement."

"I didn't say that exactly." Tim sat back. He was finished eating. "I mean most people that I meet in P.I. work aren't the kind I want to know personally. They're all deadbeats, or jumped parole, or cheating on their spouse, or trying to defraud their insurance company."

"But doesn't being a lawyer require more years of college?" Trisha asked. She tipped her head to one side and smiled at him. "Like being a doctor."

"I have plenty of time," Tim decided. He smiled at her.

"And plenty of money?"

"What about you?" he asked. "Are you working your way through college?"

"I always wanted to be a nurse." Trisha looked down at her hands. "But I don't like school. I guess that's why I like cleaning."

Her neat appearance and mannerisms made Tim think that cleaning had been a more natural choice than she realized.

"Are you attending college now?" she asked.

Tim nodded. "The community college here in town."

"And you think that being a lawyer will involve you with a better caliber of people?" she asked cynically.

Tim shrugged. "At least not on such a personal level."

Trisha cleared her throat and looked at the paper next to her plate. "This large office of yours on the ground floor," she continued. "Does it include a bathroom or kitchen arrangement? Describe it for me."

"Yes," Tim answered. "Now tell me your long story."

"Yes, what?"

"Yes, it includes a bathroom and a kitchen."

"Cleaning a bathroom and a kitchen will require a more routine schedule, you know." She was focused now, but Tim detected the uncertainty of a young woman new to running her own business.

"No, I didn't know that." Tim propped his arms on the small table and leaned closer to her. "What about the long story?"

"You don't want to hear the sordid details of my personal life," Trisha said with a beguiling smile.

"Those are exactly the kind of details I want to hear." Tim smiled back at her.

"That could lead to personal involvement." She looked down, finally taking her eyes from his.

Personal involvement sounded exciting when she said it. Tim's heart skipped a beat when he glanced over her head at the clock on the wall. "Holy smoke!" he said suddenly. "I have a test in twenty minutes. I didn't realize it was getting so late."

He scooted out of the booth and reached over and left a tip on the table. "We need to talk some more," he said realizing he hadn't accomplished his real purpose. "Can I walk you to your car?"

"No, that's okay," Trisha said. "You go ahead and don't be late." She started gathering her things.

"Listen. I'll call you." Tim hesitated despite his urgency. "It was really nice meeting you."

Trisha touched his hand with hers, and he felt a soft warm pressure that pulsated up his arm. "I enjoyed it too," she said.

Tim turned and left. Later he slapped his forehead in frustration. He hadn't even mentioned Mary Harris or Bernadette Higgins. And that small oversight was going to cost him another grand.

Chapter 8: The Good Lord Loves You

The case of the missing grand prize winner with the
deceased roommate came to a grinding halt, as did
everything else in Tim's life. He left a number of
questions unanswered on his Criminal Behavior test,
but passed it. He left all the questions unanswered
with his Clean & Safe-Janitorial-Service lead, and it
cost him. Trisha Garing was still his best opportunity
to probe Mary Harris' personal life, but since her
answering machine was the end result of all his phone
calls Wednesday evening and all day Thursday, Tim
decided to pursue another lead.

Mary Harris' Last Will and Testament was not yet
on file at the county court house. So he called the
lawyer firm advertised on one of the pens he'd found at
the apartment of Mary Harris and Bernadette Higgins.

"My name is Timothy MacCulfsky. I'm an
investigator with IRISH EYES Private Investigative
Service. Would you set me up with an appointment to
see Jack Rosenthall?"

Patty was busy typing at her desk. Brent signaled
Tim a thumbs-up, which meant his phone influence
was improving.

But apparently not enough to impress the receptionist at Rosenthall and Associates Lawyers Firm. "I can arrange an appointment with one of Mr. Rosenthall's associates next week. How does Thursday at ten o'clock sound?"

"I need to speak with Mr. Rosenthall himself, as soon as possible, on a matter of urgency. I would be willing to meet him on the golf course, if necessary."

"Please hold!" He was past the receptionist.

Tim pinched his knuckles and waited to see if his matter of urgency would carry any weight with an important personage such as Rosenthall.

"He can see you tomorrow at nine-thirty," the receptionist said when she returned. "Will that do?"

"Yes, thank you." Actually, he'd been hoping for an immediate audience with Mary Harris' lawyer.

The abrupt click let him know he needed to brush up on his Dale Carnegie course in *How to Win Friends and Influence People* before his next confrontation over the phone.

"How's it going, Kid?" Brent was in his usual precarious position of tipping back in his office chair, but not yet asleep.

Tim swiveled his own chair around to view the nearly empty bulletin board behind his desk. "Not much to go on, yet. But it's building. I have a couple of leads."

"I thought you'd have it solved by now."

"So did I," Tim said.

"Have you considered sticking those tacks into a voodoo doll instead of your bulletin board," Brent said with his eyes closed, "and listening for someone to scream 'ouch!'"

Patty picked up one of the heavier stuffed animal toys she had arranged across the back of her desk, a recent craze in collectibles, and tossed it at Brent.

"So that's how you solve your cases!" Tim said swiveling back around in time to watch the action. "No wonder you wanted to partner with me."

"Ouch!" Brent yelled when the Beanie Baby landed on his lap.

"Careful," Patty warned. "It's worth more than you are."

"So marry it," Brent said sitting up and landing his chair on its wheels.

"I'm not after money."

"Obviously," Brent said. "You prefer good sex and good looks."

Patty gave a hand and eye signal to Brent that Tim couldn't interpret, although it had something to do with him or his general vicinity.

"By the way, if you're free tonight," Brent directed at Tim, "why don't you...I mean, we'd like to have you over for dinner."

"Let's see..." Tim said. The light atmosphere had suddenly gone heavy with Brent's formal invitation. "I have several very important engagements," he feigned, "but for you, maybe I could break away early, if it's important."

"It's important to Patty," Brent said squirming in his chair. "And to me," he added when Patty gave him one of those looks that only a redheaded woman is capable of.

"Then I guess that settles it," Tim said, letting Brent off the hook. "What time?"

"Five o'clock," Patty answered.

"Sure," Tim said. "I get out of class today at three. I can make it."

"Bring your swim suit," Brent added. "We'll spend some time relaxing in the hot tub."

Tim tried calling Trisha Garing again. And while the phone was ringing, an airborne Beanie Baby landed in the middle of Patty's desk on some papers, causing them to scoot across and end up on the floor. Brent clasped his hands behind his head, closed his eyes, and leaned back comfortably in his chair.

Trisha Garing's answering machine clicked on, and Tim hung up. He needed to talk to her in person and, this time, he wouldn't forget his purpose. Business and pleasure don't mix, especially in the P.I. business.

Tim met Clarence and Waldo for lunch at their usual table at the Sidewalk Café. But, as soon as he was done eating, he left and drove to The Porthole. He went inside and looked down the long list of names on the sign-in sheet the hostess used for seating people during the busy lunch hour. No Trisha Garing, or Clean & Safe—not even close!

"How many in your party?" the hostess asked him.

"I changed my mind," Tim answered and left.

He took the time to stop and buy a wildflower bouquet at the florist shop on his way to Patty's house. Actually, it was Brent's house also. It didn't require a rocket scientist to discover that they were living together.

"For me?" Brent asked in mock coquetry when he opened the door. "You shouldn't have."

"I didn't," Tim said as he came inside. "They're for Patty."

"You're so thoughtful," Patty said taking them from him. "Unlike some people I know." She arranged them in a vase on the table already set for dinner. She closed her eyes and inhaled deeply. Tim had already noticed that wildflowers don't have much of a scent. "And they look so beautiful, perfect for the occasion."

The table was set for a more formal occasion than Tim had expected. Previous evenings that included a dip in the hot tub had always entailed cooking on the grill and lounging on the deck. "What's the occasion?" Tim ventured.

"Let's get in the tub and relax," Brent offered.

"Leave the sliding door open so I can hear the timer," Patty said as she took off her robe and slipped into the warm water. "Dinner will be ready in an hour."

Tim noticed a bottle of champagne cooling in a bucket of ice cubes near the edge where Brent was slipping in beside Patty. "What's the occasion?" he repeated.

"We're celebrating," Patty said smiling and wafting her hand under his nose.

Brent turned and poured some champagne into three fancy glasses and handed one to Tim.

"No thanks."

"Can't you make an exception to your teetotaling morals for a special occasion?" Brent asked. "A little bubbly won't hurt you, even if you are underage. We'll keep you here overnight, if you're so afraid of getting caught."

Tim felt a little embarrassed, but held his ground. Patty usually supported him in his moral standoffs, but she looked uncomfortable.

"Hey, I'm sorry. But I can celebrate just as well without it."

"And you wanted me to pick him for my best man?" Brent said looking at Patty.

Best man? "You're getting married?"

Patty wafted her hand in front of Tim's nose again. This time he noticed the ring with the oversized diamond.

"I didn't think you had it in you," Tim said to Brent.

"Well, I don't think you have it in you to be my best man," Brent returned crossly.

"BRENT WEAVER!" Patty reprimanded. "You were the one who said you were proud of him, like a son."

Brent avoided Tim's eyes.

"Come on! Admit it," Patty prodded.

"Yeah, okay. I said that." Brent finally softened. "It's just that I didn't realize I'd have a nineteen-year-old virgin who doesn't drink, in charge of planning my bachelor party."

Tim felt his face turn a deep blistering red.

"BRENT WEAVER," Patty yelled again. "You should be ashamed of yourself for embarrassing the best friend you have in this world. You said that too. Remember?"

Brent lowered the glass in his hand without drinking it.

"One thing I know is, I hope when my girls settle down and decide to get married, they find a good young man like Tim." Patty raised her glass in a toast.

Brent grunted and raised his glass toward Tim.

Tim took the glass that had been offered to him and poured the champagne back into the bottle. Then he raised his empty glass. "To good friends," he said.

Chapter 9: Free Life

Friday morning marked several occasions, which Tim pondered as he ran around the field track at Cleermantown High School. One week had passed since taking the Bernadette Higgins missing person case. He was at the $23,000 mark now. He'd also reached the halfway point in his summer semester classes at the local community college. And it was the morning after Brent and Patty announced their engagement. He knew they'd be late coming into work. They both drank quite a bit of champagne last night.

Brent and Patty still hadn't made an appearance when Tim came downstairs after his shower. He picked up the phone receiver at his desk and pressed the redial button. It was becoming a habit with him after two days. So much so that Trisha's voice caught him off guard when she picked up instead of her answering machine.

"You're home," he announced ineptly.

"Who is this?"

"Tim MacCulfsky."

"Tim MacCulfsky?"

"Yeah, we had lunch together the other day at The Porthole," he said.

"I remember."

Tim breathed a sigh of relief. "We didn't get much business accomplished."

"Whose fault is that?"

"Would you mind meeting with me again?"

"Listen," Trisha replied. "I get the impression you're not really interested in having your office cleaned. What do you want?"

"I want to talk to you." At least that wasn't a pretext. Tim easily pictured her face.

"You could've just said so, instead of hanging up on my answering machine two hundred times."

"You're exaggerating," Tim said enticed by her playful voice. "It was more like one hundred and ninety-nine times."

Trisha laughed.

"How did you know it was me?" Tim asked. "Caller I.D.?"

"Yeah," she replied. "Helps me weed out the weirdoes. They come with the territory."

Tim recalled the nickname she'd acquired at Clayton's Investment and Finance Corporation—Trish-the-Dish—and how her stately height and attractiveness would quite likely bring out the worst in low examples of his own gender. "Can we...talk?" he asked.

"Go ahead," she said, her voice teasing him. "I'm listening."

"No, I mean..." Tim faltered. "Not over the phone."

"Stop screwing around then. If you want to ask me out on a date, just do it. If not, say good bye."

Tim glanced around with the phone hugged against his ear. He was glad Brent and Patty weren't around to see him now. "Okay," he said. "Do you want to go out tomorrow night?"

"Sure," she answered quickly. "What time?"

"Five o'clock. For dinner."

"Fine."

"Where do you live?" he asked.

"Why don't I meet you somewhere?"

"Where?"

"I need to pick up some supplies at the Better Bio Natural Products Store. Why don't we meet there? Are you familiar with it? It's just down the street from The Porthole."

Tim was trying to hold the phone and write down the information at the same time. "Okay," he said. "I'll meet you there tomorrow at five."

"Wait. What should I wear? Where are we going?"

"Fancy?"

"Love it!"

"Good. We'll eat at a fancy restaurant and then take in a movie."

"Sounds great. See you then."

Tim hung up. He tried to convince himself it wasn't really a date. It was part of his job. But it felt like a date. He remembered the way Trisha Garing looked at The Porthole in more detail than he wanted to. It was one of the benefits that came with a job requiring highly developed powers of observation.

Tim headed out the door and met Brent and Patty coming in from the parking lot. "Will you be back later today?" Patty asked. "We need to go over your expense account."

"Sure," Tim said. "I don't have anything after meeting with Mary Harris' lawyer."

"Still haven't come up with anything solid on that sweepstakes winner," Brent observed.

"Today or tomorrow should clinch it," Tim said.

"Good," Brent said. "We got something cooking with security at the college. They're cracking down on cheating this fall and want someone to devise a detection plan for the high-tech surveillance equipment some of these rich kids are using nowadays. And also the computer tap-ins selling test answers. I recommended you. I told them you were their man."

Brent obviously wasn't taking him seriously about quitting the P.I. business and this being his last case. "We'll talk about it," Tim said.

He drove downtown and parked in the city lot where he always parked when meeting Clarence for lunch. Rosenthall and Associates Law Firm occupied one of the newly renovated, exclusive buildings not far from the Sidewalk Café.

"I have an appointment with Jack Rosenthall," Tim informed the receptionist when he entered.

She must've recognized his voice from the memorable exchange they'd carried on yesterday. "Mr. Rosenthall has been delayed in court," she said. "You may wait in his office, Mr. MacCulfsky." She led the way and then left Tim in a room that didn't look like a lawyer's office. It looked like a jungle, and he felt like he'd been abandoned in the middle of a big game hunt.

The green and brown textured wallpaper gave the impression of the inside of a grass hut. Large-leafed plants grew out of huge tubs and reached from floor to ceiling, blocking most of the natural sunlight in front of the windows. Fluorescent lighting in the ceiling made up the difference. Several exquisite life-size paintings of animals stalking in their natural jungle habitat hung on the walls and gave Tim an eerie feeling as he moved, and their eyes moved with him.

A large glass terrarium drew him to the far wall where a giant lizard was sunning itself under a bright light while clinging to a branch with its strangely shaped feet. Its eyes moved independently of each other and, without alarm, scrutinized Tim as he approached the glass. The creature was thoroughly repulsive were it not for the stunning pattern of brilliant hues on its eighteen-inch scaly body. Tim was relieved to see that its diet consisted of fruit as it hungrily gorged on pieces of banana.

Tim turned his attention to a curio cabinet filled with exotic trinkets and framed snapshots. They were not the average family-man variety of wife, kids and pets. The snapshots, instead, captured a life of adventure and danger—Mr. Rosenthall in safari attire trailing a group of native pack-carriers, Mr. Rosenthall with a rifle poised and ready, Mr. Rosenthall posing beside a vanquished beast. Surely Jack Rosenthall was not the kind of lawyer Mary would've picked. It seemed more likely that Bernadette Higgins had dealings with him. Tim was confident his luck was about to change.

"Timothy MacCulfsky." The subject of the curio cabinet snapshots briskly entered the room and helped himself to some coffee on a stand near his desk. "Would you like some coffee?" he offered and shut the door.

"No, thank you." Tim quickly sat down in a comfortable chair in front of the desk as Mr. Rosenthall stretched out and relaxed in the chair behind it.

"You, of course, don't mind if I record our conversation." Mr. Rosenthall pressed a button, and the tape was rolling whether Tim minded or not.

It seemed a bit melodramatic, but Tim nodded. This would be a simple question and answer session, lasting no more than fifteen minutes. But a man of Rosenthall's stature couldn't be too careful these days.

"And you realize, of course, that I am prepared to use anything you might say today to defend my client in court, should that possibility arise during our conversation."

"Court?" Tim never used profanity. In fact, he usually didn't even think it. But *Holy shit!* was the first thing that popped into his head when he realized who he was talking to. No wonder the name on the pen had stuck in his mind. It had struck a familiar subconscious chord, because his subconscious was the only part of his mind he couldn't keep from thinking about the Mark Lander murder. Fortunately, he didn't say what he was thinking.

"As Larry Howzinski's defense attorney, this is normal procedure any time I talk to a witness for the prosecution."

Tim felt himself perspiring, and he mentally kicked himself for having refused to stay up on the details of the murder case in which he was deeply involved. He was still in denial and hadn't yet recovered from witnessing the murder of a twelve-year-old boy.

"It's a safety measure for you, Timothy, as well as myself."

"For the record," Tim said, "I am refraining from any reference to the case you just mentioned. I'm here on an entirely different matter."

"Very well, Timothy," Mr. Rosenthall said. "Go ahead."

Tim's heartbeat was returning to normal. He took a small notepad and pen from his pocket and began talking. "I've been employed by a large international travel agency to ascertain the whereabouts of Ms. Bernadette Higgins, who is a grand prize winner in the sweepstakes they recently sponsored." While he talked, he made a note to himself at the top of the paper, *make an appointment to begin pre-trial training.*

"And you think she might be a client of mine?" Mr. Rosenthall assisted.

"I've drawn a blank on every lead. Her roommate, Mary Harris, recently died.

"I'm aware of that fact."

Bingo! Tim thought. Now he just needed to ask the right questions, which was often made difficult by client confidentiality. But since Mary's Last Will and Testament would soon be a matter of public record in probate court, Mr. Rosenthall was willing to discuss the pertinent details and the interview went smoothly.

Mary had insisted on retaining Rosenthall himself to draw up her will, despite the fact that his specialty was criminal law, not civil matters. And that was only the beginning of her eccentric wishes. Mary had no living close relatives. There was no mention whatsoever of Bernadette Higgins, which threw her questionable relationship with Mary into a different light. And the bulk of Mary's estate, which amounted to precious little in a bank account after the rest of her wishes were carried out, would transfer to the account of Trisha Garing.

Interesting, Tim decided, but not unusual, since they had a mutually beneficial business arrangement. Now Trisha Garing moved to top priority in the Bernadette Higgins missing person case for several reasons. And Tim told himself it was strictly business between them.

Mary's body had been cremated in an unattended ceremony, and her remains scattered from an airplane over the Amazon Jungle of South America. A fitting request, not as eccentric as it would at first seem to a non-acquaintance, from a person who spent so much time working alone in the night because of sensitivities and who was allergic to the primary ingredient in embalming fluid.

At the end of their meeting, Rosenthall and Tim had become congenial—a factor, Tim realized, that could work against him when they met in court on opposite sides of the witness stand in the near future.

Chapter 10: Dig In

Tim left Jack Rosenthall's office thinking about Trisha Garing. He began formulating the questions he needed to ask her. The lead-in would need to be handled with delicacy. She was expecting a date, and all he wanted was answers.

As he walked along the sidewalk, mentally rehearsing the various avenues the conversation could take, he passed a men's clothing store. He hadn't thought about what he should wear tomorrow night, not that it was a great concern. But it had been a while since his last date, more than a year ago now. He'd been going steady before his parents' fatal car crash. Everything in his life broke up after that.

Tim entered the men's store. It was better to be on the safe side, he decided. His dressing habits had slipped into a routine mode of comfort. It was time to break out of his preferred pattern and get with the latest.

In Tim's mind there were two ways to shop—take his time and buy what he wanted, or buy the latest trend in clothes, which was quicker and easier. He went with the latter choice. He picked the mannequin in the store window that looked the most like himself, and then matched everything from the shelves and the racks right down to the shoes. It was the safe way to dress for a first date, but expensive. Since this date was purely business, he could charge it to his expense account.

With no other concerns on his mind, Tim met Clarence at the Sidewalk Café for lunch as usual. It was nice having a friend that expected nothing from him except friendship. Waldo sniffed the shopping bags when Tim set them next to the table.

"What's new?" Clarence asked.

"Shopping." Tim knew he'd better explain the bags first.

"That's obvious," Clarence commented. "But when a man goes shopping, it's usually the precursor to a big event."

"Not so big." Tim smiled. The old man's keen perception was supernatural at times. "I have a date tomorrow night, but it's purely business. The missing person case I'm working on."

"All dates are purely business. Didn't you know that?"

Tim laughed. "But this one really is. Trust me. I don't have time right now to be involved in anything but school work and trying to clear up the mess this P.I. business has gotten my life into."

They ate lunch and went their separate ways.

Tim returned to IRISH EYES. Brent was asleep in his chair and Patty was busy determining their mid-year income statement. She balanced the books twice a year and it usually necessitated endless phone calls to chase down former clients who were delinquent in their payments.

Another aspect of the P.I. business he didn't like was collecting money from people who felt investigators didn't deserve it. The difficulty was in convincing people that catching their wandering spouses in the act of adultery was hard work, or that uncovering a fraud was not a volunteer service to the community.

Tim managed to get himself and his shopping bags up the stairs to his apartment without any comment from Brent. And he hung up his new slacks and short-sleeve tailored shirt to take out the wrinkles. He wasn't sure what he should do with the colorful boxers, which the clerk had told him was the latest in men's underwear. He'd wear them, but he was glad no one would see them.

Patty was absorbed in her work when he settled at his desk and prepared to spend the afternoon reading the assignment for his Forensic Science class. But Brent's snoring distracted him and Patty was frustrated. Tim wheeled his chair quietly to Patty's desk and picked up one of the stuffed toys and tossed it at Brent. The Beanie Baby made a precision landing on Brent's chest. And he responded by swiping at it with his hand and then resuming his nap.

"Need help?" Tim asked Patty.

She usually declined his offers to help. "Yes, actually," she said, "it would be a big help if you'd read off these amounts to me while I check them in the journal. I made a mistake somewhere, and I can't figure it out."

Tim spent the afternoon working with Patty until they had the books balanced. As a result, he decided not to charge his new clothes to his expense account. "Would you mind helping me with something?"

"Sure," Patty said, feeling relieved that the job was finally done. "What is it?"

"I bought some new clothes to wear tomorrow on an interview. Would you mind telling me what you think?"

Patty followed him upstairs after stretching the kinks out of her back. "What kind of interview?"

Tim shrugged. "Dinner at a fancy restaurant and a movie afterwards."

"Interview?" she said confused. "That sounds more like a date."

"Just a pretext. I need to interview the cleaning lady who worked with Mary Harris, Bernadette Higgins' roommate."

"Since when do you worry about what to wear on an interview?"

"Since the interviewee thinks it's a date, and I don't want her to think otherwise," Tim answered.

"I'll be interested to hear how you pull that off," Patty said.

Tim showed her his purchases, which she approved by holding them in front of him to visualize the full effect. "If I were just twenty-five years younger! What does this cleaning lady look like?"

"Not like a cleaning lady."

Patty nodded and Tim could tell she was restraining herself from further comment. "Which restaurant and which movie?" she finally asked.

Tim shrugged.

"Wrong!"

"What d'ya' mean, wrong?" Tim hung the clothes in his closet again.

"Girls like decisiveness. Trust me on this."

"But I want to let her help decide."

"Big mistake," Patty said. She sat down at the kitchen table and Tim sat across from her. "She won't be able to make up her mind if you leave the decision to her, first of all. What's her name, anyway?"

"Trish-the...Trisha."

"And, second of all, if the evening goes well, Trisha will think it's because she made all the decisions. Whereas, if you decide, she'll think you're very knowledgeable and sophisticated in such matters."

"And what if the whole evening sucks?" Tim asked.

"She'll blame you no matter what, if it doesn't go well. Even if she decides where to go and what to do."

"Why should I care what she thinks?" Tim asked. "It's just an interview, for Pete's sake!"

"Then why a FANCY restaurant and a movie afterwards?"

Patty had him on that one.

"Get the phone book," she instructed.

Tim got up and brought it to her.

She looked up *restaurant* in the yellow pages. "Here are your choices for a fancy restaurant. The Cattle Ranch is known for its outdoor wood-burning grilled steaks. The Seafood Inn is known for its seafood, of course. And The Japanese Garden is known for its traditional Japanese cuisine, which includes removing your shoes and sitting cross-legged on cushions on the floor. That would be a lot of fun for a date. Plus they keep you busy with all the different courses of food."

The Japanese Garden appealed to Tim's sense of adventure.

"But since it's an interview and not a date, you better go with something dull like—"

"The Japanese Garden sounds perfect," Tim said.

"Unless you have foot odor or a bum knee," Patty added. "Brent does."

"Which?" Tim asked, curious.

"Both," Patty answered.

"Bummer." Great ammunition to use against Brent if the occasion ever presented itself.

"He has other redeeming qualities," Patty added.

"Such as?"

"If you were a woman, you wouldn't have to ask."

Tim couldn't remember his mother ever talking to him like that, or offering him dating advice of any sort. He wished she had. "What about the movie?"

"A movie afterwards makes for a LONG evening," Patty teased. "You sure this is just an interview?"

"I'm sure," Tim said quickly, but a blush had already betrayed him.

"Pick the theater nearest the restaurant. Memorize what movies are playing and at what time. That will really impress her. But let her pick which movie she would enjoy watching with you."

Tim nodded and decided to use all of Patty's advice.

"Then after the movie...well, I'm sure you can figure it out from there." She looked at her watch. "It's time to take Sleeping Beauty home." She started down the stairs and turned to add, "Good luck on your...ahem... interview tomorrow."

"Thanks."

Tim heard Brent and Patty leave out the door moments later. He spent the rest of the evening working on his research paper. Homicide by poisoning was a fascinating topic.

Chapter 11: The Last Thing on My Mind

Saturday passed slowly. Any other Saturday, when he had plenty to do, time went much too quickly. But today was different, and he kept telling himself there was no reason for it to be different. He kept returning to the mirror to check himself out. But each time, he looked the same as when he checked a few minutes earlier, except a little more nervous. It was going to be hard to keep from pinching his knuckles, his nervous habit from earliest childhood.

Tim looked at his watch. One hour to go. He considered undressing and doing it all over again just to use up time and to make sure he had no reason to be nervous. Patty had a misguided faith in him that he could do nothing wrong. He checked his breath, took a whiff of his armpits, removed his shoes, and found no offensiveness.

However, with Patty in mind Tim decided to leave early and see if he could find something for her fit-into-the-wedding-dress diet she'd started. First he looked all around the Better Bio Natural Products Store to see if Trisha was there. She wasn't. So he began next, looking at the cans on the shelves in the diet section. And he quickly became confused.

A clerk came to his rescue, and Tim explained the need of his secretary. But unfortunately he became even more lost in her description of the benefits of each item. "Thanks," Tim finally said. "I think I'll just let her get what she needs herself."

"This really works." The long fingers with painted nails belonged to Trisha. "And they're convenient. Just pop them open and drink like a milkshake, just like in the commercials."

Tim was aware of her tall slim figure. And she was wearing loose slacks in a dark shade of rose, topped by a tunic-style, Japanese-print, silk blouse. One side of her dark hair was swept back and held in place by an Oriental comb. "How did you know?" he asked. The intuitive perception that all women seemed to cultivate and use to manipulate men suddenly gave him a scary sensation in the pit of his stomach. Now he wasn't just nervous.

"I've tried it," Trisha explained. "It'll really curb the appetite if you know her favorite flavor."

"No, I mean, how did you know I was planning to take you to The Japanese Garden restaurant?"

"I didn't," Trisha said. "This outfit was a gift from a friend, and tonight was the first opportunity I've had to wear it." She smiled. "Now I know."

Trisha was easy to talk to, and her voice was reassuring. "What's your friend's favorite flavor?" she asked, returning her attention to the shelf in front of them.

Tim had to think a moment as he looked over the flavors on the labels. "She likes Swiss mocha flavored coffee. But for dessert she always orders strawberry shortcake or banana cream pie."

"You know a lot about your friend," Trisha said as she pointed to the strawberry banana flavor. "This will be perfect. Replace her dessert cravings."

"She's my partner's fiancee, and our secretary," Tim explained. "And the three of us eat together a lot."

"And it's your business to know about people," Trisha added with an understanding smile.

"How many of these should I buy?" he asked.

"Just a couple until you see if she likes it." She placed the cans in his hands. "And try a chocolate flavor," she said leading him. She took the cans from him when they reached her cart. Tim pushed it for her as she walked down the aisle and put in her own groceries.

"Here's some munchies your friend can try. Full of flavor and almost no calories," she said tossing in a box. "I suppose you did a background check on me to see if I'm suitable dating material."

He could've said that was standard operating procedure in his line of work, but Tim didn't, because he hadn't. "No. I prefer you tell me all about yourself. It's more fun that way."

"I like fun," she said.

"So do I."

"Then what are we waiting for? Let's get out of here."

Tim put Trisha's groceries in the trunk of her car for her, and they drove away in his car. At The Japanese Garden the Oriental hostess asked, "Traditional seating or American?"

Tim looked at Trisha and then whispered in her ear, "Do you have a bum knee, or foot odor?"

"Neither." She smiled and turned toward him, brushing her cheek against his lips. "Is that a P.I. question?"

"Traditional seating please," Tim said to the hostess. He slipped his arm around Trisha's waist to guide her through the crowd of customers waiting to be seated. "It was a personal question," he whispered. "Just for fun."

The hostess, wearing an elegant kimono and sandals, led them with tiny steps to a screen-partitioned room. With a slight bow and a graceful motion of her hands, she said, "Please remove shoes before entering," and left them.

With his arm still around Trisha's waist, Tim's hand slipped low and he felt the strong muscles in her back when she bent over to remove her shoes. He helped her lower herself to a cushion on the floor next to a table only inches high. Then he sat down and crossed his legs on the other side.

Immediately a waiter was at his side to offer refreshment. "Sakei?"

"No, thank you," Tim responded. The table was so tiny he could almost touch noses with Trisha.

When the waiter asked her, Trisha nodded. And Tim realized that eating with chopsticks was not his only challenge for the night. The New York legal age limit for drinking placed her at least two years older than himself, something he hadn't considered until now.

But his worries quickly dissipated while they talked and ate. As they made their way through the appetizers, Tim discovered they had many common likes and dislikes. Trisha was opinionated about food, people, clothing, and politics. But she had an easy and honest way of expressing herself that he enjoyed very much.

They shared and laughed through the whole meal. And Tim found himself being drawn out of the self-imposed solitude he preferred. He hadn't expected Trisha to be someone with whom he'd enjoy spending time.

Appropriately, as the meal came to an end and they opened their fortune cookies, they were discussing their goals in life. "Read yours first," Trisha said.

"I don't put any faith in these," Tim said. But he picked up the crumpled piece of paper and read, "Your life is about to take an unexpected twist."

"Hmmmm!"

"Hmmmm what?" Tim tossed the fortune on his plate. "It's so generic, an unexpected twist could mean anything." But it made him think about the Bernadette Higgins missing person case, and the fact that it had unexpectedly led him on a date with a girl he liked very much.

Trisha pulled her fortune from her cookie and read it out loud. "To enter a room, you must first leave another."

"Hmmmm!" Tim said observing her reaction with interest. "Anything you want to leave behind?"

"Yeah, plenty!" she answered. "How about this place for starters?"

Tim stood up slowly, regaining the circulation in his legs. Then he helped Trisha to her feet.

"Can we just stand here a minute?" She clung to his arm and drew close against him. "My leg went to sleep."

Tim put his arms around her and supported her. They had been sitting and eating a long time, and his digestion went into shock from overload. "I ate too much."

"Oriental food is very heavy," she agreed.

They just stood for several minutes, and Tim could feel the warmth of her body transferring to his hands through the silky material of her blouse. "Think you can walk yet?" he asked.

She nodded and took several steps to where they had left their shoes. The waiter returned with Tim's credit card, and he signed the receipt. It was still daylight when they walked to his car, and Tim looked at his watch. He'd memorized the movie schedule of the nearby theater.

Trisha adjusted her seatbelt and he started the engine. "What kind of movies do you like?"

"Any kind," she answered quickly. "Depending on my mood."

"What's your mood?" he asked playfully. "Horror?" She made a face.

"Action-packed suspense? Thrilling drama?"

Trisha shook her head and her glossy chestnut hair glistened.

"Epic adventure?" Tim continued. "Romance?"

"Romance," she decided.

"I was afraid of that," Tim said as he backed out of the parking space and drove down the street. "Better grab some tissues out of the glove box."

"Why?" she asked. "Do you cry at movies?"

"I just might, thinking about the test I'm gonna flunk Monday if I don't study like heck tomorrow."

"Well, thanks," Trisha said icily, "for making the ultimate sacrifice."

Tim noticed the change and recalled a previous lesson in feminine psychology—unpredictable emotional impact. "Sorry," he said glancing at her while he stopped at a traffic light. "I didn't mean to spoil the evening. I won't talk about school again."

"It's okay," she said. She reached over and removed the holder that held his hair back in a ponytail. She ran her fingers through his hair and undid the top button of his shirt with her other hand. "There. Now you can relax."

Arriving at the theater an hour before the movie started, they used the bathrooms and played video games while they waited. They were at the head of the line when the doors opened, and they found seats toward the front in the middle section where the surround sound system would be the most effective.

"Did you know," Trisha said while positioning herself in her seat so she could lean toward Tim, "that movies nowadays are a complete sensual experience?"

Tim looked into her dark brown mischievous eyes, enhanced by the dim lighting, and wondered if she was setting him up for a joke or something else entirely.

"Subliminal suggestion is unethical," she continued. It makes everyone run out to the concession stand for popcorn and coke. But if you really pay attention during a movie, you'll notice smells that are released through the ventilation system."

"Really?" Tim said positioning himself comfortably. He put his arm on the back of her chair.

"During a New York City street scene, you can smell essence of air pollution. During a picnic-in-the-forest scene, you'll smell essence of pine and moss. A restaurant scene, you'll smell food. A shooting scene, you'll smell—"

"I get the idea," Tim interrupted. He knew all too well what an actual shooting scene smelled like, having survived one. "How do you know this kind of stuff?" he asked skeptically.

"I read it somewhere."

The previews of the upcoming attractions started and Tim settled his arm around Trisha's shoulders. Halfway through the movie he became aware that she was groping for his other hand in the dark, so he held her hand. Then she snuggled close and laid her head against his neck. He decided not to interpret any meaning from the signals she relayed by gently squeezing his hand now and then throughout the rest of the movie.

"I told you to bring some tissues," Tim said after the movie was over.

Trisha sniffed. "I never cry at movies."

The soundtrack played as the credits rolled on the screen.

"Must be essence of onion in the ventilation system," Tim said leaning over her and helping her to her feet.

Trisha playfully punched him and, when he bent over to protect himself, she kissed him. It caught him off guard, and he stood momentarily savoring her taste and wondering what to do next.

He led her out the theater door, and they got in his car. He turned on the engine and the headlights, and, all too quickly, he'd driven back to where her car was parked in front of the Better Bio Natural Products Store. He got out and opened Trisha's door for her.

They stood together just beyond the circle of light cast by the lone streetlight at the corner.

"I had a good time," Trisha said starting to move toward her car.

"I did too," Tim said. He caught her hand and walked slowly beside her. "I need to talk to you again tomorrow."

She smiled. "You sound desperate." Then she added, "What's wrong with tonight?"

"Not tonight," Tim said realizing he'd given her an unintentional meaning by his actions and words. His purely-business date that was supposed to be an interview had taken an unexpected twist. It had gone in the wrong direction, but he was enjoying himself too much to spoil it. "Lunch tomorrow at The Porthole?"

"Okay." She unlocked her car door and Tim opened it.

He didn't like having to leave her at the door of her car instead of the door of her house. "Do you want me to follow you and make sure you get home safely?"

"I'm a big girl," she said. "I work the night shift. I do this all the time."

He pulled her close and touched her lips lightly with his, but he could tell she wanted more. They kissed again, and it lasted for several minutes. They parted breathless.

Trisha fondled his hair. "Tomorrow." She got into her car, and Tim watched her drive away.

Chapter 12: I've Been This Way Before

Trisha was the last thing Tim thought about
Saturday night before drifting off to sleep. And she was
the first thing on his mind when his alarm clock
roused him Sunday morning. He felt apprehensive that
his feelings for Trisha were increasing so fast. And at
the same time, he felt relief when he didn't think about
anything else. Nevertheless, the pressures of his life
were inescapable.

Tim needed a shower when he returned from his
morning run at the high school field track. But he
noticed the blinking light on his answering machine.
So he pressed the play button and listened.

"Hi. This is Dennis Lakey at Clayton's Investment
and Finance Corporation. We talked last week about
Mary Harris. And, remember, you said if I heard
anything to let you know." There was a brief pause.
"Well, something came up. I had a private meeting
with Mr. Clayton and the vice-president of the board
today. I can't give you all the details over the phone,
but Mary Harris' name was brought up in connection
with the embezzlement I uncovered. Mr. Clayton wants

to keep a low profile and do an internal investigation, since Mary Harris is...dead and no longer poses a threat to the company.

But I gave Mr. Clayton your business card and suggested you might be a good choice, since you're already familiar with the person involved, and there might be a possible connection with the woman you're looking for. So, Mr. Clayton might give you a call Monday morning. But, if he doesn't, I thought you ought to know about it anyway. Just don't let it leak out to anyone else."

The message had been left Saturday evening while he was out. He hadn't noticed it until now. He hadn't noticed much of anything since last night with Trisha. Tim hurried through his shower, dressed, and went to church. After the service he drove to The Porthole. He looked around first, and then sat in the booth where he and Trisha had sat before.

He saw her coming in the door, and her eyes were immediately drawn in his direction. Tim stood and Trisha greeted him with a kiss on his cheek. She scooted to the inside of the booth and he sat next to her. *So far, so good,* he thought. She hadn't surprised him this time. Now, if he could just concentrate on business, for a change.

"You know," she said, "when I woke up this morning I thought I had dreamed everything that happened last night."

"Oh?" Tim said bewildered. Apparently more had happened between them when they kissed than he was willing to accept responsibility for.

The waitress took their orders.

"I have a confession to make," Tim said. He felt uncomfortable when Trisha suddenly placed her hand on his thigh under the table. But she wasn't the one to blame for his thoughts going astray. "I had ulterior motives when I called you that first time and asked to meet you. I didn't really want a janitorial service for my office."

"I guessed that." She smiled at him.

"No, I mean...I needed to ask you some questions about a case I'm on."

"What?"

"I'm working on a case and...I still need to ask you those questions."

"Is that the only reason you wanted to see me?" She shoved him hard and he nearly fell off the edge of the seat in her attempt to get past him. "You've been leading me on all this time to get information?"

Other customers were beginning to look in their direction. Tim blocked her escape, but Trisha was strong, and his legs were starting to hurt from the strain. "It was only a pretext at first. I meant everything."

"Meant what?" she demanded.

"Asking you out on a date."

Trisha stopped pushing him.

"And enjoying it," he continued.

"Really?" she asked indignantly.

"You said you did too...didn't you?"

The waitress delivered their food, and Trisha looked as if she couldn't make up her mind whether to leave, or stay and eat. Tim began eating tentatively.

"Don't ever do that again," she demanded.

"No more pretexts," Tim agreed. One of these days, he told himself, he was going to learn that girls don't like to be tricked. He'd experienced that painful reality with Rhonda last year.

"No, I mean, don't ever try to control me." Trisha picked up her fork and stabbed her salad. "It makes me hostile."

"I noticed."

They ate a while in silence.

"Okay. What questions?" Trisha asked impatiently.

"About Mary Harris. How well did you know her?"

"I knew her," Trisha said curtly. She ran her index finger down the side of her glass, and the condensation collected into a big drop that rolled down and soaked into the paper place mat. "That's about it."

"You knew her better than anyone else did," Tim said. "You had a working arrangement."

"Oh that," Trisha said. "You want to know about that?"

"That and anything else that might be helpful in tracking down her roommate."

"Her roommate?"

"Yeah. Bernadette Higgins." Tim watched Trisha's face to see her first reaction to the name. Women weren't usually good at poker faces. He was hoping perhaps Trisha was privy to a secret about Bernadette going into hiding, or some such revelation. But Trisha's face betrayed no hint of secret knowledge about Bernadette Higgins.

"She's news to me. Never heard of her." Trisha was almost finished with her lunch.

"You gonna eat your fries?" Tim asked.

"No. You want them?"

He took one and ate it.

"That's typical of Mary though. She didn't let anyone get close to her. She was hard to get to know."

"So how did you get to know her well enough to have a working arrangement with her?"

Trisha sighed. "You're determined to know the story of my life one way or another, aren't you?"

"Just the facts, Ma'am," Tim said in his best Sgt. Friday impersonation.

Trisha laughed and leaned forward to finish off her glass of Coke. Tim leaned back in the booth and positioned his arm so that when she leaned back his arm was around her shoulders with his hand touching her bare arm.

"A few years back, I was having some problems in school," she began. "So I dropped out. I was depressed and just laid around a lot. Mom—she's divorced—she decided I'd been mooching off her long enough. So it was either pack my bags or get a job.

"I couldn't afford to move out, so I got a job. Waitressing at a hamburger joint near home, so I wouldn't need a car. The hours were rotten, the pay stunk, and I was always in a lousy mood. So one day, I mouthed off to a customer and got fired. I got another lousy job and did the same stinking thing. I drifted around that way, and Mom was pretty fed up."

"Hard to believe," Tim couldn't help observing.

"Believe it." Trisha drew closer and looked into his eyes. "I was pretty messed up for a while. Then I hired on at a janitorial service. Believe it or not, I liked it. Well, not the work really. But it was like being on my own. I worked by myself most of the time when no one else was around, after regular work hours when everyone had gone home. I cleaned up my act. And...I was getting over breaking up with...a guy. The hours were good for me, so I could use Mom's car when she wasn't using it. And pretty soon I could afford my own car."

"Do you still live with your mother?" Tim suddenly realized he'd been rubbing his thumb up and down her bare arm, and he didn't know why. But it was better than pinching his knuckles.

"Yes." Trisha turned toward him and her breath was warm on his ear. "I didn't mean to bore you."

"I'm not bored," he assured her. However, he was determined to stick to his business this time. "This leads up to Mary Harris."

Trisha had been playing with the condensation on her glass, using her finger like a squeegee, Tim noticed with amusement.

"Mary had a chronic case of allergies. She couldn't even tolerate being around people because of their colognes and after-shaves, things in their clothes, things in the air. She had it bad, so she worked most of the time when no one else was around. She had the kind of job, she could do that, computer consulting and set up. So...one night there she was, working in the office I was supposed to clean.

"She started coughing and wheezing and got all upset. She grabbed a spray can from me and ordered me to stop cleaning at night when she was working. I told her...well, I told her some not so nice things she could do about it. I was equally upset, because I thought she was just being uppity. You know, thought she could boss me around because she had a better job than me. I let her know she wasn't my boss.

"That's when she started telling me about the hazardous ingredients in cleaning products. I told her I didn't give a rip. She said I ought to, because I was killing myself, as well as everyone around me. She asked me if I ever had headaches. And when I stopped to think about it, I realized I'd been having headaches and sinus infections since I hired on at the janitorial service.

"Then she came on like a commercial for ecologically safe and natural cleaning aids. She had my attention, but I told her I was stuck using what the company gave me to clean with. She advised me to try reasoning with my boss.

"Yeah, right! That went over like a lead balloon. I lost a lot of sleep, and nearly lost my job the next day. The company wasn't about to spend more money on the good stuff, when they could get the name brand commercial products at wholesale." Trisha paused.

"Then what happened?" Tim prompted her.

"I told Mary about it the next time I saw her, and that's when she made me a deal I couldn't refuse. Although, if I had really sat down and thought about it, I might not have done it. It involved quitting my job—vacation pay, insurance benefits, security, and all—and investing the money I'd saved in my own cleaning equipment and supplies. And there was no guarantee. I had to trust Mary to do what she said she'd do. Which was, every time a client hired her to do their computer makeover, she'd see to it that they'd hire me also to do their janitorial work.

"Mary was a brilliant business person. She helped me decide on the name **Clean & Safe**. Clean tells exactly what I do. And Safe is my selling point. The letter 'C' puts me at the top of the alphabetical listing in the yellow pages here in Cleermantown. Did you know that's why a lot of businesses call themselves ABC whatever? It puts them at the top of the listings where they hope people will see them and call them first."

"No, I didn't know that," Tim said thoughtfully.

"The rest is history," Trisha concluded. "I now have more business than I can handle. Mary and I had what she called a symbiotic relationship. I made her work environment safe. And she made sure I had plenty of work. We got along pretty well, except when she tried to give me advice about my personal life. We differed in that area."

"She never mentioned a roommate?" Tim asked.

Trisha shook her head.

"Or the name Bernadette Higgins?"

"Nope."

Tim was satisfied that Mary Harris was justified in leaving her meager life savings to Trisha in her will; that didn't need any further explanation. And Mary's unusual chronic illness, which her insurance didn't cover, explained why her life savings had been meager. But what DID need explaining was Bernadette Higgins and what Mary Harris would've called their kind of shared relationship.

"Want to go for a walk?" Tim asked.

"Sure," Trisha said.

Tim scooted out of the booth and took her by the hand.

"Your turn," she said, turning toward him when they were outside in the bright sunshine. "And I want to hear every last juicy detail."

"You don't really want to hear about my life," Tim said as they walked hand in hand.

"Include all the girls you've ever known," Trisha said stopping and stepping in front of him. "So I can mentally annihilate them."

Her mouth was within easy reach. Tim had never dated a girl who was nearly as tall as himself. And before he realized it, he kissed her. "Funny," he said taking a breath, " I can't remember any of them." Trisha was not only a handful physically, his hands were around her firm hips, but she filled his mind and displaced every other thought when he was with her. And he could feel himself wanting to be with her as much as possible.

They walked quietly for a while. "C'mon," Trisha encouraged him. "Start talking."

"Where should I start?"

"The beginning. As far back as you can remember."

"That could take all afternoon."

"Then you better get started. I have to go to work early tonight. Tomorrow is Monday, the beginning of the work week for everyone else."

Tim began his life story, being careful to avoid mentioning the year of his birth, since Trisha was older. He told her about the kidnapping when he was only three. And how a lawyer named Harry Spears had arranged for him to have a new identity with a new family and home, instead of fulfilling the death order of a crime boss named Almighty. And how only a year ago he'd found his real family after being chased around the countryside by killers. It troubled him to talk about it.

It was the first time Tim had shared the details of the harrowing experience with anyone. His own family didn't even know the whole story, for their protection.

Brent knew—he'd been instrumental in his rescue. Clarence Drib knew—he'd been a newspaper reporter covering the story from the time of the kidnapping and faked death, to the conclusion when Tim had been reunited with his family. And Rhonda knew, of course, having lived through it with him. But Tim didn't mention her in his story to Trisha, or any other girls he'd ever known, for that matter. Trisha was the only one he wanted to remember from now on as she comforted him with sympathetic kisses.

Chapter 13: Walk on Water

When a missing person can't be located, it's usually because they don't want to be found. How and where Bernadette Higgins disappeared was a mystery. But, Tim decided, maybe now he should concentrate on WHY she would want to disappear. She didn't leave a paper trail. That should've been his first clue.

Brent was in the office when Tim came in from running at the high school field track.

"Why do you waste your energy doing that?" Brent commented.

"Doing what?" Tim wiped the perspiration from his face.

"Running! Running in circles like a chicken with your head cut off. It wastes time. You don't get anywhere."

"Exercise," Tim answered. They'd been through it all before, and it was useless to explain. "It gets my heart pumping. It clears the sleep out of my head. And it prepares me for the day ahead."

"Sex does all that, and better." Brent tipped back in his chair.

"I'm not married."

"And, at the rate you're going, you never will be. How many girls do you meet in a day? Do you ever think about talking to one of them?"

It was a comfort to know Patty hadn't spilled the goods on him about his Saturday night date. "No," Tim said. *Where is Patty anyway?* he thought as he glanced around the office.

"Take my advice, Kid. Play it smart. Don't get married when you're old."

"Like you?"

"Don't wait until her parents are on Social Security and can't afford a wedding," Brent continued. "This whole thing is gonna cost me a fortune, which I can't afford either. I thought she'd be satisfied with an expensive ring. She's out right now ordering an expensive wedding dress and making all kinds of expensive arrangements. Do you know she's planning a honeymoon?—like it'll be our first night, or something."

Tim spurred him on with, "Really?" and felt no remorse.

"And she even wants a church wedding. Can you believe it? After spending every last penny I have on it, she wants to get married in front of God and everybody."

Tim shook his head to keep from bursting with laughter.

Brent, believing he had a sympathetic ear, added, "My first marriage was quick and simple. Just a justice of the peace. No flowers. No cake. No invitations. No nothing. Now that was a wedding!"

"You're divorced," Tim reminded him.

"And another thing, Kid," Brent said. "Don't ever get divorced."

"Like you?"

"Lousy divorce cost more than a wedding. And the payments never end."

"Thanks for the lesson," Tim said as he went upstairs to take a shower.

When he returned Brent was working, actually working at his desk, instead of sleeping. Tim started to sit down at his own desk so he could study while waiting for the call from Clayton's Investment and Finance Corporation.

"Come look at this, Kid," Brent said. "Tell me what you think."

Tim walked over and stooped down to get a closer look at the photo Brent was holding. "Is he someone you know?" It was a dead man's nude body at a crime scene.

Brent used to be in charge of homicide at the Cleermantown Police Department, but his work with IRISH EYES involved surveillance of live bodies for over a year now.

"A friend at homicide dropped it by. We have a serial killer on our hands, and the lab boys are completely clueless."

"THEY have a serial killer on THEIR hands," Tim corrected, filling in the familiar words he knew Patty would've said if she were here.

"But just look at it," Brent urged. "How can a man die of a snapped neck while lying nude on the floor on his stomach...with the biggest smile on his face you ever saw?"

"You have a dirty mind," Tim said. "I'm sure you'll come up with it." He didn't like looking at dead bodies. Still, the intrigue of the situation piqued his curiosity.

"But just think about it...on his stomach." Brent turned the picture to a different angle.

"Fond memories," Tim suggested.

"Broken necks happen during a fight or a struggle. This guy's practically laughing his butt off."

The phone rang and Tim picked it up. It was Mr. Clayton arranging the meeting that Dennis Lakey had told him about during the answering machine message.

"I'll be there in an hour," Tim replied and hung up.

He prepared to leave, but something about the dead man's picture, all of a sudden, conjured up a fond memory of his own. "How old is that picture?"

"I don't know," Brent said. "Could be minutes. Maybe hours. He was found this morning."

Tim began searching frantically through a storage shelf for the equipment he would need. "Get on the phone," he shouted to Brent. "Tell the boys not to touch his back when they move him. Transport him just like he is. Then call the morgue and tell Dr. Morgan to prepare her camera to take footprints with a laser light. We have to hurry."

"Footprints?"

"Were the other bodies found the same way?"

"On the floor, nude, with big smiles on their faces," Brent confirmed.

"Look at the picture again," Tim said.

Brent looked.

"Now think about the smile on your face when Patty gives you a back massage."

The light came on in Brent's head. "Footprints? On the floor?"

"Japanese style." Tim was sure he was right as he recalled Rhonda's remedy for his aching back after driving all day, for days on end, last year. Rhonda would never know how helpful she'd been to him, or that she'd provided a possible clue in solving a multiple murder case. But only if they were in time.

Tim was a few minutes late for his meeting with Mr. Clayton, having spent the hour with Dr. Morgan finding footprints in the skin of the dead man's back. And just to make sure, he'd gone with Brent to the murder scene, where he was able to lift a good print from the bathroom floor also. He just wished he could be there to see the killer's face when confronted with the footprints after being so careful not to leave fingerprints at the scene.

"Sorry to keep you waiting," Tim said as he took his place in the chair in front of Mr. Clayton's desk. Dennis Lakey, sitting in a chair next to the big desk, nodded to Tim.

Mr. Clayton went into his fingertip exercises as he began talking. "We have a little problem we need to clear up, and Dennis here suggested that you might be able to help us do just that."

"I'll help, if I can," Tim said.

"My first concern is confidentiality," Mr. Clayton emphasized. "The investment and finance business is very volatile, and I would hate for clients to become unnecessarily concerned about the state of their investments and potentially make a run on our corporation that could hinder profitable operations."

"No problem," Tim responded. "The reputation of IRISH EYES is dependent on client discretion."

"Since it would serve no purpose to press charges against a...deceased employee, I see no reason to involve legal authorities in the matter."

"What exactly is the matter we're talking about?" Tim asked.

"A small discrepancy that Dennis uncovered in the records department. Two accounts that can't be accounted for."

"And there might be more by the time I'm done," Dennis Lakey interjected.

"Why don't you explain the whole thing to Mr. MacCulfsky just like you explained it to me, Dennis," Mr. Clayton said.

"Ever tell a teacher your dog ate your homework?" Dennis asked.

Tim shook his head.

"Trust me, they don't buy it. They also don't buy it when you say your computer ate your homework. It happened to me quite a lot back in college, before computer makers overcame that bad little habit by adding the 'auto save' function. Now, when something goes wrong or the power goes out while you're working on a computer, you can retrieve your work unharmed and complete up to the point where the auto save last kicked in."

Tim couldn't help giving him a "what's your point?" expression.

"That's WHY I discovered what Mary Harris did," Dennis explained. "I never got over my lost trust in computers. I'm always careful. Computers may be quicker and make fewer mistakes, but when a mistake is made, it's perfect. And it's never discerned as a mistake. In fact, the computer is a perfect instrument to make a mistake with, because then you can ask it to show you all the discrepancies the mistake has caused. And then you can fix all the discrepancies and hide the mistake."

"I follow you," Tim said. "Mary was making mistakes, on purpose, and you discovered a discrepancy she missed. All because you don't trust computers."

"Here's exactly what I found." Dennis punched in some codes and brought up a listing of names and numbers on the monitor screen at the end of Mr. Clayton's desk. "A discrepancy or error involving this date," he said pointing to the numbers. It was a simple error I could've changed without even checking. But I checked. I called the representative whose name is listed as handling the account. He had no recollection of the account at all. What struck me, was that if I hadn't bothered to check on it, years would've gone by without any need to ever check on the facts—thanks to computers. And by that time, the representative would've handled so many accounts in the interim, he wouldn't be expected to remember an account from years ago. After all, that is why we use computers, isn't it?"

"You've made me a confirmed skeptic," Tim said.

"That's not even the best part," Dennis said relishing the intrigue of his discovery. "The best part is this." He held up a disk and inserted it in the computer's disk port. "This is a backup disk that Mary didn't know about from the old system. And the account is not there. It never existed before, and the representative doesn't remember setting it up less than two weeks ago. In fact, he was home in bed with the flu that day, and his entry logs for the last two weeks don't show it anywhere. I spent time running a comparison through the before and after systems. I found another one.

"You know what's scary? Mary Harris would've gotten away with it, if she hadn't died. She would've found the discrepancies herself and corrected them. Also, if she'd had the opportunity to train me like she was supposed to, I wouldn't have been feeling my way through and learning most of it by trial and error, which is why I discovered the mistakes.

"By the way," Dennis said looking at Mr. Clayton, "some of the shortcuts she implemented will improve the efficiency of the department many times over."

"I'm glad to hear that bit of good news," Mr. Clayton returned.

Tim sat back and thought for a moment quietly. The other two men waited in silence. "I don't see where you need my help. You've done a good job of uncovering and documenting foolproof evidence. I assume you're taking the steps necessary to eliminate any future problems. The only other measure you might need to take is to alert Mary Harris' previous employers of the possibility of tampered accounts, which you're in the best position to do yourself since you have her work history. Of course, if they didn't take the same precautions you did, they'll be hard pressed to uncover anything." Tim shrugged and got to his feet. "Good job," he said sticking out his hand toward Dennis.

Dennis shook his hand.

"But we do need your help, Mr. MacCulfsky." Mr. Clayton stood also. "You see, one of the accounts has been drawn on, AFTER Mary's death."

Tim paused and sat back down. "Better give me a copy of the names on those accounts," he said. "Also any pertinent information such as addresses, phone numbers, etc. Have you done anything to the accounts?"

"Not yet," Dennis said.

"Good. Leave them open."

Dennis and Mr. Clayton looked at each other.

"So far, the accounts have caused a minor recoverable loss to the company," Mr. Clayton said. "But you must understand, Mr. MacCulfsky, we stand to lose quite a substantial amount if the accounts are emptied. And if there are anymore that Mr. Lakey hasn't uncovered yet,..."

"I understand," Tim said. He was pinching his knuckles. "But if you close them now or put a freeze on them, you could alert whoever it is that's partially responsible for them. Mary obviously wasn't working alone on this."

"How long will it take you to solve this situation?"

Tim took out his electronic date book. It not only contained a list of appointments and his class schedule; it kept a running tally of the days remaining in his contract with the travel agency. There were twenty days remaining, and his contingency fee now stood at $20,000.

"At the most," Tim calculated, "twenty days. That's when my contract with the travel agency ends. And, if I haven't found her by then, she's out of reach and you can close out the accounts."

"In the meantime," Dennis added, "I can tag the accounts in the computer, and we'll be alerted immediately if they show any more activity."

Mr. Clayton nodded his head. "It would be very gratifying if I could present this situation with a positive conclusion at the next board meeting."

By the time he left, Tim had formalized an agreement to work the investigation for Mr. Clayton. Dennis left with him to go to lunch. "I'll be in touch with you," Tim said. They parted, and Dennis walked the short distance to his reserved parking space. Tim walked to the visitors' parking lot. Now he had an idea why Bernadette didn't want to be found. Trouble was, she was hiding right under his nose somewhere.

121/RIGHT UP YOUR ALLEY

Chapter 14: Done Too Soon

Life is full of the unexpected. People going about their daily routines and then suddenly—death in the prime of life, bankruptcy in the midst of so much prosperity, failure after a long run of success, winning a million dollars while committing grand larceny. Life is like that sometimes.

Brent spent the rest of the day at the Cleermantown Police Station basking in the lime light created by their stunning resolution to the "Leave 'em Smiling" serial murder case. And why not? Tim didn't mind. Brent deserved it. After all, Tim had his own caper with which to deal, tracking the accounts of Florence Miller and Faunecia Neinhouse, aka "Flora" and "Fauna."

Naming her aliases as the representatives of plant and animal life of a particular place or period was only the beginning of Mary Harris' witty embezzlement scheme. She had given birth to it, quite literally, in the vital statistics department of the county courthouse where she'd been hired to convert the data of living souls to entries in a computer system. A couple of nonliving souls to fulfill her needs had gone unnoticed.

From there, Mary Harris had nurtured Flora and Fauna with job histories at various places of employment and had provided them with retirement benefits and pensions from companies matching her own recent work history. The checks were being funneled to a postal service box number, which Tim had no difficulty in locating. It was an elaborate scheme, and Tim would be spending weeks following up and meticulously documenting each unwary participant along the way—unraveling the threads in a giant anthropomorphic doily, as it were, which she had worked into a thing of beauty to adorn her crowning treasure, just as her hobby had been crocheting the little doilies crowned by the porcelain figurines in her apartment.

But for now, Tim had to jump into the middle of it and nab Bernadette Higgins before she grabbed the treasure and ran out without leaving a thread to follow. It would require a careful plan to catch her with her hand in the cookie jar, which was actually a postal drop box in downtown Cleermantown. If he were dealing with Mary, he had no doubt that she had backup systems in place to alert her of his meddling in her fraudulent affairs by computer. Bernadette, he wasn't so sure. Still, she warranted the same kind of kid-glove treatment, just in case.

Tim had some time to kill before lunch, so he drove to the apartment building. A quick look revealed that Bernadette's red Corvette was exactly as before, and he drove past. He was acquainted with the dispatcher at Cleermantown's one and only taxicab service, which got him a peek at the logbook for the previous two weeks.

Being tall came in handy at times, once Tim
learned that he could easily look over other people's
shoulders without appearing to be nosy. And his
speed-reading course more than paid for itself in
unexpected ways also. There was no record of a pick
up at or near the apartment of Bernadette Higgins.

The logbook at the chauffeured limousine service
was kept on computer, and a privacy filter protected
the screen. Being tall was no help to Tim here. It didn't
even help him to gain the confidence of the young lady
at the keyboard. A pretext was the only way to get
information under such security.

Nevertheless, Tim left the chauffeured limousine
service with the almost certain knowledge that
Bernadette had never resorted to the extravagant
conveyance. Finally he drove to the city parking lot
nearest the Sidewalk Café.

Their customary table was waiting, and when he
sat down, Tim saw Clarence and Waldo round the
corner from the opposite direction. It was a toss-up
who walked slower, the overweight Pekingese attached
to the leash or the elderly journalist who held onto the
unnecessary restraint. The dog and his master made
the trek to the Sidewalk Café everyday at the busy
lunch hour, even when Tim didn't. During the winter,
and on rainy days, the café's charm was moved
indoors. But its real appeal was the quaint atmosphere
in the open air on warm summer days, such as today.

Clarence sat across from Tim and held out a folded
newspaper. "You made the front page again."

Tim noticed the now familiar picture of Mark
Lander. "I'll read it later." He refolded the newspaper
and set it aside.

"Any new leads on the present case?" Clarence asked.

"Not a thing," Tim said, feeling a little depressed in spite of his productive morning.

"Yes, sir," said the waiter, who mistook Tim's words to mean he didn't wish to eat. "And you, sir?" he said directing his full attention at Clarence.

"I'll have my usual beef on whole wheat with lots of mustard and onion, and a Pepsi with no ice. Just water for my dog, and..." Clarence restrained his mirth. "...my friend would like his usual beef and cheese on white toast with lettuce, tomato and mayo, and give him a very large root beer."

The confused waiter left to place their order.

"He won't get a tip from me," Tim remarked.

"He's new," Clarence justified.

"What makes you think I want root beer instead of milk?"

"The atmospheric conditions are such that the movement of air is causing the moisture in the ground to evaporate at a faster than normal rate for the temperature that exists, due to the brightness of the sun on this cloudless summer day."

Tim coughed. "Huh?"

"Just a lucky guess."

While they ate, Tim filled Clarence in on the fact that Mary Harris had been cooking the books at Clayton's Investment and Finance Corporation, and the fact that a co-conspirator was still reaping the benefits after Mary's death.

"And, naturally, you believe the second party to the crime is your missing person, Bernadette Higgins, winner of the million dollar grand prize," Clarence surmised.

"Why else would she disappear? It seems the logical conclusion."

"Yes," Clarence said rubbing his chin. "It does, doesn't it?"

"I have a plan for trapping her though."

"Good," Clarence said approvingly. "Such a shame," he mused. "She didn't know that tomorrow was the day of her miracle, because she gave up a day too soon."

Tim nodded.

"Life sucks!" Clarence quoted the short, first line from his favorite mystery novel.

"That about sums it up for me too," Tim agreed.

The rest of the day Tim spent at the shooting range practicing more survival techniques, and at afternoon classes that went later than scheduled. Brent and Patty were gone, so the first thing Tim accomplished when he arrived home was to leave a message on Trisha's answering machine.

He listened to her voice, and unexplainably faltered when he spoke. "Sorry I couldn't see you today..." He realized he sounded desperate, as she called it. "I have a busy schedule, but...are you free this week? Would you like to...What would you like to do? Call me!"

Tim hung up and microwaved a dinner. He skimmed through the front-page story of the newspaper Clarence had given him at the Sidewalk Café. Instead of slipping into quiet disregard so the scales of justice would swing in the right direction, his former case was growing in infamy. Now Jack Rosenthall was alleging that some of the evidence had been mishandled by the police, which meant, if the defense attorney got his way, the burden of proof would fall squarely on the shoulders of eyewitnesses.

Unfortunately, Tim was the only eyewitness who had seen the murder. And that meant Jack Rosenthall would do everything he could to discredit him on the witness stand. And if he succeeded...Tim would just have to make sure he didn't succeed. Brent had recommended that Tim distance himself from the case, in order to get over the emotional trauma. Now it was time to prepare for what lay ahead of him.

Brent had warned him about emotional involvement. But it was hard not to be emotionally involved with the missing people he was hired to find. Emotion was inherent in such cases. Emotional need is most often the motivating factor in missing person searches.

Tim ate and worked at his desk late into the night. But his mind refused to concentrate on the textbooks he was reading and kept pulling him toward the mixed up case of Bernadette Higgins, the missing million dollar winner, and Mary Harris, the deceased eccentric embezzler. He turned around and stared at Bernadette's enlarged image tacked to the bulletin board. He'd recognize her anywhere the moment he saw her, as well as her unique set of fingerprints. And there'd be no love lost between them when he turned her over to the authorities.

Chapter 15: The Time is Now

Tuesday morning Tim was anxious to bait a trap and put his plan into action. And he needed Patty's help to pull it off. He waited until he heard snoring from Brent's corner. Then he rolled his chair to Patty's desk and sat next to her.

"I want every last detail." Patty leaned back and crossed her arms, waiting. "Don't hold anything back!"

Tim looked at her.

"Your date, silly. How was your date?"

He cleared his throat. "Perfect!"

"Which movie did she pick?"

"Romance—"

The telephone interrupted before he could finish, and Patty picked it up. "Just a moment, please." Patty covered the mouthpiece and whispered excitedly, "It's her, Trisha Garing."

Tim rolled back to his desk and picked up his extension. He turned his back toward Patty and said, "hello," when he saw her put down her receiver.

"Got your message." Trisha sounded relaxed or, Tim decided, tired. "Let's do another dinner and movie. I really enjoyed it."

"How about tonight?" Tim rushed in.

"I'd really love to spend the night with you, darling...but I'm working tonight..." a deep breath that sounded like a yawn. "...and tomorrow night, too."

"You sound tired," Tim said with concern. He was suddenly aware that the snoring across the room had stopped. He glanced around and saw Brent staring in his direction. He felt his face turn red.

"I just got home...haven't been to bed yet."

A pause and then Tim asked, "Do you work Saturday?"

"I'll need to get some sleep in the morning, but I'm free the rest of the day."

"Okay then, Saturday it is!" Tim glanced around again, and Brent was pretending to work at his desk. Brent's desk was a pretext. He was actually eavesdropping. "Same time?"

"Same place, too. I'll need to pick up some more supplies."

Tim felt elated. "See you Saturday at five!"

"Can't wait," she breathed.

"Good night." Tim listened to her hang up before he turned around and put his own receiver down.

"How come your partner is always the last to know?" Brent said sadly shaking his head.

"Know what?" Tim asked innocently.

"That you have a love life."

"Because my partner has a severe lack of discretion."

"I knew," Patty said proudly.

"How'd it happen, Kid?" Brent continued.

Tim couldn't help noticing that Brent referred to Trisha as if he'd caught a disease or had been involved in a terrible accident. "She's the janitorial service at Clayton's."

"Clayton's Investment and Finance Corporation?" Brent's voice went serious. "That's the place you went to find out about the dead roommate, isn't it?"

Tim knew he was about to hear another lecture on personal involvement.

Patty coughed and loudly cleared her throat, which meant she wanted Brent to drop his present line of questioning.

Brent took the hint. "What's she like, Kid?"

Tim and Patty looked at each other and smiled.

"That serious, huh?" Brent sighed.

"We've only dated once...officially," Tim added after recalling that he'd been with her nearly every day since they met.

Brent sighed again and repeated, "That serious, huh?"

With friends like Brent and Patty, there was no such thing as a private life. His affairs were an open book. "She's five-eleven, slender, brown hair, brown eyes, beautiful skin, sexy voice, wonderful personality, lips like a goddess..."

"That serious, huh?" Patty sighed dreamily.

"By the way," Tim said, "Trisha recommended these dietary drinks for you." He pulled open his desk drawer and handed the cans to Patty. "They come in all flavors, but she thought you would prefer these."

Patty examined them. "I like her already," she said. "When do we get to meet her?"

"Yeah, that's what I want to know," Brent said leaning back and assuming his precarious nap position again. "When do we meet her?"

"She's very busy," Tim confided. As he thought about Trisha, the eventuality of having a steady girlfriend began to play in his mind. He could definitely get used to the idea.

Later, instead of meeting Clarence at the Sidewalk Café, Tim ate lunch with Brent and Patty, because it was raining. They sat in the office eating pizza for an hour. At least, Brent and Tim ate. Patty drank one of her new diet drinks.

The pouring rain outside produced a cozy atmosphere inside that Brent found irresistible for napping. Tim found it impossible to concentrate. And Patty was too distracted to work. She looked at Brent snoring in his chair with his feet propped on his desk, and smiled in a way that saw more than was visible to the eye.

"You know what I feel like doing?" she asked.

Tim shook his head. "No telling."

"C'mon. Let's go shopping."

"It's raining!"

"That's why they invented malls."

Tim began to brighten at the prospect. "What about him?" he asked observing Brent's unsuspecting peaceful expression.

Patty opened the top drawer of Brent's desk and reached between his ankles. "Don't worry about him. He's better off sleeping through it. The only part of Brent I need at the mall is this little thing." She withdrew his petty cash stash and slipped it into her purse.

"Actually, this is a great idea," Tim said as he helped Patty with her raincoat. "Because I need your advice on picking some bait for a trap I'm going to set."

"Cheese works well on mice," Patty said as Tim shut the door behind them, and they ran in the rain to his car.

"I'm after bigger game than mice," Tim explained as he opened the passenger door for Patty. He closed it and went around and got in on the driver's side. "And this game has very rich taste."

"Sounds intriguing!"

Tim started the engine and they drove toward the mall. "I need to buy a small gift that can pass through the mail easily, small enough to be left in a mail box. But enticing enough that a person wouldn't just toss it as junk mail."

"Man or woman?"

"A woman," Tim answered.

"A small bottle of cologne. No, wait. Jewelry," Patty decided.

"Then, it needs to be wrapped in something that can be spotted from a surveillance car when she carries it outside the building."

"A tube-shaped mailer, the kind documents are stored in."

"Too big." Tim was deep in thought, and the car behind him honked to let him know the traffic light had changed. He drove on.

"Not if it's only six inches long," Patty said. She liked the idea. "And then wrap it in orange paper. Unusual shape. Unusual color. You won't miss it, even if you're sound asleep when the mark walks out. The package will scream at you as she walks by."

"Okay, good," Tim agreed. "Then, I need you to type a message to put inside. Something to the effect that she has won the gift in a contest and needs to contact a person. You can give your name and use the IRISH EYES phone number as a contact."

Patty smiled. "Does that make me IN on this baby?"

"If you want to be," Tim answered. "I was hoping you would. I'll need some help with the surveillance while I'm in classes."

Brent and Tim had never used Patty's assistance in the field. It was an understood agreement between them to never involve her in the actual work. But this wasn't dangerous. In fact, it was so simple he didn't want to disturb Brent's sleep over it. Patty was perfect for the few hours he'd need her to fill in for him. And her insatiable itch to shop for the wedding would put her activities above Brent's suspicion. He'd never know.

Chapter 16: A Modern Day Version of Love

Tim was on pins and needles the rest of the week. Surveillance at a postal drop box was not his idea of life on the wild side. Patty, on the other hand, was having the time of her life. Her first adventure in the field of P.I. work was like a tryst. She parked her car behind Tim's blue Tracker at one-thirty Wednesday afternoon as agreed, giving him plenty of time to make his two o'clock class. Tim drove away and left her to watch until the business closed at six. He'd been there since they opened at nine, and right now he needed to grab a quick lunch at the nearest fast-food drive-through and to use the bathroom at the college.

Patty was a novice, considering she was the secretary of a P.I. service and engaged to a retired police detective. But she was willing to do whatever Tim told her. She didn't realize there was more to doing a surveillance than just watching for the mark to walk out the door with the bait.

"For one thing," Tim had told her, "don't drink before you go on watch."

"Of course I won't drink," Patty said. "I'll be driving!"

"No, I mean, don't drink anything. You won't be able to go to the bathroom until after six. You can't just leave when you need to."

"Oh," Patty said. "Right. Don't worry! I won't take my eyes off the door for a minute."

"Actually," Tim said beginning to worry, "you shouldn't just stare at people going in and out. The idea is NOT to look like you're watching."

"I know that," she said. "I've watched spy movies before. I just meant I would do a good job. You can count on me to do this right."

"I know you will," Tim said to reassure himself as much as to affirm his trust in Patty. "The main thing is to turn on the video cam when you see the bait. Get as good a shot as you can of her face, keep her in the viewfinder all the way to her car, get a full-length of the car, and a shot of the license plate. It doesn't matter if the shot blurs or how quick it is, just get the license plate."

"Then I beep you on the pager, and try to follow." Patty made it sound exciting.

"After you turn off the video cam."

"Oh, yeah."

"Don't worry about getting burned. She's not expecting a tail."

"Burned?" Patty looked confused.

"Discovered," Tim explained, "while you're following her. Most people never know they're being tailed. Wild speed chases only happen with cops and in the movies. Anyway, if she burns you, don't worry! That's why you get a shot of the license plate."

"Ten-four," Patty said.

"That's not necessary."

"Okeydoke."

Tim sighed. "I'll call you on the cell phone. You describe the car, and pinpoint your exact location and heading, and then hightail it home as soon as you see my blue Tracker."

"Okay," Patty said confidently. "But what if it happens right in the middle of one of your classes?"

"Then I'll be spared a boring afternoon."

Patty smiled.

"The only glitch you need to worry about," Tim had told her Tuesday when they planned the whole strategy, "is if Brent starts to suspect you're up to something and decides to throw a monkey wrench into the works."

"I know," Patty said. "Then I just beep your pager and you miss your class."

"No big deal," Tim said with a shrug.

Everything went like clockwork for two days. On Friday, Tim spent the whole day outside the building. He didn't have classes, and they decided Patty should spend the day with Brent, so he wouldn't have reason to suspect her absences during the previous afternoons were planned.

And besides that, Tim expected the bait to be taken on Friday. He came prepared with sandwiches and snack cakes enough to last the day. But the inactivity of surveillance was taking a toll. He fought the temptation to get out of his car and stretch or do some deep knee bends. That would tip off anyone to the fact that he'd been sitting there all day. And the force of gravity would bring on the urge to use the bathroom.

Finally the long day came to an end without seeing a single soul leave the building with anything that resembled a document tube wrapped in orange. As a last ditch effort, Tim went to the door and knocked just as the manager was locking up and hanging the closed sign. He waved Tim away and pointed to the clock. Tim persisted. The man relented and unlocked the door.

"Hey man, thanks," Tim said breathlessly. "I think I lost something when I was in earlier." He glanced around. "I think I might have thrown it away by accident. Mind if I take a look?"

The man nodded, but he made it clear his patience was ebbing.

Tim rummaged the trashcan filled with junk mail items and paper refuse. No sign of orange wrapping, but it gave him an idea. If they hadn't spotted the bait by then, he could check the dumpster in the alley Monday night, which was the night before trash was picked up in Cleermantown. The orange wrapper was a beacon, and that way he would know if the bait had been snatched without his seeing it.

"Thanks anyway," Tim said and left. He drove home.

He returned next day when the postal service opened and spent Saturday morning watching the coming and going of local citizens. Drop boxes are mostly used by home-based small businesses to look more official, by people in transition, and by people who don't want to be located at their homes for various and sundry reasons. The business closed at noon, but patrons could pick up their mail for another two hours in the outer lobby.

Tim was disappointed at the end of the shift. The bait had been a splendid idea, but it wasn't foolproof. A lot of unknowns could've gone wrong and resulted in failure. A woman with a large enough purse could've simply stashed her mail inside out of view. The package could've been opened inside the building, in which case the enclosed letter with a contact number was his only backup. Or Bernadette Higgins could've just vanished without a trace. And he wasn't even sure Bernadette Higgins was the perp they were looking for in this case.

At any rate, he preferred to believe the bait hadn't been taken yet. Which meant, more sitting in his car next week. And Patty would have to continue relieving him on the sly, so he could go to his classes.

As he drove to their meeting place, Tim realized he hadn't put much thought into planning his second date with Trisha. He'd told her dinner and a movie, but sitting in theater seats lost its appeal after several days of surveillance from his car seat. Even with the expectancy of her kisses and putting his arm around her.

"Where are we off to tonight?" Trisha greeted him.

"I was hoping you had some ideas," Tim said. He was on safe ground letting her make the choices this time, since his choices last time had turned out so well.

"I have a lot of ideas I want to do with you," she said kissing his nose.

Tim happily noticed that her tight revealing dress was not meant for sitting.

"Let's start at a German diner where I've eaten once before. I just love their food and the atmosphere is unbeatable."

Tim bought some more diet drinks for Patty when Trisha checked out, and he put Trisha's supplies in the trunk of her car. Then they drove away in his car.

"It's called The Brat," Trisha explained on the way. "It's spelled B-R-A-T, but it's pronounced with a short O instead of an A sound."

The Brat was a cafeteria-style restaurant serving food with German names and offering beer to wash it down. Tim took a tray and flatware wrapped in a paper napkin and made his way down the counter behind Trisha. He followed her example and tried the bratwurst on a homemade roll with a side of potato salad and a bean dish of some sort. She took a piece of pecan pie for dessert, he took the bread pudding. She asked for and received a large frosty mug of beer. Tim declined and filled his mug with root beer at the soft drink dispenser.

When they reached the cashier Tim paid for their meals. Trisha went ahead and found a small table in an out-of-the-way corner. The place was loud, but the cozy atmosphere was invoked by the necessity to sit very close in order to carry on a conversation. And it just seemed natural that their hands gravitated to each other.

"How did you find me?" Trisha whispered against his ear.

Tim was breathing hard and he realized it wasn't from having to raise his voice in order to be heard. His mind was completely off track. "What do you mean?"

"The first time you called me," Trisha continued, "and said you needed a janitorial service. How did you find me?"

"I picked up your business card at Clayton's Investment and Finance Corporation."

"What did you mean when you said I wasn't what you expected?" Trisha had turned completely around to face him and rested both her hands on his thighs.

"I didn't expect you to be so..." Tim stood slowly and lifted her with him. He needed to get outside where it was cooler, hopefully without spoiling the moment. "...so wonderful." They walked out with their arms around each other.

"Where do we go from here?" she asked.

"Lady's choice," he reminded her.

Trisha held his arm up with both her hands and looked at his watch. "The night's still young. Do you like dancing?"

The thought of holding her close and moving in synch was tantalizing. "Sure," he answered. "As long as you don't expect any Michael Flatley moves."

"Good," she said giggling. He opened her door, and they drove away.

"I forgot to use the bathroom before we left," she said meekly. "Can we stop off at your place for just a minute?"

"No problem." Tim pulled into the parking lot, and they were walking to the door before he noticed the van sitting with its lights off. He quickly unlocked the door, practically pushed Trisha inside ahead of him, and then looked out the window before turning on the lights. He was right. The local news station was cruising for Saturday night tidbits.

Trisha looked around. "Nice place."

"It's over here," Tim said leading her to the full bathroom that was part of the downstairs office arrangement.

She didn't take long. And when she came out, Tim was made uncomfortably aware that her original intention had been to spend time alone with him.

"We better go," he said interrupting her progress. He needed to have a long talk with her later about their relationship. Right now he needed to make sure his private life was kept out of the local news.

"Want some free advertising?" he asked.

"How?" Trisha frowned with skepticism.

"Just walk out the front door and tell that nice lady with the microphone all about Clean & Safe Janitorial Service." Tim pointed to the woman and her cameraman standing in the parking lot. "Smile real big and walk real slow toward the car. I'll meet you there."

"Sounds like fun," Trisha said agreeably. Tim opened the door for her and then shut it. He ran upstairs and let himself out the bathroom window. His fear of heights was less of a problem in the dark. Besides, he was willing to go out on a limb for Trisha, quite literally.

He cautiously climbed down the branches of the maple tree in the fenced backyard. Then he opened the gate, making sure to silence the chime at the bottom with his foot, and then swung it shut silently. He sneaked around the side of the building, caught sight of the frustrated news team returning to their van, and climbed into the driver's side of his Tracker the same moment Trisha entered on the passenger's side. He started the engine and they quickly drove away.

"How do you rate?" Trisha asked.

"Newsworthy case," Tim replied.

"I knew there was more to you than just a sweet smile," she cooed.

Trisha's directions led straight to the nightclub district of Cleermantown, and Tim parked on a back street. Together they walked into a place called The Black Widow's Web. Trisha was at ease placing her

order for a white wine spritzer. Tim pinched his
knuckles. "Just some ice water for me," he said. The
waitress repeated the order and dubbed Tim's
refreshment a "frigid virgin," saying it with particular
emphasis.

Trisha smiled sympathetically. "Do you really prefer
virgins or are you afraid of getting carded?"

Tim's moment of truth had arrived.

"I can take care of you, you know. I'm friendly with
the door keep."

"I am...I'm underage," Tim admitted. "But I really
prefer not to drink. I'm a Christian." He felt like a
hypocrite knowing that she'd given him the go ahead
when she'd caught him earlier looking down the front
of her dress.

"I admire a man with principle," she said taking his
hand in hers. "I really do."

He felt unsure of himself, but Trisha didn't allow
his moment of embarrassment to spoil the night. "Let's
dance."

The music was loud, the air was polluted with
smoke, and Tim felt intoxicated without imbibing. He
felt wonderfully liberated now that Trisha knew his
secret and it didn't matter to her. He held her close,
and they danced late into the night.

Chapter 17: Sunday Sun

Sunday, August 2 (day $14,000 In the Bernadette Higgins missing person case), dawned with a cold front making its way south across Cleermantown, New York. Tim was up early, in spite of his late night with Trisha, and ran around the high school field track as usual. The sun and the ominous dark clouds vied for dominance. The clouds finally won, and Tim headed back home before the faltering raindrops turned into a heavy downpour. It was a cleansing rain without wind, the kind that farmers pray for in the middle of a hot, dry summer. The crops would be good this year, if the trend continued.

Tim checked the answering machine as he walked past on his way upstairs to take a shower. No messages. He knew there wouldn't be. Too early. Trisha would sleep late today. She worked tonight.

He came back downstairs later with his hair still wet. Still no messages. He sat down at his desk and opened an interesting book about famous cases of murder by poison. *In olden days the ability to administer poison was a skill as highly cultivated as any art form and it was part of the highly respected profession of the apothecary.*

Tim stared at the phone as if by wishing he could make it ring. *Shakespeare made good use of death by poison in his famous tragedies, "Romeo and Juliet" and "Hamlet."* Tim pondered Romeo and Juliet, the most famous fictional lovebirds in history with probably the shortest history of lovemaking in fiction, cut down in their youth.

He picked up the telephone receiver and listened to the dial tone. He set it back down. She needed her sleep. He'd wait a while. He picked up his pen and tried to summarize what he'd just read. But his mind was elsewhere.

Tim picked up the receiver again and this time he punched in Patty's number. It rang a couple of times and Brent answered.

"Hi. Is Patty there? I need to ask her about a report she typed last week." He was getting good at pretexts.

"Yeah, Kid. Just a minute."

Tim heard the TV playing loudly in the background. Then he heard a click and Patty's voice. "I got it," she called.

There was another click and Tim knew Brent had hung up his extension.

"The bait wasn't taken," Tim informed her. "Are you on for Monday?"

"I guess so," she replied.

"You know I have practice at the shooting range. It'll be a long day."

"I know."

"Thanks, Patty."

"No problem. I'm glad to be able to help. It's different being in the field. Now I know what it's like."

"Not always fun, is it?"

"It's a change," Patty said.

There was a brief pause and Tim opened his mouth to say good-bye.

"How was it?" she demanded. "Your second date? Do I have to wheedle it out of you?"

Tim smiled. "Sorry. I didn't know you were interested."

"Of course I'm interested."

"It was okay."

"Just okay?" she demanded. "You two on the rift already?"

"Okay then,...does great sound better?"

"Don't leave me hanging."

"We went to The Brat for dinner. Ever heard of the Brat?"

"Nope."

"German food. Crowded and noisy. Then we went dancing."

"Where?"

"The Black Widow's Web."

"Oh..."

He knew she'd heard of it. "Mind if I ask you something, Patty?"

"What?"

"How does a Christian reconcile lifestyle differences with a non-Christian?"

She hesitated. "That's a hard one. I'm still trying to figure it out myself."

Tim fidgeted. "What should I do?"

"You mean about you and Trisha, right?" Patty didn't wait for an answer. "Don't compromise, Dearie. Stand your ground and do what you know is right. No matter what." She hesitated. "You're asking the wrong person, you know. I tend to let my emotions get in the way."

She was referring to her relationship with Brent.

"You have to live with your choices the rest of your life. So make the right choices, Dearie. Listen, I gotta go now. The game's only half over, and Brent wants me to pick him up another six-pack."

Tim said good-bye and hung up. But concentrating on his research paper was hopeless. He looked out the window and the rainfall blurred into an impenetrable layer of gray mist and a dull hum in his ears. A streak of lightning, followed by a loud rumble, broke the monotony. The storm was moving away. And Tim noticed the box that had been sitting on the back of his desk long enough to be overlooked, but today it seemed out of place and beckoned to be dealt with.

It was the box from his first visit to Clayton's Investment and Finance Corporation containing Mary Harris' personal belongings. He disregarded the eerie feeling of touching the possessions of a dead person.

He withdrew the white mug with her name in big black capital letters emblazoned on the outside. Three yellow #2 pencils of the wholesale variety rolled across the bottom as Tim tipped the box to get a good look at the rest of the contents. A bottle of prescription eye drops.

Tim removed her photo I.D. badge. He worked with his computer scanner until he had reproduced an enlarged color copy of Mary's image the same size as Bernadette Higgins' photo tacked to the top left corner of his bulletin board. He tacked Mary's to the top right corner. He stared at one and then the other, the two women somehow related in an evil scheme that was reeking havoc even after the death of one and the disappearance of the other.

The box also contained a glass jar of herbal tea leaves, good for stimulating the immune system, according to the enclosed instructions. An expensive-looking glass bottle with a pump dispenser bore an elegant label describing the contents as soothing, medicated hand and body lotion. A spool of ivory crochet thread was stabbed through with a silver crochet hook, and the beginnings of an intricate web-like doily dangled from the protruding end. Under it was an instruction booklet of crochet patterns. And the last item was a business card from the Leeland Family Planning Clinic, offering counseling and services, and guaranteeing the client's complete privacy and discretion with handling insurance claims. In other words, an abortion clinic.

Tim smiled and turned in his chair to view the bulletin board again. "My! My!" he said out loud. "You two have been up to no good, haven't you?" But after a few minutes and pinching his knuckles, he came to the conclusion that the business card might've been included in Mary's box of possessions by accident. It probably belonged to someone else. Still, he considered, either one was not beyond the possibility. Love has a strange way of blooming when you least expect it or want it.

Clarence was seated at their usual table when Tim arrived at the Sidewalk Café. "Good," he said as soon as Tim was near enough to hear. "You didn't let the storm this morning keep you away. I thought I would have to eat alone again." He lowered his bald head and peered underneath the table. "Sorry, Waldo," he added, "but I've suspected of late that you've been sleeping instead of listening to me."

"Sorry," Tim said. "I've been on daytime surveillance with this crazy missing person case."

"I figured as much."

"I have all the information I can scrounge up from every source I can think of," Tim said frustrated, "but nothing leads anywhere. Just dead ends."

Their food came and they began eating.

"Now I'm stuck sitting in my car day after day waiting for the bait to be taken at some stupid postal drop box they came up with," Tim continued.

"Sounds pretty smart to me," Clarence observed.

"Yeah," Tim agreed. "Would've been the perfect caper if Mary hadn't keeled over just when they were about to dig out the mother load."

"Why don't you just drop it, and let the authorities handle it?" Clarence commented offhandedly. "You have school and a sweetheart to think about. You don't have time for this."

"What?" Tim said in disbelief. "I...I have to finish this last one, and then I'll quit."

Clarence chuckled and Waldo poked his head out to see what the merriment was about. "You won't ever quit," he said. "You're hooked for life. Admit it. You're a P.I. junkie and you love it."

Tim didn't like being the butt of a joke.

"One day you say you're going to quit the P.I. racket. The next day you can't be talked into quitting, because you can't resist the urge to finish the puzzle. You love the puzzle. The more pieces, the more you love it."

"I don't love it," Tim argued. "And I will quit. Just as soon as I solve this one. Besides, I have plenty of time to decide on a better career choice."

"Oh, to be nineteen again," Clarence mused. He peeked under the table again. "That's two and five-sevenths in dog years," he added for Waldo's benefit. "Did you know," he continued, "that family counselors recommend placing a jigsaw puzzle on the dining room table as a means for families to stay in touch?"

"No, I didn't know that." Tim was finished eating and he was waiting for Clarence.

"It's the rare individual who can walk past a partially constructed jigsaw puzzle and resist the urge to stop and slip in a piece or two, and most often linger at the pastime beyond expectation. And it's the gifted individual who chooses a career that involves turning life's jigsaw puzzle pieces right-side-up and trying to fit it all together into a beautiful picture."

Tim pinched his knuckles and reflected. That was why Clarence had an undying and unreasoning admiration for the former police detective, Brent Weaver. And that was why Clarence had chosen a career that followed detective work so closely. He liked watching a master jigsaw puzzler piece life back together. That was why he was a newspaper reporter.

"I hate jigsaw puzzles," Tim lied. "And I'm no good at detective work."

Clarence lapsed into silence and finished eating.

"God be with you!" Clarence called as they parted.

Tim headed toward the parking lot. He almost turned around, but remembered it was Sunday and Clarence had spent the morning in church. Still, *why did the old man always say that—just before something bad happened?*—he wanted to know.

Chapter 18: Streetlife

Monday morning Brent and Patty arrived early while Tim was out for his morning run. It was probably Patty's idea, Tim realized, so she could make up for some of the work she'd missed while doing surveillance for him.

"I can't wait until this wedding thing is over," Brent said when Tim jogged through the door. "So everything can get back to normal." Brent settled himself in his chair and tipped back. "All this planning and window shopping has got to stop. It's driving me crazy! I'm not a rich man."

"Maybe there won't be a wedding," Patty retaliated, "if you keep it up."

Tim felt responsible for the tension and looked from one to the other.

"And what are you looking at, Kid?" Brent yelled at him. "Why don't you solve a case once in a while?"

One of Patty's stuffed toys made a high arc through the air.

"Incoming," Tim warned. But he was too late and it hit Brent on the side of the head.

Brent gave Patty a look that meant trouble was brewing behind those beady brown eyes of his. Tim ran upstairs to take a shower before the trouble hit.

"Now see what you did?" he heard Brent chiding. "He doesn't like our company."

"Can you blame him?" Patty flared. "You don't play nice with others. And you keep calling him Kid."

"He loves me," Brent returned confidently. "And so do you."

Someday, Tim thought, *he's going to get too cocky and tip too far in his chair.*

"It's taking so long to find a cake decorator," Patty was explaining when Tim returned later, "because I can't find one who has an enraged groom figurine eating crow to set on top of the cake."

Tim tried to sneak out the door without eliciting comments from Brent.

"And where are you off to all the time?"

"Working," Tim answered simply.

"Working on what?" Brent continued. "How come the dead broad takes up more room on your bulletin board than the one you're supposed to be looking for?"

Tim looked at the bulletin board and shrugged. It was true. He had enough information on Mary Harris to fill the right side of the bulletin board and almost nothing on Bernadette Higgins. He could've explained that it was easier to track a dead person—the trail ends here, so to speak. But that wouldn't improve Brent's mood. "They're connected."

"Well, unless they're Siamese twins," Brent said sourly, "you better get a new lead and find her before your fee dwindles down to diddly-squat."

"That's what I'm about to do." Tim shut the door and left. Maybe a few extra days of all-day surveillance was a godsend meant to spare both himself and Patty from Brent's tension over the wedding. Unfortunately the big day was still more than a month away.

Patty showed up just after noon and parked a few car lengths down from Tim's car. He decided to get out and talk to her. She rolled her window down.

"Did you already have lunch?"

She shook her head.

"You're early. Do you want me to pick you up something?"

"No, Dearie. I'm not really hungry."

Tim had a feeling she often went without lunch. And he wanted to tell her he thought she would look great in her wedding dress, even without skipping desserts. But he didn't know how to politely word his observation. "I'm sorry this is causing you conflict with Brent. I shouldn't have asked you to do this for me."

"Don't worry, Dearie. That's just Brent. We get along better than it looks like on the surface. We've known each other too long...a long, long time. Speaking of time," she interrupted herself, "you better get along and grab a bite before practice."

Tim nodded and left. He decided he'd have to come up with a really great wedding gift to make up for all the trouble he was causing.

His classes lasted later than they were supposed to, but he was growing accustomed to that. He returned home. No phone messages. No messages from Patty either. Nothing. When nothing is happening, Tim decided, it's time to make things happen. He put his supper in the microwave and returned downstairs to use the phone.

Tim punched in the number of the Leeland Family Planning Clinic from the business card tacked to Mary's side of the bulletin board. He pretended to be an insurance claims processor. And, in a matter of minutes, he was transferred to the person in charge of matters that the phone-answering secretary was not qualified to handle.

"We have no patient by the name of Mary Harris listed in our records," she assured Tim. "Perhaps if you give me the date and time of her most recent visit, I could check our appointment log."

"This is most disconcerting!" Tim faked an attitude and pretended to be flustered. "Would you do me the kindness," he asked, "of also checking under the name of Bernadette Higgins?"

This gave the woman at the other end of the line cause to pause. "Due to the...ahem...confidential nature of the services we perform, we are not in the habit of giving out information about our patients over—"

"Ms. Harris has previously duped our company by turning in claims that actually belonged to her sister—Bernadette Higgins, please?"

"Just one moment while I check." He was put on hold and held auditorially captive by the local country and western music station. Then, "We do not have a patient listed by that name either."

"Sorry to have put you to so much trouble, Ma'am," Tim said. "I'll just stamp a big 'denied' across this form and recommend her policy be reevaluated and dropped. Thank you." He hung up and tossed the business card in the trashcan by his desk.

Next, he punched in the now familiar number of Clean & Safe Janitorial Service. The voice on her answering machine was business-like and Tim wavered while he listened for the tone. His heart won out and he spoke slowly and softly, hoping his voice sounded sexy instead of betraying that he was scared spitless about pursuing a serious relationship.

"I really enjoyed Saturday night...we need to get together again and talk. I mean we need to talk more. I'd like to get to know you better. Call me, when you get a chance. And let's make plans...to get together more." Tim hung up before his rambling turned imbecilic. And he fished the business card out of the trashcan and returned it to its former spot on Mary Harris' side of the bulletin board.

He ran upstairs and removed his supper from the microwave. While he ate at the little kitchen table, Tim formulated his plans for after dark. He changed into dark clothes, so he wouldn't be conspicuous; the oldest ones he could find, in case things got messy. He waited for night to fall and noticed that his calendar indicated there would be only a thin sliver of moon in the sky tonight.

When he was ready to leave Tim suddenly remembered one of Brent's rules—not that Brent followed a rule book when it came to being a detective, but he had a few of his own that he called his "staying alive" rules. And the one that came to mind was: "When on the job after dark, always wear a bullet-proof vest. The crazies come out after dark, they carry guns, and they shoot at anything that gets in their way."

But what Tim was about to do wasn't really "on the job." And Brent only gave him rules so he could feel blameless if anything happened to Tim. Besides, if Brent followed his own rules, he'd be wearing the Kevlar vest himself. Tim reconsidered when he thought about all the good things he had going for him right now.

He opened the bottom left-side drawer of Brent's desk. Brent was either not on a job tonight, or he'd decided the vest was too hot to wear on an August night. The shoulder holster containing Brent's Smith & Wesson revolver scraped across the bottom of the drawer. He'd never be on a job without his weapon either. Tim slipped the vest on over his shirt. No one was going to see him anyway. He was going to pay a visit to a dumpster in a downtown alley. The one behind the More Than Mail postal service. How dangerous could that be?

Tim saw the van sitting across the street, just in time, before he opened the door. *You'd think in a city the size of Cleermantown, something newsworthy would be happening elsewhere.* Tim climbed out his upstairs bathroom window, which was harder while wearing the bulky bulletproof vest. He got in his car, gave the slip to any possible tails, and ended up at his destination alone at 11:13.

It wasn't the first time he'd ever picked through garbage to get the information he needed. Nevertheless, it was a humbling experience. There was no dignified way to climb into a dumpster. He just pulled himself up with his arms and slipped over the edge and made a soft landing in mostly paper.

He took the penlight from his pocket and shined the beam back and forth across the surface looking for something orange and shiny. When he felt something moist and squishy while using his hands to get to another layer, he realized businesses discarded things other than paper, like lunch leftovers and bathroom refuse. And more than one business made use of this particular dumpster. The task took a while, but he rummaged to the bottom in as methodical a fashion as possible, and was satisfied that the orange wrapping he and Patty had used to tag the bait was not anywhere in the dumpster.

Tim looked around and found a fairly clean piece of paper to wipe his hands on, before turning out his penlight.

"Get out of there slowly with your hands up."

The voice startled Tim, but he immediately began thinking up a pretext that would somehow justify garbage pilfering in an alley. "I have to use my hands to climb out."

"Just get the hell out!" The tone of the voice was ominous. And it didn't sound like a policeman. In fact, it sounded like—

"Right now! Damn it!"

—a woman. "Okay! Okay!" Tim said trying to sound cooperative. "Just give me a chance. I can explain everything."

"Shut up!"

Tim jumped down to the ground and the gravel crunched under his running shoes. Normally his next move would've been to take off like a jackrabbit and then veer sharply in case his adversary was armed and dangerous. But it was a woman. And he could make out in the dim light that she was about half his height. And she was old. The husky voice had fooled him.

"You're in my territory," she said furiously. "No one butts into my territory and gets away with it."

Tim looked around and noticed a beat-up, old shopping cart nearby, and the woman was clutching a big cloth bag in one hand. "I wasn't trying to get away with anything." Tim had heard there were homeless people and bag ladies living in Cleermantown, but he'd never confronted one before.

"I said shut up!"

Tim felt sorry for her despite her offensiveness. Her appearance was humorous, were it not for the fact that she was wearing everything she owned and nothing matched or properly protected her. Tim stepped forward to apologize for being a bother, a bad move in anybody's book.

Her foot swung upward with surprising agility and Tim was left with the agonizing reality that there was no longer a woman alive who wouldn't resort to the cinema-popularized version of self-defense. As soon as he bent over, she struck him a side blow to the head with her bag. He was on his hands and knees in the dark crawling aimlessly when his mind finally registered consciousness. And he headed in the direction he believed and hoped he'd find his car. The pain was excruciating when he stood up and unlocked the door of his Tracker.

It seemed longer driving home than it had taken him to get to the alley. Thank God the van was gone when he parked. He slowly made his way inside and up the stairs. He turned on the light in the bathroom to assess the damage.

Her bag must've had a bowling ball in it, because his head felt like he'd been hit with one. His left eye was swollen shut and his ear was bleeding. He leaned down painfully in the sink and splashed cold water all over his face. He felt like getting in bed and sleeping, but he was afraid he might not wake up again. He decided he'd better let someone know he wasn't feeling well.

"What time is it, Dearie?" Patty asked when she heard his voice on the phone.

Tim squinted at his watch. "About one o'clock. Sorry." He felt exhausted and he could hardly talk.

"Why did you call? Is something the matter?" She was getting an inkling from his voice. "What's the matter, Dearie?"

"What's good for a swollen eye?" His main concern was having to explain to everyone for the next several weeks of his life how he got a black eye. It would be embarrassing to admit he got mugged—by a little, old bag lady.

"I've heard that raw steak is good for a black eye."

"I just got all the blood washed off," Tim argued feebly. "I don't want to put a piece of bloody meat on my face."

"How bad are you hurt, Dearie?" Patty sounded concerned. "Do you want me and Brent to come over and take you to the emergency room?"

"What happened, Kid?" It was Brent's voice and Tim knew he'd grabbed the phone from Patty as soon as he learned he was hurt.

"Just a scrape," Tim lied.

"What's this about a black eye? It sounds like more than a scrape."

"I got beat up."

"Beat up! How bad? Do you want us to come over?"

"It's not bad. I'm okay. Honest."

"I'm coming over. Hang on!" It was Patty who had wrested the phone from Brent now.

"No, don't do that! I'm okay," Tim said weakly. "I just wanted to check in with you guys."

"Okay, Dearie. Get some sleep. We'll be in early to check on you."

Tim made it to his bed and fell asleep in his clothes on top of the covers.

Chapter 19: I'll Come Running

"Don't ever do that again." A deep voice boomed overhead, and Tim woke up and nearly jumped out of his skin. He felt Brent lift him off the bed by the Kevlar vest he was still wearing. "Do you hear me, Kid?" He shook Tim until he responded by opening the only eye he could see out of. His left eye was swollen and throbbing with pain from being jerked upright so abruptly.

"Okay. I won't," Tim mumbled relying on Brent's strength to hold him up.

"You nearly scared Patty to death when she saw you, Kid."

Tim remembered last night and groaned involuntarily.

Patty came up the stairs and hurried into his bedroom. "Here hold this on your eye." She positioned it and then placed Tim's hands over it. "Lay him down," she instructed Brent.

Brent let go of the vest, and Tim fell back on his bed.

"Gently, you big dumb oaf!"

"What is this?" Tim asked trying to see her with his good eye.

"A scraped potato poultice," Patty answered proudly. "It's an Irish cure for bloodshot eyes."

"Figures," Tim said. But he couldn't quite muster a smile.

"What were you trying to do?" Tim could feel Brent's hot breath against his face. "If you were getting into something dangerous enough to wear a bullet-proof vest, why didn't you ask for backup? I would've come."

"I know." Tim opened his eye and looked at Brent. "But I didn't think it was important enough. And I wasn't really expecting any trouble." Tim sighed. "I was just checking the garbage before trash pick-up day to make sure the bait didn't get tossed. Clayton has a lot at stake, I can't afford to miss. The dumpster just happened to be the territory of a very hostile homeless person."

"What?" Brent yelled.

"What part don't you understand?" Tim yelled back. His head throbbed with pain. "The part about the hostile homeless person?"

"Yeah." Brent raised his voice a few more decibels. "You mean to tell me a bum flattened you and gave you that black eye?"

"Is it really black?" Tim asked raising himself on one elbow. The pain almost made him vomit. But the humiliation would be even worse if Brent ever found out the bum that flattened him was a little old lady with steel-toe shoes.

"You lay back down and take it easy today," Patty said. She shoved Brent out of the way and tried to coax Tim back into bed.

"No, I can't," Tim insisted. "I have to be there when it goes down. I can't miss it." He was already dressed. All he had to do was make it to his car and spend the morning outside the postal service building. He was sure he would feel better by noon when Patty came to relieve him for classes. He stood up and waited for the world to stop spinning.

"Actually, it's more of a purple," Brent said dwelling on the negative.

Tim stopped at the bathroom for some pain relievers and slipped the whole bottle in his pants pocket for later when it wore off. Then Brent and Patty followed him downstairs.

"By the way," Patty said quietly. "I took a message for you a few minutes ago."

Tim raised his eyebrows but it hurt.

"I didn't have time to write it down." She cleared her throat.

Brent helped Tim remove the Kevlar vest.

"Trisha says she would love to do something Saturday with you. And, if it's okay with you, she'll make all the arrangements. She'll meet you here at five o'clock."

Tim blushed and that hurt too.

"Here?" Brent was seated in his chair now.

"This is where Tim lives," Patty said.

"Yeah, but...here?" Brent continued. "Why not meet her at her place?"

"She lives with her family," Tim said.

"So, go meet her family," Brent said.

Patty sighed, and Brent became docile again. "Tim has a private life."

"Then he better get a private phone upstairs in his place."

Tim hadn't thought a phone line of his own was necessary, since he didn't have a social life. That was before he met Trisha. "That's a good idea." He walked out the door and arrived at the postal service building just as the manager was opening for business.

Tim scrunched down in his seat and propped his forensic science textbook on the steering wheel. His focus was a little off with only one eye. He held Patty's Irish home remedy on his swollen eye and surprisingly the stinging sensation stopped. Being able to watch the door of a building and read a book at the same time required skill and concentration, and two eyes with sufficient peripheral vision. Tim tried, but gave up and just watched the building.

He was having a hard time staying awake an hour into the watch. Then he saw someone who made him sit up and take notice. Trisha got out of her little dark Mercury Continental and walked into the building. Moments later she returned carrying a white business envelop in her hand.

She didn't look in his direction, so Tim was about to honk his horn to get her attention. Then he remembered. His black eye was appalling, even to him. And he hadn't taken a shower since crawling around in the garbage last night. He ran his tongue over his teeth and realized that if she came over and greeted him with her customary kiss, all his attempts to impress her would do a swirly down the toilet. Instead, he scrunched down even lower when she drove past, oblivious to his presence.

Shortly after noon, Patty drove up and parked. She quickly got out and came to Tim's window. "Are you okay, Dearie? I've been worried sick over you."

Tim felt terrible that he'd caused her so much trouble. "I feel much better now. Please don't worry. See I can even open it now." He made a valiant attempt and ignored the pain, and actually opened his left eye for the first time today. The bright daylight made it water.

He didn't feel like going to class, but he went and sat in a desk as far from the front as possible without drawing attention to himself. That didn't prevent the instructor from calling on him several times to answer questions. Then, to make matters worse, his beeper went off. He fumbled in his pockets and dropped the bottle of pain relievers on the floor before turning it off, then mumbled an apology as he got up and left.

He hurried to the nearest pay phone and punched in the number of the cell phone. Of all days for the bait to be taken, Tim thought, why did it have to be the day he couldn't see well?

He waited anxiously, for Patty to pick it up, then he heard a voice. "IRISH EYES," Brent said sleepily. "How may I help you?"

"I need to talk to Patty."

"She's not here, Kid. She's off on another one of her wedding preparation sprees."

"Oh," Tim said.

The realization that Patty hadn't checked to make sure the cell phone was under the car seat, where Brent usually stashed it, definitely put a damper on his ability to follow the mark. He just hoped and prayed Patty remembered to turn on the video cam and zoom in on the shots he would need to track her down.

"Talk to you later," Tim said and slammed down the receiver.

He ran to his car and made record time pushing the speed limit and accelerating through yellow lights. And when he got there, Patty was sitting in her car in front of the postal service building. Tim quickly got out of his car and ran to hers.

"Oh, Tim, I'm so sorry. I've been trying to keep my eyes on the place, but I can't take it any longer. It burns like hell! I can't stand it," she sobbed.

Tim looked confused.

"See! My hands." She held her hands out the window for him to see.

Tim's confusion turned to alarm when he saw them. Her hands were bright red and irritated. He looked around frantically. His left eye joined the activity and served to blur his vision. But he spotted a water faucet sticking out of the side of a building half a block away. He opened the car door and pulled Patty by her arms to a standing position. Then he practically carried her to the faucet where he turned it on and stuck her hands under the cold running water.

Patty yelped and tried to pull away. But Tim held her hands firmly. Whether the cold water was numbing the itch or effecting a halt to the reaction, Tim didn't know. But she finally regained a little control.

"What happened?" Tim asked.

"I don't know," Patty whimpered. She turned her head enough to wipe the tears on her shoulder. "My hands were feeling a little dry and irritated, so I decided to use some hand lotion."

"Hand lotion?"

Patty nodded. "I saw that fancy bottle of hand and body lotion sitting on your desk. It looked like it would be really good. I read the label and it sounded...it was so tempting, I tried some."

"On my desk? I don't keep any hand lotion on my...oh, yeah," Tim said remembering the box of Mary Harris' belongings he'd brought from Clayton's Investment and Finance Corporation.

"How do your hands feel now?" Tim asked. A large puddle was forming under the faucet and threatened to flood their shoes.

"A little better," Patty said.

Tim turned off the water faucet. Her hands were still red and irritated.

"But they still itch," she said as the numbing cold wore off and the feeling returned.

Tim took a couple of pain relievers from the bottle in his pocket. "These are anti-inflammatory pain relievers. They'll relieve the irritation and prevent swelling." He placed them in Patty's mouth and then turned on the faucet again and caught some water in his cupped hands for her to drink. She swallowed the pills.

Her hands looked painful. "I'm going to take you to the emergency room now." Tim put a supportive arm around her and walked toward where their cars were parked.

"No, that's not necessary," Patty said.

"You can't drive with your hands like that."

Patty didn't waste her strength arguing. She stood by her car until Tim opened the door for her. Then she slid behind the steering wheel.

"Move over and let me drive you," Tim insisted.

"You have to stay here and watch. After a whole week and all you've been through, you can't miss it now."

She was right, but loyalty to a friend was a higher priority than any job. "You can't drive yourself!"

"Oh yeah? Watch me!" To prove her point, Patty managed to get the key in the ignition and turned it by clasping it between both hands. She clumsily shifted from park to drive and drove away leaving Tim feeling like the lowest scoundrel on the face of the earth.

He had three hours of waiting and watching until the postal service closed for the day, which gave him plenty of time to think. And he thought about what had just happened.

If the injury to Patty's hands was caused by the hand lotion from Mary Harris' box of belongings, then that meant...what?...Why would someone known to have severe allergies use a hand lotion that caused burning and itching? Why would a hand lotion, supposedly made from all natural, hypoallergenic ingredients, cause injury to a person's skin? It didn't make any sense.

Unless...it wasn't accidental. And if it was on purpose, then someone had intentionally...a bizarre thought occurred to Tim...tampered with the hand lotion. But who? And why? He didn't want to believe what his mind was telling him.

Who better than her roommate, knew Mary had severe allergies? And who better than her roommate, was in a position to take advantage of the embezzlement scheme at Clayton's? And who had a better motive for getting Mary Harris out of the way?

Could it be...murder? Using her own hand lotion? Could it really be true that Bernadette Higgins was a partner in a scheme with the potential to rob several local companies of millions of dollars? Could it also be true that she saw the chance to rid herself of the one person who stood between her and the whole take? Greed?

Tampering with her hand lotion for the purpose of killing Mary was not only murder, it was murder of the worst kind—premeditated. And the genius of it was, homicide by poisoning that took advantage of Mary's severe allergic condition was virtually impossible to prove.

Chapter 20: I'm a Believer

After the postal service closed for the day, Tim quickly drove home. Brent and Patty were gone. He'd been thinking about the tainted hand lotion and what it could mean. In a court of law, he didn't have anything on which to hang a conviction. It was called merely conjecture based on circumstantial evidence. His only real evidence had been compromised—he himself had removed the bottle of hand lotion from the scene of the crime, and the chain of command necessary for evidence to be used in court, had been broken by leaving it on his desk.

Still, it never would've been discovered if Patty hadn't been tempted to use it. He knew, even if he couldn't legally prove it, the hand lotion had been used as a murder weapon, in a death that never would be ruled a homicide. All he could do is point out the suspicious circumstances surrounding Mary Harris' death.

All of which only fueled his determination to penetrate Bernadette Higgins' secret hideaway. He needed to nail her for the embezzlement conspiracy.

That could be proven in a court of law. And he knew
Clayton would hire the best lawyer money could buy.

As of midnight, Tim had eleven days remaining
under contract to find Bernadette Higgins. But he'd
spend the rest of his life, if necessary. In fact, now that
he thought about it, he'd prefer finding her after her
contest eligibility expired, so she couldn't afford a good
lawyer. However, any delay in finding her now, might
allow Bernadette to escape the repercussions of the
heinous crimes she'd committed. For Mary's sake, he
had to find her. And the sooner the better. But how to
find her posed the problem. He needed more bait to
draw her into the open.

The first thing Tim did was to dispense a small
amount of the lotion onto a piece of cardboard without
touching the bottle. It took only seconds for the telltale
odor of formaldehyde to reach his nose and overwhelm
the, at first, flowery fragrance. There was no doubt
now!

Tim decided to check for latent fingerprints. The
paper label was his best chance, since several people
had handled the bottle. And prints were more likely to
smudge on the smooth glass surface anyway.

Developing latents on paper was NOT one of the
fun aspects of fingerprinting, because it required the
use of a chemical that could cause severe headaches
and even chemical pneumonia. However, the fact that
paper can retain fingerprints virtually forever, makes it
a useful tool for scientists, as well as investigators,
allowing them to fingerprint the writers on papyrus
found in ancient Egyptian tombs.

Tim ate his supper first, so he wouldn't be working
with the nauseating smells on an empty stomach.
Then he checked the parking lot to make sure the local

TV news anchorwoman wouldn't accost him. He carried the bottle, by its dispenser, outside and set it in the middle of the parking lot. It was the time of day just before sunset and not yet dark enough for the streetlights to activate.

He knelt down and held the aerosol can of Ninhydrin at arm's length from his body and about a foot from the label. He sprayed, then stood up and moved away quickly to avoid breathing the fumes. While he waited for the unpleasant metallic odor to dissipate, he realized the stillness and the heaviness of the air, just before a storm, would prolong the job.

It had been rainy the night Harry Spears was gunned down in this very parking lot. And the thought gave Tim a chill as he recalled stumbling into the middle of Brent's homicide investigation a year ago.

A lot of good resulted from that chance encounter. He'd found his birth parents, and a family of siblings, all of whom he dearly loved. He'd returned Rhonda Ghent safely to her home and family. He'd met Clarence Drib and Waldo, without whose help and encouragement he wouldn't be alive today. And, of course, Brent was the one responsible for making him believe he'd someday make a good P.I. Brent became his mentor, who taught him the rudiments of day-to-day survival in this nasty world he now found himself caught up in, a long way from the quiet little town in Michigan where he grew up.

And the price he paid for this wonderful life was the memory of staring down the barrel of a handgun just before getting a hole blasted in his shoulder, of watching people die all around him, and of being so terrified he'd peed his pants and cried like a baby. The nightmares and anxiety attacks weren't as often now

as they had been a year ago, but there were times
when he was convinced Almighty, the underworld
crime boss, was watching him, ready to clean up the
remaining loose end in his identity crisis. The one
thing that had helped Tim through it all was the
certainty that God was God, and Almighty was just a
man, no matter what he chose to call himself.

Tim stopped pinching his knuckles and walked
back to where he'd left the bottle on the ground. He
picked it up by the dispenser and went inside. A little
applied heat would make the fingerprints materialize
more quickly. It usually took up to forty-eight hours
for Ninhydrin to react with the amino acids contained
in all perspiration, a natural component left behind in
fingerprints. Tim hung a blow dryer from the edge of
his file drawer, plugged it in, and directed the heated
air onto the label.

In the meantime, Tim worked on the final draft of
his research paper covering the fascinating topic of
poisoning as a means of homicide. It was even more
fascinating to him now that he had first-hand
experience dealing with it. In fact, it was a personal
issue with him now to gather as much evidence as he
could get his hands on, summarize and set forth the
details, and wrap it up and solve it with Bernadette
Higgins' confession to the police—signed, sealed and
delivered, and ...in his dreams!

Tim finally succumbed to the urge to sleep. He
checked the lotion bottle and turned off the blow dryer.
No fingerprints had appeared yet. When his alarm
woke him Wednesday morning, he lay in bed trying to
convince himself that Brent was right about the futility
of exercise, and tried to go back to sleep.

But he was awake and his mind was running, even if he wasn't. He quickly dressed in shorts and a T-shirt and his sneakers. He felt disappointed that no fingerprints were visible on the label as he set out for the high school field track to do his morning laps. More time was needed, that's all.

"'Bout time you hauled your scrawny keister back in here." Brent *sounded* upset.

Patty *looked* upset. Not a good sign!

"We're going to have a talk...when you're dressed." It wasn't a request. It was more than a command. More like a threat to his life.

Tim opened his mouth to suggest that maybe it shouldn't wait, since he was...dressed. But Patty caught his eye and gave him a signal that seemed to confirm the advisability of doing exactly what he was told to do. Brent sometimes thought he was still in charge of a police unit, and he was used to having his orders obeyed.

"Yes, sir," Tim snapped. He suppressed the urge to also give a salute and hurried upstairs.

When Tim came back downstairs the atmosphere hadn't changed. Brent wasn't even tipped back in his chair. He was sitting tall and alert.

"Don't ever do that again." Brent enunciated each word slowly.

"You said the very same thing yesterday morning," Tim said, attempting to sound jovial. "And I didn't...do that again...I don't think." Then he added, "What was it I did anyway?"

"You want another black eye?"

"Oh, yeah. The black eye." Tim unconsciously touched the left side of his head. "I know I didn't do that again."

"I'm talking about breaking the rules," Brent said releasing his pent up anger. "The rules we operate by. The ones we live by, and die by if we break them."

Tim had a feeling he should know what Brent was talking about, but he didn't. So he stood quietly waiting and began pinching his knuckles.

"You used Patty on a job!"

Uh, oh!

"You NEVER use Patty on a job. She works in the office, not in the field. She's not a P.I. or a trainee."

Tim swallowed and glanced at Patty. She looked miserable and her hands were still red and irritated.

"You put her in danger, and I don't know if I can ever forgive you for that."

This was serious, Tim thought, and shifted nervously under Brent's glare. "It wasn't..." Tim was about to tell him it wasn't dangerous, but that posed a difficult burden of proof, since Patty was the one who'd discovered they were actually trying to track a murderer. "It was supposed to be just a simple surveillance. She was just filling in a few hours for me, so I could go to class. She was going to page me if the mark took the bait."

"And now you know how easily simple plans can go wrong. And it doesn't change the fact you put my wife in danger."

"Sorry," Tim said. It was all he could say.

"You're not cut out to be a P.I. You think it's a game. I don't want you for a partner."

Patty gasped. "That's not true. Why don't you quit browbeating him and treat him like your partner, for once?"

Brent stood up, angry.

Patty got up and stood right in front of him with her hands on her hips and her head tipped back so she could look at Brent eye to eye. "And besides, I'm not your wife yet. And maybe I won't be, if you keep thinking you can order me around and control me to keep me out of danger. I make my own decisions. I chose to marry you. And I chose to help Tim. It was my choice, I wanted to do it. After all, I work for him too, since he's your partner. I've asked to go with you on surveillance, remember? And you wouldn't let me. I want to learn the business you're in. I love everything about you, including what you do. I want to be with you."

Brent deflated like a punctured balloon and ended up kissing Patty and holding her in a long embrace. He turned around and faced Tim. "You're not off the hook, Kid."

"I know."

"I'm going to have to think about all this, come up with some guidelines," he said thoughtfully.

Tim nodded.

"And another thing, Kid. You better pray that girlfriend of yours isn't Irish."

Patty put her hands on her hips and gave Brent a look.

"On second thought, pray that she is." He kissed Patty with obvious passion. "Makes life exciting."

Tim looked down at the lotion bottle sitting on the floor in front of his file cabinet. *Talk about exciting!* Pink lines of fingerprints were beginning to appear on the paper label.

Chapter 21: Flight of the Gull

Tim checked his watch. He didn't have time to wait for the prints to fully develop. He'd check them later. And, if his theory was correct, he already knew whose fingerprints he'd find on the label. Right now, he needed to find out where exactly Bernadette Higgins, the million-dollar-grand-prize winner and embezzler-turned-murderer, was hiding. She had some explaining to do. And, if he laid out the groundwork very carefully, she'd have some confessing to do in front of the proper legal authorities.

Tim took the long way and drove past the parking lot of Clayton's Investment and Finance Corporation. He couldn't explain his need to know where she was. But when he didn't see Trisha's car and felt disappointed, he decided it served him right for succumbing to a ridiculous emotional impulse.

Tim drove on and parked across the street from the postal service building as the business day in Cleermantown began. He was finding each unfruitful day of surveillance harder to take. And now that he had the added responsibility of trying to nab a murderer, he could barely sit still.

Patty made her appearance at one o'clock and parked behind him. Tim got out of his car and got in on the passenger side.

"I wasn't sure if Brent would let you come anymore," he said.

"Don't worry about Brent."

"He's right, you know. I shouldn't put you in danger."

Patty sighed. "I don't believe this! I just finished straightening out his male chauvinist mindset, and now I have to deal with you."

"That hand lotion thing yesterday threw this missing person case in a whole new light."

"I couldn't help it. Brent woke up when I got back, and he saw my hands. It just slipped out when he asked where I'd been and what I was doing," Patty explained. "I'm sorry I let you down."

"It's okay," Tim said. "It's not that. I feel better now that Brent knows. I should've never asked you to sneak around behind his back like that."

"I almost got away with it." Patty smiled. "He didn't know for a whole week. And he's a detective."

All women were born sneaky, Tim knew that. But Patty sounded like he'd created a monster. "What I was getting at about the hand lotion," he said returning to his original thought, "is this case has gone from a simple missing person, to grand larceny, and now to homicide."

"Homicide?" Patty's green eyes grew bigger.

"So you can see..." Tim fidgeted. "...I should stay here the full time. It's too important, and too dangerous, for you to handle."

"Homicide?" she repeated.

"The hand lotion was tampered with. Mary Harris was extremely allergic to formaldehyde. And someone put formaldehyde in the hand lotion, knowing that she used it every day."

"And now you think I can't sit here and watch for that someone," Patty said, "even though I've already been doing it for a week." Her anger increased. "Now all of a sudden I'm incapable? I'm supposed to let you flunk out of college, just because I made a stupid mistake and let you down one time? Now you don't trust me? You think I'm stupid enough to screw this up?"

"No, you're not stupid!" Tim braced himself for impact. She was going to get physical at any moment. He didn't know which area of his anatomy to protect from her Irish temper. "In fact, if you hadn't used the hand lotion, no one would've ever known. She would've gotten away with murder. And she still might get away with it, if I can't prove it. That's why...it's important. I can make up the class time I miss and get notes from another student," he added.

Patty had been watching the building during the whole conversation and now she watched closely as a man came out the door, empty-handed. Her jaw stiffened. "I can do it."

Tim quit watching Patty and turned away. "Okay," he said. "You can do it." He got out of her car, but turned to add, "Just be careful. Don't take any chances. Not any," he emphasized.

He walked to his car and drove to the campus parking lot for his first class. Brent would kill him if anything else happened to Patty. This extra stress was just what he needed! And being called on to give an impromptu speech in class made his bad day even worse.

Tim stopped at the office long enough to check the fingerprints that had developed on the hand lotion label. They were mostly incomplete or overlapped, but he found one good clear print of a left thumb that precisely matched the thumbprint he'd lifted from Bernadette Higgins' makeup compact. It was all the proof he needed. Unfortunately, it wasn't enough to hold up in court. And it didn't provide any clues to where she was hiding.

When Tim arrived at the morgue, Dr. Morgan was on duty, sitting at her desk and filling out a report.

"Sorry to bother you so late," he began.

She finished what she was writing, and then set her pen down and looked up at him. "It's always a pleasure to talk with a handsome young man." She smiled.

Tim took the compliment in stride. In Dr. Morgan's line of work, she would take pleasure in talking to anyone with a warm body and a peart complexion. "I need your expert advice in a missing person case I'm on."

Dr. Morgan let her reading glasses drop to her chest on the chain around her neck and gestured at a chair facing the side of her desk. "Still haven't found the lady in the photograph?" she asked.

Tim sat down and shook his head. "She's more than missing. She's completely vanished, on the heels of discovering she's a thief, and now I believe she murdered her roommate."

"Murder is a strong accusation, Timothy."

"That's why I need your advice," Tim said. "I need to know how to go about proving it."

"Timothy," Dr. Morgan smiled uncertainly, "I advise you to go to the police if you have reason to suspect murder."

"I plan to do just that." Tim began pinching his knuckles. "But I'm afraid it's not that simple. I believe she poisoned her roommate by inducing a severe allergic reaction."

Dr. Morgan straightened in her chair. "Are you sure?" She had a nervous habit of rolling between her fingers the chain that held her glasses. Tim was a student of nervous habits, since his own nervous affliction had been the vehicle that led to his true identity and the whereabouts of his birth parents a year ago. "Are you sure you're not just allowing your fascination with your research topic to fabricate the possibility?"

"I'm positive." Tim told her everything he'd discovered thus far.

Dr. Morgan nodded. "This has the earmarking of a classic textbook case of homicidal poisoning. By the time someone recognizes it for what it really is, as you did, the evidence has been lost or, as in your case, compromised to the point of uselessness in a legal indictment."

"So what should I do?" Tim asked.

"Take it to the police," Dr. Morgan repeated. "And include this, just for good measure." She looked up the case file on Mary Harris, flipped through it, and handed Tim a piece of paper. The death certificate with the autopsy findings. "I can release the whole file to the proper authorities, but I don't think they'll find it helpful."

Tim read the cause of death. Cardiac arrest and asphyxiation by accidental environmental poison due to a severe allergic reaction.

"Because it was an unattended sudden death at her place of work, my associate performed a medical-legal autopsy. Unfortunately, a limited autopsy was ruled sufficient, because the deceased had been under the care of a physician for a known medical condition, which contributed to her death."

Tim looked at her, disappointed.

"One thing's for sure," Dr. Morgan continued, "this case is right up your alley."

Tim winced at the recollection of Brent saying the exact same thing three weeks ago. "Why do you say that?"

"Doing a research paper on the topic of homicide by poisoning has made you somewhat of an expert in a less than popular specialization."

"I specialize in missing person cases, not homicide investigations," Tim reminded her.

"Still, you have the specialized knowledge to contribute to this investigation. And citing a first-hand case history in your research paper is sure to win you an excellent grade and a place on the dean's list."

Tim stood to leave. "Thanks for your advice, Dr. Morgan."

"By the way, Timothy," Dr. Morgan remained seated, "that was an excellent piece of investigation in discovering the footprints in the 'Leave 'em Smiling' serial murder case."

"Just lucky," Tim said as he left.

Tim unlocked the door and entered the office of IRISH EYES. He saw the blinking light on the answering machine before he turned on the lights. He

was anxious to take a post-morgue-visit shower, but
he was even more anxious to hear Trisha's voice. He
pressed the play button and started undressing. But
he stopped to listen closely when he heard Dennis
Lakey's voice.

"Thanks for the update."

Tim had sent by registered mail a summarized
report of his findings, which included his plan to bait a
trap and do surveillance at the postal service, the
address given on the bogus accounts. It hadn't
included his suspicion that Mary's death was a
homicide.

"I hope you're closer to finding Mary Harris'
roommate now. I need to warn you. Mr. Clayton is
getting impatient, because today one of the tagged
accounts registered some activity. The monthly
dividend check we sent to the usual address was
cashed."

Tim turned and slammed his fist against the stair
railing. She was going to get away with it if he didn't
do something. And he had to do it NOW! Once he
alerted the police to what he suspected, he wouldn't be
allowed within ten feet of anything to do with
Bernadette Higgins. And the case would go
UNSOLVED without admissible evidence.

Chapter 22: Song Sung Blue

Being a private investigator didn't give a person any authority above that of the average citizen. There was no difference where it concerned legal matters. Private investigators are bound by speed limits in a car chase, they aren't entitled to a search warrant no matter how much probable cause they come up with, and they put everything on the line when they make a citizen's arrest. But sometimes the need to perform above the normal call of duty of John Q. Public kicks in. And therein lies the difference.

As he stood in the shower, Tim thought about how it could've happened. How had Bernadette Higgins slipped through his fingers? It wasn't a foolproof plan, but it should've worked. He and Patty had been watching every single minute the postal service was open for business. Except...

The chance that Bernadette Higgins had made her appearance during Patty's episode with the hand lotion, the few minutes when they'd both been preoccupied with relieving her burning and itching hands at a nearby water faucet, was too uncanny to believe.

He hadn't seen a woman with a purse large enough to conceal the bright orange document tube, and he'd alerted Patty to the possibility. Perhaps someone had been inside long enough to unwrap it and discard the bright orange signal after the night he checked the dumpster. But that was unlikely also.

The only other likely possibility was that the mail for the accounts was being forwarded to a series of one or more postal drop boxes at different addresses before being picked up by Bernadette Higgins. That even sounded like something Mary Harris would think up and arrange.

Tim stepped out of the shower, dried off, and dressed in dark clothes. He couldn't help remembering the last time he wore them when he looked in the mirror and was made aware that his black eye was improving, but still visible.

When he returned downstairs the light on the answering machine was blinking again. *What now?* Tim pressed the play button and listened while he retrieved what he needed from the locked cabinet where he and Brent stored their expensive and less-used equipment. It contained surveillance cameras and binoculars for day and night observation, eavesdropping devices, countermeasure kits, voice analyzers, and the item Tim was going to have the opportunity to try out for the first time, their new electronic lock pick gun.

"Hi. It's me. Trisha. I wish I could ever catch you at home, instead of leaving a message." She sighed.

Tim sighed. *You and me both!* As soon as he had the time, he decided, he was going to have a private phone line installed upstairs in his apartment.

"I got your last message. I'm looking forward to Saturday. I wish I didn't work such odd hours, so I could be with you more." The answering machine clicked and rewound after Trisha hung up.

Tim visualized her beautiful brown eyes and realized he was losing focus on his objective. Tonight was not the night to be thinking about romance. He needed to concentrate. He tacked Mary's death certificate to her side of the bulletin board.

But there was a chance Trisha might still be at home. Tim looked at his watch. A quarter to six. She began work at six. He quickly punched the numbers. It rang. Once. Twice. Too many times. When he heard the familiar sound of her recorded voice, he hung up. He'd missed her call while in the shower.

He took a deep breath, checked for parked vans and roving reporters in the parking lot, and then plunged out into the moonless night. He made one stop at an electronics store that was open late where he purchased the smallest answering machine attachment they had available. He drove past Clayton's Investment and Finance Corporation, and his heart raced at the mere sight of Trisha's dark blue Lincoln parked under the light in the parking lot. She was on the job, and so was he.

He needed to concentrate. His life might very well depend on his ability to keep Trisha out of his thoughts tonight. He parked a block away and walked to within sight of the apartments and the red Corvette sitting like a sore thumb in the parking area. It hadn't been moved.

He crept to the porch in front of the door, thinking the whole time that it was useless to sneak. A guy his height toting a backpack couldn't help drawing attention if someone happened to be watching. Apparently, no one was. He slipped the business end of the electronic lock pick in the keyhole. It took longer than he expected. For some reason, he always associated the word "electronic" with the word "speed." Nevertheless, it was better than trying to get in through a window.

Once inside, Tim quietly closed the door and looked around with his penlight to get his bearings. Everything was just as he remembered it, except for the layer of dust he would try not to disturb. He had taken the precaution of wearing gloves, since the police would probably follow close on his heels with their own investigation once he turned the case over to them.

B and E's were not his preferred method of investigation. His first break in and illegal entry had been discovered by, none other than, Brent Weaver, who mercifully withheld the charge to protect Tim's immaculate police record. And now he owned the building that had begun his life of criminal investigation. It was IRISH EYES Investigative Services and it housed his upstairs apartment.

Tim's first order of business was to check the telephone and the table on which it was sitting for latent fingerprints. He shined his penlight on the surfaces from several angles. But the passage of time and a layer of dust had obliterated any clues that might've once been there. He lifted the receiver and checked the underside. He dusted it, just in case, with no results.

Then he set to work connecting the answering machine. He plugged it into a nearby outlet, switched the phone cord to a double jack attachment he'd purchased at the electronics store, and channeled it through the answering machine. He popped in a celebrity answering tape, and then made sure it was all properly installed by listening for a dial tone and hoping he knew what he was doing. The last step was to make the answering machine less conspicuous by duct taping it securely underneath the table.

Next, Tim entered the bedroom and carefully searched for fingerprints with his penlight on all the furniture and smooth surfaces. He pulled out the drawers of the heavy wooden dresser, creating a stair-step effect, so he could view the contents of each simultaneously.

The right-side drawers belonged to Mary, if his assessment of the opposite personalities was correct. They contained white cotton undergarments, and an assortment of socks and nightgowns completely void of bright colors and lacy trim. One drawer contained gloves, white handkerchiefs with crocheted edges, and a plain jewelry box filled with the always-in-good-taste strand of pearls and a selection of outdated pins and brooches.

The left-side drawers would've been the envy of any Victoria's Secret model. Bernadette made up for the lack of business Mary afforded the popular lingerie company. Tim noted the colorful, sheer, and skimpy array—no ankle-length cotton gowns or support hosiery for Bernadette.

Tim made his way into the adjoining bathroom, a treasure trove of smooth flat surfaces where, in most cases, he was sure to find latent prints. It took time to check and dust the tub, the toilet, the trashcan, the medicine cabinet, mirrors, brushes, shaver, and all the toiletries that might still bear the user's prints. He lifted all he could find and carefully labeled and stored them in his backpack, along with paper cups and other paper items that had been used and discarded in the trashcan.

When it came to personal identification, fingerprints were the best. Makeup, clothes, and other physical aspects could all be changed, but there wasn't much a person could do about fingerprints, except try not to leave any.

Tim decided to check inside the closet when he finished in the bathroom. Once again, Bernadette's belongings occupied the left side, Mary's the right. Dark unflattering suits, white blouses, plaid pleated skirts, plain waisted dresses, all of expensive fabric, made up Mary's wardrobe hanging on the rack. The shelf above was stacked with cotton cardigan sweaters. A neat row of dark shoes lined the floor, all of the flat heel and oxford variety. Tim made a note of the sizes.

Bernadette's side of the closet was a conglomeration of the latest fashions and colors. Jeans, shirts, sweaters, suede and fur vests, dresses of the night-on-the-town variety, belts, and purses, lots of them, hung in no apparent order and threatened to encroach on Mary's side. Tennis shoes, hiking boots and heels of every color imaginable littered the floor. Tim noted the sizes. Plastic storage boxes lined the shelf above. Inside were wigs in an assortment of hair lengths, and colors ranging from salt-and-pepper gray, to platinum blonde and bright red.

The idea that Bernadette might be a master of disguise with numerous false I.D.'s at her disposal, didn't surprise Tim. Obviously, she'd provided the flesh and bones manifestations for Mary's inventions whenever legally required. The two women formed an odd partnership, a harmonious marriage of completely opposite personalities, living and working together toward a common goal of amassing a small fortune for themselves through false identities, deceptive disguises, and embezzled front money. But, as in any partnership, it only worked as long as they cooperated. Somewhere along the line, whether greed, a power struggle, or a silly disagreement, the communication had broken down and spelled Mary's untimely demise.

A set of expensive luggage formed the dividing line in the floor of the closet. The utter completeness of Bernadette's disappearance prompted Tim to remove the large heavy canvas suitcase and lay it flat on the floor. He unbuckled the heavy center strap and unzipped the three sides of the lid. He flipped it open and checked all the compartments. A slightly smaller suitcase filled the inside and Tim was encouraged by its zipped and buckled façade. He opened it also and checked the compartments. Next came the garment bag. Tim removed it, so he could unsnap it to full length. He unzipped it and removed the toiletry bag. When he unzipped that, Tim pulled out the matching cloth laundry bag. The drawstring was pulled tight and knotted, but he knew he was close to pay dirt. In sequence, he removed three shoe bags, each knotted with a drawstring and stuffed inside the previous one. His trouble was worth it when at last he dumped the contents on the floor.

Bernadette Higgins' passport lay in the heap, along with a wallet containing her driver's license, a library card, and several credit cards naming her as a user of Mary Harris' accounts. For all practical and legal purposes, Bernadette Higgins was dead also. Her new alias was the mystery now. She'd cut all ties to this past life. And somewhere, whoever she really was, she believed she'd gotten away with murder.

The keys to Bernadette's red Corvette lay on the floor also. Tim picked them up. He'd love nothing more than to check the interior of the sports car for fingerprints. But courtesy lights and warning buzzers in an apartment complex of this size was all the detriment he needed to convince him to leave that task for the police to do when he turned the case over to them.

Tim carefully redid the luggage the way he had found it, as well as making sure the apartment looked the way it did when he entered. He thumbed through the mail piled on the coffee table, and found nothing revealing. No hobby supply catalogs, except the one addressed to Mary concerning crocheting. Steaming open the envelope of the telephone bill would serve no purpose, since Bernadette had formulated her plans long before the latest invoice was tallied. And she wouldn't have any reason to call home. At least, not yet. Not until he gave her a good enough reason. That was a job for tomorrow.

When Tim arrived home, he sat down immediately and drew a sketch of the apartment. He added every detail and placement of furniture he could remember. And then he tacked it to the middle of the bulletin board.

Then he listed personality and physical characteristics for each of the two women on separate sheets of paper. He included details down to the size and color of their underwear. But a bulging dossier wouldn't help him find the one who had murdered the other, unless he knew how to put the puzzle together.

Chapter 23: High Rolling Man

"Dean's a good friend of mine," Brent said. "And he holds the current department record for the most solved homicides. Although he'll never come close to matching my record," he bragged.

"But," Tim said, "has he ever handled a case of homicidal poisoning?"

Brent stared thoughtfully at the bulletin board. "Murder is murder. And Dean has a sixth sense when it comes to understanding the criminal mind."

"So...you think I have enough to prove a case for homicide?"

"You should never make positive assumptions," Brent said. "The evidence is still open to another interpretation."

"The way I see it," Tim asserted, "there's no other way to interpret it. Bernadette's fingerprints were all over the bottle of hand lotion that Mary used at work. And the hand lotion contained formaldehyde, which Mary was severely allergic to. Bernadette was Mary's roommate, so Bernadette knew Mary's allergy was severe enough to kill her if she didn't receive medical attention. Bernadette also knew that Mary worked alone. And, most importantly, Bernadette was the one person who stood to benefit from Mary's death as a partner in the embezzlement scheme."

"Hold your horses," Brent said loudly enough to cause Patty to look up from her desk with an alarmed expression. "Those are all viable assumptions, but don't close your mind to the less obvious." Brent paced back and forth with his hands clasped behind his back. "What if...Mary committed suicide?"

Tim laughed. "No way! Why would she do that?"

"It's not as messy as cutting her wrists or shooting herself," Brent remarked. "It goes along with her personality characteristic of being neat."

"But Bernadette's fingerprints are on the hand lotion bottle."

"That can easily be explained away by simply saying Bernadette used her roommate's hand lotion before Mary took it to work. Maybe she bought it for her. After all, you said yourself that Mary's fingerprints were less prevalent in the apartment, because she wore gloves all the time to keep her skin allergies under control."

"Mary wouldn't have committed suicide when she was on the verge of pulling off the heist of a lifetime. She spent years laying the groundwork for those bogus accounts."

"What about the possibility that someone where she worked discovered what she was doing and decided to get in on the action? Anyone at Clayton's had access to her hand lotion and knew she had allergies."

"Not really," Tim said. Actually, the possibility had crossed his mind before all the evidence began pointing to Bernadette Higgins. "None of them knew her very well, because she worked alone on the computer system at night when everyone else was gone."

"And you believe what everyone tells you, Kid?" Brent stopped pacing and looked at the bulletin board.

"No," Tim answered. "But how do you explain Bernadette's sudden disappearance when Mary died?"

"That's my point," Brent emphasized. "Stick to finding Bernadette Higgins. Whether she's innocent or guilty, dead or alive, doesn't matter. And I'm sure you'll find most, if not all, the answers to your questions. And let the police handle any suspicions of homicide."

Brent was right, Tim decided. His only two jobs were missing person cases. The first, to find a contest winner. The second, to find out who was drawing on bogus investment accounts. If they turned out to be one and the same person, he would end his stint as a P.I. trainee on a successful note. And he'd leave the question of Mary's death to the police.

"So...you don't think I have enough to prove a case for homicide."

"All I'm saying is, a lot of holes need to be plugged to prove anything."

Tim nodded. "Okay," he said. "Call and tell Dean I'm on my way."

Patty handled the message while Brent settled himself and tipped back in his chair. "Dean will meet you in an hour," she informed Tim.

Tim picked up his own receiver and dialed the number of the empty apartment where Mary Harris and Bernadette Higgins had once lived. It rang six times before the answering machine picked up. He smiled at the recording of the famous comedian's joke on the tape. When he heard the beep, he left a test message to ensure that the machine was working properly, and to program it so all future calls would be answered after only two rings. Then he tested the remote retrieval, and heard his message played back. He hung up, satisfied that his second attempt to bait a trap for Bernadette might be the one to draw her out into the open.

His meeting with Dean was interesting, but Tim knew he hadn't impressed the new homicide detective at the Cleermantown Police Station. Being Brent's partner was more of a handicap than an edge when he entered the highly competitive world of cops. And it didn't take long to turn over all his information. He didn't have much that could be called concrete, based on sound evidence of a provable nature.

The job done, Tim visited several of the businesses in town that had been frequented by Mary Harris and/or Bernadette Higgins. A stash of paper and plastic shopping bags in their apartment had revealed several. Receipts and wrappers in the trashcans added to the list. And the ads on the barrels of pens in the desk and on magnets clinging to the refrigerator gave him more places to visit. He was looking for a pattern and, if he got really lucky, a face in a crowd with Bernadette Higgins' features.

By lunchtime Tim had worked up an appetite and noticed a subtle pattern of behavior. One or both of the women had a deep appreciation for luxury and the

kind of personal attention and convenience that came
with shopping and recreation at exclusive places—a
full-service filling station, a grocery store with carry-
out attendants, a health spa that provided amenities
for every grooming desire, a women's clothier shop
with personal sales representatives who could
purchase any foreign or domestic ensemble for a price,
and, of course, a travel agency that sponsored a
million dollar sweepstakes annually and could afford
to hire a private investigative service. Rich taste,
considering Mary Harris drove a black Toyota and
worked as a computer consultant.

Tim arrived at the Sidewalk Café, as Clarence and
Waldo were making themselves comfortable at their
usual table, in time to place his order after Clarence.

"Where you been keeping yourself?" the retired
journalist wanted to know.

"Where every gumshoe wastes his life away," Tim
answered.

"Surveillance." Clarence peeked under the table at
Waldo. "Didn't I tell you he was on surveillance?" He
returned his attention to Tim. "Waldo was convinced
you'd given us up for female companionship."

It bothered Tim that Clarence sometimes carried on
conversations to and through the dog. "You should
maybe seek out some female companionship yourself."

"I have all the companionship I need, including that
of a wet-behind-the-ears gumshoe." Clarence laughed.

Their food came and they began eating.

"Did you get what you were looking for?" Clarence
asked.

Tim shook his head. "She was too smart to get
caught with her hands in the mailbox."

Clarence nodded.

"And she's smart enough to get away with murder."

Clarence frowned. "I smell an exclusive feature coming my way."

"It's yours," Tim said. "But first, I need you to do something."

The old man set his sandwich down and listened.

"I need you to place a classified in all three of the local papers. Make sure it's a showstopper, an eye-catcher. Double outline, boldface type in giant capital letters, two columns wide. Whatever it takes."

Clarence had a pen and pad in his hands so fast, Tim didn't see where they came from. "And what would you like the ad to say?" he asked.

"Bernadette, where are you? Please call home! Mary."

"That'll stop her dead in her tracks," Clarence said when he finished writing.

"Let's hope so," Tim said.

They finished eating, and Clarence looked at his watch. "If I hurry, I can maybe pull enough strings to get the ad in tomorrow's editions."

Tim watched as Clarence headed home, and he thought he detected Waldo adjusting to a bustling, instead of a shuffling, pace.

Now there was nothing to do but wait. On Friday morning, Tim was at his desk studying for a test when Brent and Patty walked in, arguing as they always seemed to be doing lately.

"I was going the speed limit," Brent said.

"It's foggy out," Patty argued.

"So?"

"Speed limits are the speed you should go when conditions are ideal, not when it's foggy."

"I know these streets like the back of my hand. I could drive around blindfolded. I was a cop, remember? My job was to know the streets."

"You're a typical cop," Patty said vehemently. "You think you own the streets."

"I DO own the streets," Brent said settling into his chair. "I'm a tax paying citizen, and a servant of the community."

"You're an egotistical maniac, who—" Patty's voice trailed off as a look of horror came over her face.

Tim followed her stare to her noticeably bare desk. He glanced at Brent, whose mischievous smirk contradicted his peaceful, closed-eyes expression as he tipped back in his chair.

"Where are they?" she demanded angrily. She was referring to the stuffed animal toys that normally lined the back of her desk. She even cast an accusing look in Tim's direction, and he felt his insides shrink.

"I didn't touch them," Tim said. "I never touch them," he added to emphasize his innocence.

But by now, Patty had turned her gaze on the obvious culprit.

Brent was unmoved.

Patty mumbled something about getting even. "Just you wait!" she enunciated. And then more mumbling about getting what he really deserved.

Tim slammed his book shut. "I've had enough of you two fighting. I'm trying to study."

Patty quit mumbling, but stared at Brent. Brent opened one eye and looked at Tim.

"We're not just a partnership," Tim continued. "We're friends. And what affects one, affects all of us. Brent is nervous about getting married. And when he's nervous, he behaves childishly."

"He behaves childishly all the time," Patty said under her breath.

"And you're irritable, because you're worried about fitting into your wedding dress," Tim said.

"I'm not worried about it," Patty said irritably.

"And you're both doing a lousy job of pretending not to be interested in my personal affairs...I mean, life...my personal life," Tim corrected.

"I'm not interested in your sex life, Kid," Brent interjected just for fun.

"Social life!" Patty yelled in Tim's defense. "And yes you are! You gave me the third-degree after I talked with her on the phone."

"When did you talk with her on the phone?" Tim asked.

"Okay! So I care who the kid hangs with," Brent argued. "Someone's gotta watch out for him when he goes gaga over some girl."

"I'm not gaga," Tim said, bristling. "And when did you talk with her on the phone?"

"So what if he goes gaga!" Patty returned. "You're the last person he needs watching out for him with his girlfriend."

"I'm not gaga! And when did you talk with her on the phone?" Tim repeated, tired of being ignored.

"And he's right!" Patty said. "Stop being childish and give me back my toys."

"No," Brent said firmly, closing his eyes. "I don't have your silly toys."

"Liar!" Patty yelled.

"I'm going to the library," Tim said jumping up and grabbing his books. "Page me if you have anything intelligent to say."

"I just don't get it," Brent said without opening his eyes. "He's been so edgy ever since he met that girl, what's her name?"

"Trisha," Patty shouted. "Her name is Trisha." She grabbed the closest thing at hand, a mail holder, and threw it at Brent. "Shut up! And give me back my toys."

Chapter 24: Kentucky Woman

In spite of turning the search for Bernadette Higgins, missing person turned murder suspect, over to the police, Tim couldn't just let it go. It wasn't the money. The money had turned as elusive as she was, disappearing by increments of a thousand dollars with each day that passed. And $30,000 had dwindled down to $8,000. His bulletin board was still covered with a layer of disheveled bits and pieces of information and fingerprint cards that were more confusing than illuminating.

When Saturday arrived, he tried to relax. He could now switch his focus to more pleasant thoughts, which included another evening with Trisha. In the shower he rehearsed what he wanted to say to her. His hidden agenda was to establish an open and honest relationship, to find out where he stood with her, and to let her know how he felt about her and a lot of other things in his life.

He dressed in comfortable clothes, the kind he liked to wear and not something he hoped would impress her. If Trisha didn't like his faded jeans and oversized T-shirt, well...then they'd have something to discuss. Afterwards, he put on a load of laundry to wash and ran the vacuum cleaner over the carpet. He didn't have sloppy habits, so there wasn't much to do. But Trisha's line of employment was janitorial service, which he kept in mind as he cleaned his apartment.

When he returned downstairs with plenty of time before Trisha's arrival, he sat down at his desk. He wanted to void his mind of anything to do with school and missing persons, as well as murdered persons. But when he turned around, the faces of Mary Harris and Bernadette Higgins stared back at him from the bulletin board. He pinched his knuckles and stared. "Okay, ladies," he said out loud, "tell me, in your own words, what happened. Start at the top."

In his mind he imagined both of them blurting out their own version of the tragic story, trying to justify what they did before the other had a chance to be heard.

Tim held up his hand to silence the bedlam and clear the confusion. "One at a time, please."

They both stared back at him. Mary seemed to sulk with her tight-lipped bitter expression. Bernadette smiled at him, deciding to keep her secret locked behind those all-knowing eyes of hers.

"Well?" Tim insisted as he stood up. *My God,* he thought. *They're driving me crazy! I'm talking to pictures on a bulletin board, for Pete's sake!* He stared at them. *And I'm gaga over a girl I don't even know!* He scrutinized the bulletin board and spotted a business card peeking from beneath the edge of a piece of paper.

He removed the **LEELAND FAMILY PLANNING CLINIC** business card. It didn't belong. He'd tossed it in the trashcan once before and changed his mind.

This time he took it outside, along with the aerosol can of Ninhydrin. He sprayed and waited for the fumes to dissipate. Then he carried it back in and propped it on edge to dry and to await any fingerprints that might appear.

At precisely five o'clock the doorbell rang, and Trisha stood bearing two grocery bags, one in each arm, when Tim opened the door. He took them from her and she closed the door giving him a front and back view of the honey-colored, softly clinging, one-piece jumpsuit she was wearing.

"I hope you don't mind," she said as her eyes swept over him with similar approval. "I brought some stuff for making a home-cooked meal. And since it's raining, I thought it would be nice to just stay inside tonight and watch some videos I rented."

"That sounds..." Tim noticed tiny beads of moisture on her hair and arms. And when he glanced out the window, it had indeed started to rain. "...like a great idea." He led the way upstairs, carrying the bags of food, to his attic apartment.

He set the bags on the kitchen counter, and Trisha set her purse next to them.

"You didn't give me a proper greeting," she said coming close and sliding her long slender arms around him.

"I didn't have a chance—"

Trisha gave him a long kiss.

"Hello," he said slowly releasing her.

Trisha looked around the kitchen, beginning with the refrigerator next to the entryway. She opened the door and her eyes scanned the contents. "I need to get a feel for your kitchen," she said. She opened the freezer compartment, looked in, and shut it. Then she advanced to the cupboards and drawers, opening and shutting, and assessing his wares.

Tim stood by, watching, amused. Trisha was the spice of life he craved.

She made her way around the kitchen and ended up on the other side of the entryway where the microwave stood on the counter.

"Typical bachelor," she pronounced, shaking her head. "How do you survive on nothing but frozen dinners?"

"I eat out a lot," Tim said feeling embarrassed that she'd found him typical and his kitchen inadequate.

"Good thing I brought everything I need." She began taking things out of the bags and placing them on the counter.

"Sorry." He'd always thought of himself as a fairly competent cook, until Rhonda complained about his meals last year. Now his confidence was totally shattered. "I don't have time to be domestic."

"And the arrangement is all wrong," Trisha continued. "Your microwave shouldn't be here next to the door on the opposite side of the kitchen from everything else."

"I eat on the go."

"Spoken like a true bachelor." She put her hands on her hips and studied various aspects of the room. "With a relaxed arrangement, you'll enjoy cooking and eating meals in here."

"No time," Tim countered. But he knew it was a losing battle.

"The microwave should be..." She turned. "...over there," she said pointing. "Close to the refrigerator with counter space between."

Tim sighed, unplugged the microwave, and moved it according to her bidding.

"And the table should be in front of the window," she decided, "so you can hear and watch the birds in that lovely tree while you eat."

"Only bluejays come around here," Tim said. He began moving the table and chairs. "And they sound terrible."

Trisha smiled and helped move the last chair. Tim took the opportunity to place his hands on her waist while she was near enough. She turned and kissed him. "Of course, that means we'll have to move the dishes and silverware, so they're closer to the table." She kissed him again, lingering this time. "But we can do that after we eat." She moved away and began unwrapping the groceries on the counter.

Tim sighed heavily as he watched her.

She smiled. "The best thing about this meal is that it only takes fifteen minutes to cook, and it's very healthy and tastes absolutely scrumptious." She measured some vinegar, peanut oil, soy sauce, and ginger powder into a small bowl. "It doesn't have to go from the freezer to the microwave to be quick and simple." She laid a large salmon filet on the broiler and spooned some sauce over it before closing the door. "If you'll set the table, it will probably be done by the time you're finished."

Tim used his nice china and glassware instead of the unmatched plastic dishes he was accustomed to using for his everyday quick meals. Trisha boiled rice and microwaved a dish of carrots. When the steaming dishes were on the table, he lit the candles and turned out the overhead lights. He pulled out her chair, and she took his hand as she gracefully lowered herself.

He positioned the chair comfortably close to the table for her. He sat down and dished up her plate, and then his own.

He didn't dare speak as their eyes met, for fear the moment would end. The food looked and smelled tantalizing. As did Trisha, only she was more so.

"Taste," she said softly.

He chewed, slowly at first, and then with enthusiasm.

She smiled and lifted the pitcher, which she'd brought in her shopping bag, and poured the amber liquid into his glass of ice cubes and then her own.

It smelled vaguely familiar. "What is this?" he asked.

"Sun tea," she said. The flickering candlelight made her eyes sparkle. "It's a family tradition I haven't been able to forsake."

Iced tea had been responsible for many of his sleepless nights while traveling through Kentucky and Arkansas last year. "Okay," he said, "your family background is southern. But I can't place the broiled salmon dish."

Trisha paused from chewing and laughed. "Don't even try to figure out my ethnicity from my cooking."

Her smooth dark chestnut hair and brown eyes left him clueless as well.

"It's rebellion cooking, but I'm not a confederate rebel. I call it 'I hate my mother's artery-clogging, heart-stopping, southern-fried cooking'."

Tim laughed. "That definitely brings back memories. What part of the South is your mom from?"

The rest of the meal was spent reliving Trisha's girlhood memories of summers spent with her grandparents in Tennessee and of growing up with divorced parents in perpetual conflict.

When they had finished eating, Tim helped clear the dishes and put them in the sink. Trisha proceeded to run the water and add dish soap.

"Just leave them," Tim suggested.

"They'll only take a minute to wash." She was standing next to him at the sink. "Then I'll serve up dessert." She slowly traced her index finger back and forth across his stomach. "And I'll make sure you're completely satisfied."

Tim cleared his throat and grabbed a dishtowel.

Chapter 25: I'm Glad You're Here With Me Tonight

"May I look around?" Trisha asked when the dishes were done. "Or do you have skeletons in your closets?"

"Be my guest," Tim said making a wide sweep with his arm. "My life's an open book."

She turned right at the kitchen door and Tim followed her to the balcony style living room that overlooked the IRISH EYES office area. "I like this," she said walking around. Tim held back as she neared the railing. "It's so open and airy!" She leaned her tall body way out over the railing and remained suspended as she surveyed the office below.

Tim gasped and felt his meal threatening to make a comeback. He dropped to his knees, and Trisha pulled herself back and rushed to his side. "Are you all right? You look as if you've just seen a ghost."

Tim got to his feet before she could touch him. "Heights," he explained taking a step away from her. "I have a fear of heights."

He didn't want her comforting him when he felt humiliated, but she drew closer and wrapped her long arms around him.

"Now you know my mortal weakness," he said trying to make light of it.

Trisha didn't laugh at him. Instead, she held his hand as he completed the tour of the rest of his apartment. She approved of his tidy laundry room, stopping long enough to comment that his detergent was responsible for polluting the earth's water supply all the way to Antarctica. She nodded at the neatness of his storage room. And his spacious well-lit bathroom received a rave review upon passing her examination. "Not bad, for a bachelor," she said. "And you even put the seat down."

She didn't ask about the closed door at the end of the hall, which led to his bedroom, and Tim didn't offer. "Can I see where you work?" she asked.

Tim hesitated, remembering Brent's offense at her even meeting him here.

"Since your work takes up so much of your time."

"Sure! Why not?" he said leading the way downstairs. "Just don't leave any fingerprints on Brent's desk. He's very touchy about his messes."

Trisha laughed. "This must be his," she said walking over to the messiest desk. When Tim joined her, he noticed a couple of screws and a small square metal plate on the floor behind Brent's chair. He started to bend down and see what it was, but changed his mind. He smiled and made a mental note to himself to be sure to be there when Brent settled in his chair Monday morning.

"And this must be Patty's," Trisha said moving to her desk. "She sounds really sweet on the phone."

"She's sweet alright," Tim said. He glanced at Brent's booby-trapped chair and smiled again.

Trisha circled to the other side of the room. "And this is yours." She affectionately rubbed her index finger across the wooden surface as if picking up vibes from his past intellectual pursuits at the desk. The chair was pulled out, and she sat down. "This feels nice," she said pulling up to the desk. "I don't have a desk and chair, but I think I'll get one. I'm successfully self-employed—I should have one," she said with conviction.

"Go for it," Tim offered.

"I will." She smiled and checked out the feel of the swivel. But when she turned completely around, she stopped still and stared with a pained expression.

Tim followed her gaze to the bulletin board and understood.

She looked shocked.

"Sorry," he said. "I guess I should've at least removed her picture."

Trisha still didn't say anything.

Tim realized it was his turn to do the comforting. He knelt down beside her and took her hand in his. "I didn't know it would affect you like this. I'm sorry."

Trisha recovered somewhat and looked at him.

"Now that I've turned the case over to the police, I should probably take it all down and file it away."

"Police?" she gasped.

This wasn't one of his finer moments of chivalry. "Um, yeah." He decided to break the news to her, since he had let some of it slip out already. "Mary Harris was cooking the books at Clayton's and some of the other places she'd worked."

"Cooking?" Trisha whispered.

"Embezzling—stealing money through phony accounts."

Trisha nodded weakly. "Oh." Her eyes took in the bottle of hand lotion tucked away in the corner by his file cabinet.

"And..." Tim added, "...I believe she was murdered."

Trisha looked frightened as she turned her eyes on him. "Murdered?"

Tim rubbed her hands and helped her to her feet. He drew her close. He recalled hearing somewhere that people in shock should be kept warm, and he gladly accommodated some of his own body heat. "We don't have to let this spoil the evening, do we?" he asked hopefully.

"No," Trisha said recovering. "Let's not spoil the evening." She held up Tim's arm and looked at his watch. "We have plenty of time to watch movies."

Tim placed his hands around her waist to lend support going upstairs.

Trisha picked a movie and slipped it into the VCR and sat down on the sofa. Tim sat next to her and peered uncomfortably over the back of the sofa. Although he'd moved it away from the railing, it still felt too close to the edge for comfort. He tensed.

Trisha looked at him. "This isn't where you spend time and relax, is it?"

Tim shook his head. He'd gone along with Brent's open-air floor plan for the living room, but he didn't spend any time enjoying the view below.

Trisha switched off the movie with the remote control on the coffee table and stood up. She headed straight for the closed door at the end of the hall. She opened it, and entered after turning on the light. She nodded approvingly, and Tim breathed a sigh of relief that he'd made the bed and picked up his dirty laundry from the floor. "This is where you relax. I can tell. It lacks a woman's finishing touch, of course, but it's so you! I love it," she pronounced. "Let's move the TV and VCR in here."

Tim marveled at the ease with which he'd managed to get Trisha in his bedroom for the evening. And he wasn't even trying!

Together, they made the transition. And afterwards, they ended up sitting cross-legged in the middle of his bed with their shoes off eating large servings of angel food cake topped with strawberries and whipped cream.

"How do you do it?" he asked when she finished eating.

She took his bowl and set it with hers on the nightstand. "Do what?"

"Stay so slim."

Trisha smiled and positioned her knees around his hips and raised up. As their lips met and her hands applied gentle pressure on his chest, his natural inclination was to drift back against a pillow with her on top. But he resisted and felt embarrassed by his unpreparedness.

Tim got off the bed and walked around the end to the nightstand. Trisha had set their bowls on top of his latest email from Rhonda, which included a color printout photo of her. He carefully removed the two-page letter and wiped off the moisture rings from the sweating bowls.

"Sorry," Trisha said. "I didn't realize it was something you wanted to keep." She got up and stood beside him. "Who is she?"

"Just a friend."

"I see." Trisha's tone was skeptical.

"No, really." It was hard not to convey the fondness he felt for Rhonda. "She's a friend. She's one of my cases I succeeded in returning home safe and sound. Actually, Rhonda was my first...case, that is."

He suddenly realized Trisha had begun reading the letter, and he quickly shoved it in the drawer of the nightstand. "Unfortunately, she developed a chronic case of puppy love for me," he explained.

"That's understandable." Trisha smiled. "You're quite a hunk for a little girl like her to handle."

Tim felt he should defend Rhonda's virtue, but the opportunity slipped away as Trisha fluffed a pillow and propped it against the headboard. She settled herself on the bed and leaned against the pillow. "C'mon let's watch the movie." She pressed the buttons on the remote control to turn on the TV and then to begin the video.

Tim settled on the bed, being careful to leave a respectable space between them, while previews of soon-to-be-released videos flashed across the small screen of his portable TV.

Trisha reached up and dimmed the lamp, a feature Tim had never had occasion to use before. "Just like at the theater," she said. From the grocery bag beside the bed, she produced a container of popcorn.

Tim laughed. "You thought of everything."

"I try to," she said. She reached again. This time she produced a can and popped open the top. Then she handed it across to him.

He reached for it and read the label. "No thanks," he said when he realized it was beer.

"You can drink in your own home," Trisha urged. "You're not going to be out driving around or anything. Besides, it's only beer."

"I just don't want it," Tim said. His conviction didn't come across as courageously as he wanted, but it was a firm conviction, nevertheless.

"It's one of those fancy flavored kind," she continued. "It doesn't even taste much like beer. Try it." She held it out toward him.

He sat, silently mortified, but refused to be pressured. Trisha turned off the VCR when it reached the beginning of the featured attraction, and a loud commercial blared over the TV. The whole situation had a dampening effect, and Tim started to get up.

Trisha laid her hand on him to prevent his moving away. "How old are you?" she asked.

"It has nothing to do with my age," Tim said evasively. "It has to do with the fact that I'm a Christian, and I live by certain principles I believe in."

"I believe in certain principles, too," Trisha said. "But they don't prevent me from experiencing life. There are just some things you have to try in order to know what it's all about."

Tim desperately wanted to ask her about the life experiences she was referring to, but he let it pass. And she dropped the issue and settled back on her side of the bed.

"Do you still want to watch the movie?" she asked, "with me?" The last question expressed the uncertainty he had caused her to feel.

"I'm sorry I'm a little edgy," he explained. "It's just that...the case."

"Forget the stupid case, and just try to relax," Trisha said snuggling against his arm. She removed the band holding his ponytail. "All you have to do is watch the movie and relax. Don't worry about a thing."

Tim pressed the remote, which started the movie. Trisha ran her hand through his hair and ended with a tantalizing tickle at the nape of his neck. He enjoyed being with Trisha more than he was able to explain, even to himself. She took a sip from the beer can on the nightstand, and they finally settled into watching the movie and eating popcorn.

Chapter 26: Hanky Panky

It wasn't his favorite kind of movie, Tim preferred action and suspense thrillers. But Trisha was a romance buff. And she took several opportunities to fan his ardor and completely distract him from the storyline. One hour into the movie the lights and the TV screen flickered off and on.

Tim reached over Trisha to the nightstand and turned off the movie with the remote control. Across the bottom of the TV screen a tornado watch and a severe thunderstorm warning were posted along with the affected counties. The electrical power flickered tenuously and the TV crackled with static. He turned it off.

"I better get a candle," he said getting up. Trisha followed him holding onto his hand. He led the way out the door and down the hall to the kitchen. Without turning on the light, they watched out the window. A flash of lightning lit up the sky and revealed a tumultuous wind and driving rain. He turned on the light. "Maybe you better call your mom and let her know you're safe."

"She knows not to worry about me," Trisha said.

Tim rummaged through a drawer and found a box of matches. "Still, it would be nice to let her know." He found a candle on top of the refrigerator.

"I live with her," Trisha explained, "but I'm self-sufficient."

The wind rattled the window and, for a moment, Tim thought it might succeed in ripping through the building as the floor shook under their feet. His stomach felt queasy. The storm was in full force, and it was supposed to last until morning. "Won't she mind if you don't...come home?" Under the circumstances, he had no choice but to let her spend the night.

"She's not expecting me," Trisha answered.

They headed back toward the bedroom. Tim stopped. "Maybe it's safer downstairs," he decided.

"Is this another one of your mortal weaknesses?" She kissed him and the lights flickered. He put his arms around her and the box of matches dropped and spilled on the floor.

"No," he said kneeling to pick them up. "But you are."

Trisha smiled as she knelt and helped him.

In the bedroom, Tim set the candle and matches next to the lamp, ready for the moment when the electricity might go out completely. They took their respective positions on the bed, and he waited with the remote while Trisha opened a can of beer, her third for the evening. She took a long swig, set it on the nightstand, and took the remote control from his hand. "Let's make our own movie," she said.

Tim hesitated. "Let's talk," he said.

"We can talk afterwards." She began kissing his forehead, beginning at his left temple and working across to the other side.

Kissing was perfectly harmless, he told himself. He knew his own limits. And, as long as they kept their clothes on...

She slowly zigzagged back and forth down his face, spending extra moments on his ears and nose. She bypassed his mouth and began kissing his neck.

So far, so good, he decided. And he was enjoying it.

Trisha scooted down on the bed, so that it became necessary for him to lean over her. He kissed her and stroked her hair gently. She pulled him down on top of her, and her strong firm arms embraced him.

The lamp flickered one last time before everything went completely dark and silent. Tim stopped still and listened to Trisha's rapid breathing. His own breathing was keeping pace with hers. He felt her lift his T-shirt up and over his head. Then he heard the zipper on the front of her jumpsuit. He stopped her midway with his hand and felt her soft skin. "We need to talk," he said.

He sat up and felt for the nightstand. He found the matches and managed to light one and used it to light the candle.

"I can teach you," she said, "if that's what you're worried about."

"It's not," he said sitting on the edge of the bed. He turned and looked at her in the candlelight, lying exposed on the bed. He reached over and covered her. "I'm worried about our relationship being long-term."

She didn't say anything for a few minutes. "It's that Christianity thing of yours, isn't it?"

"Yeah." He sighed.

"Is it always going to stand in our way?" Trisha knelt behind him on the bed and laid her head against his neck. She encircled his bare chest with her arms and kissed him.

She knew all the right moves. But if his moral ethics wouldn't allow him to change his lifestyle, would she be willing to change hers? He could really love her—he already loved her. But it was all happening too fast. He realized that. And yet, she seemed to fall into place in his life. She fit like a puzzle piece that had been missing until now.

Tim turned and gathered her in his arms. He gently laid her back on the pillow. "You sleep here," he said, softly kissing her. "I'll sleep on the sofa." He stood up. "Don't forget to blow out the candle." He walked out and closed the door. He slowly felt his way to the living room aware of the possibility that he might inadvertently get too close to the balcony railing. For the first time in his life, though, falling over an edge would've been welcome, compared to the profound sadness he felt in his heart.

The storm continued to rage outside, and it was still night when Tim awoke to an unfamiliar sound. Someone was at the door. The security system would surely prevent someone from breaking in. He sat up suddenly on the floor in front of the sofa, remembering where he was, but not remembering what would happen to the security system during a power outage. Someone entered downstairs, none too quietly, letting the wind catch and bang the door violently against the wall.

"Tim!" He recognized Patty's voice, and he could hear her bumping into things downstairs in the office.

Tim's eyes adjusted to the dark, and he leaped up and bounded down the stairs. "What's the matter?" He caught hold of her. "Stand still!" He stubbed his toe on the corner of his desk and let out a yelp. He found a flashlight and shined it in Patty's direction.

She was thoroughly drenched and her wet auburn hair was plastered around her face. "Oh, Tim! Clarence had an emergency and tried to call you. The phone lines are down on this side of town. So he called us. Brent's with him now."

"What happened? How bad is he?" Tim felt panic overtaking his senses at the thought of losing a friend.

"It's Waldo," Patty said. "He's had a stroke or something. The vet's not sure."

Tim felt a rush of relief. "Waldo?" But he knew Clarence needed him as much for the bereavement over his canine companion as he would if he himself was stricken.

He looked down and realized he was standing in his underwear in the dim glare of the flashlight. "I'll get dressed," he said handing the flashlight to Patty.

"Anything I can do?"

They both looked up and saw Trisha standing at the balcony railing with a sheet draped loosely around her unclad form. She leaned forward holding the candle in her hand. Tim gasped as his fear of falling kicked in vicariously.

He caught Patty's incredulous expression as he turned and rushed upstairs. He gathered his pants from the living room, and tripped over things on the bedroom floor until Trisha joined him with the candle. "I have to go," he explained. "I don't know how long I'll be."

She let the sheet drop and helped him find the rest of his clothes. She raised her arms and slipped his shirt over his head. Then she sat next to him on the bed while he worked at getting on his shoes. "I'll be gone when you get back," she said. "I have a Sunday account."

Tim glanced sidelong at her unabashed nakedness. She had beautiful dark skin. "Okay," he said. "I'll call you." He joined Patty downstairs and together they drove to the veterinary clinic.

When he saw Clarence's red Mercedes in the parking lot, Tim braced himself for bad news, but prayed for good news. Patty knocked on the door, and a very tired-looking young man in a white lab coat let them in. He led them down a hall and into a room where Brent was pacing nervously. Clarence was holding a silent vigil at Waldo's side and, when Tim entered, they hugged.

Brent, always eager to avoid emotional displays whenever possible, looked relieved to see Tim. Brent gave Clarence a reassuring pat on the back, which the old man recognized as a farewell. "Thanks for coming."

Brent nodded. "Any time." He and Patty glided out the door leaving Tim to comfort his friend in need.

"I would've come sooner," Tim said, feeling guilty that he'd been so thoroughly enjoying himself in Trisha's company during his friend's darkest hour, "but the phone was out."

Clarence was too distraught to pay attention to Tim's explanation. "I couldn't let them put him to sleep," he said with emotion. "I just couldn't do it, even though the vet said he probably won't recover."

Tim looked down at the hairy little bundle lying motionless on the covered metal table. *This doesn't look good,* he found himself thinking. He needed to think positive thoughts.

"If...when...he regains consciousness, then the vet will know the extent of it...how much paralysis... whether it's life-threatening, or will cause him to suffer."

The young man in the lab coat entered at that moment and began checking Waldo's vital signs.

"Let's sit down," Tim suggested as he eased Clarence out of the way toward some nearby chairs in the room. Clarence sat down on the edge of one without taking his eyes off Waldo.

When he finished, the vet joined them and pulled a chair around to face them. "I don't want to hold out any false hopes—the prognosis doesn't look bright—but," he said qualifying the idea he was about to offer, "if you could bring some of his favorite toys and things from home, it would minimize the trauma of waking in an unfamiliar place, if he does rally."

Clarence visibly brightened in spite of the negative outlook.

"Letting him smell you and hear your voice wouldn't hurt anything either," the vet said as he left the room.

"I'll get the stuff," Tim offered.

Clarence had already set to work letting Waldo hear him call his name and putting his hands in front of his nose to replace the disinfectant smell in the air with his own scent. "His old blanket is at the foot of my bed," he said fishing his keys from his pants pocket and handing them to Tim. "Bring one of my old socks," he continued. "He loves my socks. You'll have to look for his chew toys under the couch. His favorite is the squeaky rubber bone."

Tim hurried out into the waning storm, but he knew it was going to be a long night.

Chapter 27: Brother Love's Travelling Salvation Show

Tim left the veterinary clinic the next morning in time to take a shower and dress for church. Waldo was stable, but remained unconscious. Clarence was dozing fitfully. And Trisha was gone. The church he was planning to attend was one he'd never visited before.

Having been a Christian for only a year now, Tim had never felt the need to experiment beyond the full Gospel church of his own choosing where he was an avid member of the congregation. But attending the church of a missing person often sheds light on their whereabouts, since religion tends to be a stabilizing factor in most people's lives. He was grabbing at straws—pen barrels, to be more exact, where he'd found the name, address, and phone number of the church, which he hoped had a strong influence on Bernadette Higgins' system of beliefs and practices.

If Bernadette Higgins appeared in the flesh at church this morning, it wouldn't be the first time he'd found the subject of his investigation in a congregation of Christians. A church was where he'd found his birth sister a year ago. Or rather, Kathy had singled him out from among the crowd because of his odd nervous habit of pinching his knuckles.

Tim tightened and adjusted his tie before getting out of his car and slipping inside the church building. It was impossible to slip unnoticed though, as most of the early crowd appeared to be women. The last-minute crowd, no doubt, would consist of families and the husbands who were huddled outside the backdoor smoking their Sunday morning last cigarette and praying church would let out before the big game on TV.

Tim sat down at the end of the middle section of pews closest to the back, so he would have a good view. He scrunched down and read the church bulletin, hoping to preserve his anonymity.

A woman approached him, and Tim politely stood to shake her hand. Unfortunately, she was short. And by the time her eyes slowly traveled up his above-average height, surveyed his broad shoulders, and took in his long hair; she stood enraptured with her mouth open, and her formal welcome speech long-forgotten.

"Good morning," Tim said firmly clasping her hand.

The woman's eyes fell to about waist-level when she stopped craning her neck. "You're new to our church," she observed. The implication was that she would've noticed him if he had ever been there before.

Her reaction, which wasn't uncommon to Tim after adding six more inches to his height since graduating from high school, was something he still found difficult getting used to. And his stature gave him yet another reason to believe he wasn't cut out for detective work. He just didn't fit the job description. He was too easy to identify and he stood out like a sore thumb when he was supposed to blend into the background while doing surveillance or undercover. "Just visiting," Tim said.

"Are you visiting with some of our regular members?" The woman looked around for likely candidates, but seemed to come up short on genetic possibilities.

"Actually," Tim responded, "I'm looking for someone. Maybe you know her. Her name is Bernadette Higgins."

"The name doesn't ring a bell," the woman said shaking her head. "But I've missed a few Sundays. I had surgery on my gall bladder. I wasn't at all well, and my doctor said I should take it easy."

"What about the name Mary Harris?"

"I've never heard that name either," the woman said thoughtfully. "Did she have gall bladder surgery too?"

Tim smiled. "Excuse me. I think I'll stretch my legs." He set his bulletin and his Bible down to save his seat.

"There's coffee, tea and pastries in the anteroom off the left side of the narthex," the woman called after him.

Tim made his inquiry to several of the women as he ate a muffin and tried mingling among the small group. Finally, a woman made her way over to him.

"Did you know Mary?" she asked after shaking hands and introducing herself.

"No, ma'am," Tim replied. "I'm a friend of her family."

"I was sorry to hear about her death," she said sympathetically. "How did it happen?"

"Allergic reaction," Tim answered. "Did you know her very well?"

"No, I didn't know her at all. I made a point of saying 'hi' to her whenever I saw her. But, other than that..." She went on to explain. "She was always alone and sat away from everyone else. She only came once in a while."

"Did she ever talk about her roommate, Bernadette Higgins?" The question was a little more abrupt than he wanted to sound, but Tim noticed people were filtering out of the room and beginning to take their places in the main sanctuary.

"Mary didn't actually talk about anything. She wasn't sociable. She was very odd, always wearing gloves, dressing like she did." The woman sighed. "She'd sit in a dark corner and only remove her sunglasses when church started. She acted like she had a disease. No, I take that back. She acted more like everyone else had a contagious disease, and she was afraid of catching it."

Tim stood listening, aware the room had emptied, and a man waited impatiently at the door.

"She dressed perfect to a fault." The man at the door caught her attention and motioned for her to come, but the woman continued. "Very expensive looking clothes, but drab and colorless. She always looked like she was attending the funeral of a loved one. Once, I noticed during the hymn singing, she was wiping her eyes with a fancy crocheted handkerchief." The woman drew confidingly close to Tim and touched his sleeve.

Tim bent closer.

"If you ask me," she whispered, "I think she was a movie star in hiding. Maybe recovering from substance abuse, or some other tragedy." She nodded knowingly and walked away to join her impatient husband at the door.

Tim waited a few minutes, and then walked in and took his place unnoticed at the back of the sanctuary while everyone was standing. During the singing, he methodically observed, and eliminated as a possibility, the face of each female blonde in the congregation. During the prayer time and the short sermon, he turned his attention to the women with other colors of hair, since Bernadette had a penchant for wigs.

He finally spotted a likely candidate with long black hair on the other side of the church. But when everyone stood to sing the closing hymn, he realized she was too short to be Bernadette Higgins. And her Oriental eyes and complexion confirmed it.

After the service, Tim decided to once again join a small group of people in the anteroom for refreshments. He took the opportunity to approach several women who appeared to be Bernadette's age. He mingled and listened to snatches of conversation. But no one had ever heard the name Bernadette Higgins or seen the face in the photograph he was hesitant to show, because she could quite possibly be in disguise.

The group dwindled quickly as the noon hour approached. Tim tossed his Styrofoam cup in the trashcan and picked up his jacket. He made a stop at the restroom on his way out. While standing at the urinal farthest from the door, Tim heard someone enter with slow footsteps. He looked up as a man approached and stood next to him. Much too close for comfort. Intentionally, Tim realized.

"If you ever come to this church again, you'll be welcomed with closed fists, instead of open arms."

Tim was caught completely by surprise.

"Do I make myself clear?" The man wasn't talking loudly, but his presence was overbearing.

"Loud and clear!" Tim answered, trying to hurry. "I didn't know churches had bouncers."

"This church watches out for its womenfolk," the man warned. "And we'll take action if you ever step inside this church again."

"Wait a minute," Tim said smiling and zipping his fly. He knew now what the misunderstanding was all about. "I'm looking for a woman..."

"We're not a match-making service for perverts, like you. You were caught eyeing up every female in the place."

"I can explain!" Tim backed away toward the sinks and turned around to wash his hands only after he had the man's reflection centered in the mirror. He was a tall middle-aged man. Well-built, but Tim could take him on in a fair fight.

Tim didn't bother to dry his hands as he watched, in disbelief, the man shove his sleeves above his wrists. "I'm a private investigator." Tim whirled around to face the enraged man. "I'm looking for a particular woman, who looks like..."

"I don't care what your sexual preferences are," the man hissed as he propelled his fist toward Tim's face.

Tim had been reaching for the photograph of Bernadette Higgins in his pocket, but he managed to duck the punch. Just for good measure, he tackled the man's knees and sent him sprawling on the floor.

Tim scrambled for the door. He turned around to view his adversary, who was starting to pull himself to his feet. "I'm not a pervert," Tim said angrily while holding the door open. "I'm just trying to do my job." He let the door shut behind him and swiftly left through the nearest exit.

The gravel crunched under his shoes as he walked across the parking lot. "And I'm a Christian," he muttered under his breath while he drove away.

Tim stopped at the clinic to check on Clarence. One look at his face told the news. Waldo was conscious, but the ordeal was not yet over. The Pekingese was confused as to how to cope with the paralysis of part of his body. And Clarence was coping with his canine companion's mixed reactions to the traumatic physical changes.

Waldo excitedly sniffed Tim's extended hand. His tail refused to do anything but droop, but his brown eyes brightened as more and more familiar things were reintroduced into his life.

"I forgot to tell you before," Clarence said. "Your ad is in the papers. I can renew it for another week, if you let me know before Friday."

"This time next week," Tim said turning at the door before leaving, "the case is officially closed. Thanks for your help."

Clarence rushed forward and hugged him.

Tim tried hard not to feel awkward as he stooped to hug the short bald man who'd become his loyal friend. The whole situation prompted another one of those "life's-too-short" revelations that Tim always found emotionally draining.

Chapter 28: You Are My Love At Last

The first thing that caught Tim's eye when he
walked in the door and looked at his desk, was a piece
of paper with handwriting on it. He picked it up with
trepidation, not knowing how he'd react if it were a
"Dear John letter" from Trisha.

It began with "Dearest Darling Tim" and when he
finished reading it, he was sure he'd reached the
pinnacle of poetic passion. Trisha not only knew what
to do, she knew exactly what to say to fan his ardor.
He set the love letter down on his desk after rereading
it several times, and took a long, deep breath. Brent
would have a heyday if he ever got his hands on this.

He picked up the telephone receiver and punched
in the now familiar numbers. He waited for the beep to
leave a message while listening to the voice he adored.
"Tell me the truth," he said in a feigned outrage.
"You're a romance writer, aren't you?" Then he added,
"Yes, I love you," and hung up.

He hesitated trying to mentally shift gears.
Emotions complicated matters. It would've been much
simpler if Trisha Garing had rejected him, cold as ice,
and said she was engaged, or busy, or some other

excuse for not seeing him after that first meeting. But instead, she'd received his attentions warmly. And now, he found himself reorganizing his priorities to accommodate his growing need for her.

He punched in the numbers to retrieve messages from the answering machine that he'd installed at the apartment. The only message was his own, which he'd used to test the machine. Does Bernadette know the newspaper ad is a trap, he wondered? Did she know the bait at the postal service was a trap? Perhaps she'd only benefited from Mary's built-in precautions when they cooked up the embezzlement scheme. Or, maybe, he decided, it's just too soon to expect results from the ads in all the city's papers.

When he hung up, he swung around and noticed the forgotten business card, now bearing visible imprints. Disappointingly, some of his own fingerprints were superimposed over the former ones. But there were enough original prints to pick out at least one belonging to Bernadette. He was more than convinced of her guilt. But getting provable, court-admissible evidence was the challenge.

Tim picked up the receiver again and punched in more numbers. He waited.

Patty answered. "How's Waldo?" she asked right away when she heard Tim's voice.

"Conscious, but confused."

"Clarence must be relieved."

"Yeah," he agreed. "But the vet is trying to determine if the paralysis is permanent."

"Poor Clarence," Patty said with sympathy.

"Is Brent around?"

"You mean the mesmerized blob in front of the TV watching the game?"

"Is there more than one?" Tim asked, humoring her.

"Fortunately, no," Patty answered.

"Then he's the one."

"Disturbing him now would be like waking a bear during winter hibernation," she warned.

"It'll only take a minute!"

"A bullet through the head would be quicker and less painful."

Tim was reduced to begging. "Please!"

"Only if you make it worthwhile." And Patty was not above blackmailing him. "Give me ALL the details."

He knew what she wanted, but he decided to give her a toned down version of his home-cooked, candlelight dinner with Trisha. "It was very romantic."

"That much I could see, Dearie," Patty said impatiently. "I want specifics!" She sounded like Brent conducting a police interrogation.

"As you know," Tim said getting to the point, "Trisha ended up spending the night because of the storm. But what you don't know is, I slept on the couch...alone."

A brief silence followed.

"I knew that," Patty said quietly.

"How did you know?"

"You ever watch a cat stalk a bird?"

"Yeah," Tim answered wondering.

"Ever see the look on the cat's face when the bird flies away?"

He didn't answer.

"You had that look...Um...It's commercial break. I'll intercept Brent while he rushes to the bathroom, so you can talk to him."

Tim wanted to object, but the background noises were such that he knew it was too late. And he really wanted to talk to Brent.

"What's up, Kid? You know my Sundays are off-limits." Another one of Brent's unwritten rules.

"I just wanted to know if you've heard anything... you know...about the case."

"Once you turn it over to homicide, Kid, you're officially off. You know that! You're supposed to throw the ball and get out of the way. Let someone else make the play."

Brent, of all people, knew how hard it was to do that. Once it's your case, Tim realized, you have to follow it through to a conclusion—sort of like closure.

"Is that all you wanted?"

"Yeah," Tim answered with a shrug.

"You know police are too busy to issue an update to every concerned citizen in every case that comes across the desk."

"This isn't your everyday homicide!"

"None of them are, Kid...but I'll ask."

"Thanks," Tim said. "And, by the way, Irish women get even."

"What's that supposed to mean?"

"Just a warning from a friend." Tim smiled and hung up.

That taken care of, Tim made his way upstairs with his tie draped across his shoulder. He reached out to turn on the news, which he liked to listen to while eating, and suddenly remembered that his TV was no longer in the living room. He unbuttoned his shirt as he continued to the kitchen. He made a plate of leftovers from dinner the night before and set it in the microwave, which was now on the opposite side of the kitchen away from the door. And Trisha had made good on her plans to move the dishes and flatware closer to the table. The new arrangement would take some getting used to.

Tim walked into the bedroom and turned on the TV. The bed was made and the blinds were open to let in sunshine. He listened to the news while he changed clothes and hung up his pants and tie in the closet. He stopped at the bathroom on his way back to the kitchen, and once again noticed the signs that Trisha had showered before him earlier that morning.

He retrieved his meal from the microwave and returned with it to his bedroom. Funny, he thought, that he'd missed out on the fact that eating in bed was fun. His mother never would've approved. Patty would probably disapprove, too, if she knew. But Trisha had some valid ideas about fun.

He changed channels and started watching an old John Wayne western movie. After eating, Tim felt tired and decided to take a short nap. He'd been awake most of the night keeping vigil with Clarence.

He set his empty plate on the carpet, pulled down the covers, and fluffed a pillow. As he snuggled down and pulled the covers back up over himself, his nose picked up the faint, but unmistakable, scent of Trisha. He raised up on one elbow and sniffed while he repositioned the pillow to where it was strongest. Then he nestled against it and took no time drifting off to sleep.

Tim awoke early Monday morning and was already at his desk working when Brent and Patty arrived. They walked through the door in the midst of a heated argument.

"You better give me back my Beanie Babies, or else..." Patty looked at Tim and checked what she was about to say.

"Or else what?" Brent baited her with a smug grin.

She looked again at Tim, and tried to restrain herself. "Or else...all Hell will break loose!"

"All what?" Brent tormented her mercilessly.

"You heard me." Patty slammed down her purse on her desk. "Give 'em back before it's too late."

"You know how to get your toys back," he teased. "All you have to do is apologize for saying I'm childish."

"Never!" Patty yelled. "I won't apologize for saying something that's true."

"True or not," Brent sat in his chair, "you'll never see your Beanie Babies until you apologize."

"When I get through with you," Patty trilled, "you'll be apologizing to me and begging me to take them back."

Brent laughed heartily. "Impossible!" He tipped back slowly in his chair. "I have a collector lined up who's willing to pay me enough for your Beanie Babies to cancel all the debts this wedding thing has cost me."

"WEDDING THING?" Patty was enraged. "COST YOU?"

Tim gripped the edge of his desk and peeked from behind closed eyelids.

It was one of those moments in time when everything seems to occur in slow motion. The tension was heavy and the silence impenetrable. Brent hung in midair for what seemed an impossibly long time before his chair broke in two and slid out from under him. He landed on the floor with a bone-wrenching thud.

"Yes!" Patty yelled triumphantly.

Tim stood and gave her a high-five before walking over and helping Brent get to his feet with the same hand.

Patty continued celebrating with an Irish jig and several victory shouts.

Brent brushed himself off and, as dignified as he could under the circumstances, reclined on the sofa by the door to take his nap.

The remainder of the morning was quiet. Tim studied for a test, but he couldn't help wondering what Brent was thinking—whether he was going to tempt fate and continue badgering Patty into submission, or surrender and return the toys that she used as ammunition to fire at him when he least expected it.

Tim knew the answer when he opened the door to leave, and the noise caused Brent to instinctively roll off the sofa and crouch on the floor in a defensive stance with an expression on his face as if his worst nightmare had just come true.

Chapter 29: The Boat That I Row

With final exams at college in less than two weeks, and his grand jury deposition in the Mark Landers murder case scheduled for the same week, Tim felt less compelled to think about Bernadette Higgins. In six days both contracts would expire—one with the travel agency, and the other with Clayton's Investment and Finance Corporation—leaving him with more time to devote to his personal interests, which included finishing college and a meaningful relationship with Trisha.

Nevertheless, he couldn't bring himself to remove the items from his bulletin board. Not yet, anyway. And he couldn't quite put it completely out of his mind. Monday came and went without any results from the classified ad in the newspapers. Not even a hang-up call on the answering machine.

Tim was beginning to think maybe Bernadette had finally left town, or maybe his own activities had tipped her off and she was lying low for a while. And, on top of that, the police seemed to believe Mary Harris' accidental death ruling didn't warrant upgrading to a full-fledged homicide investigation.

The pressure was on, and Tim began pre-trial training sessions with the prosecuting lawyer. He needed preparation to face the grueling questions he would be asked as the only eyewitness to the murder. One emotional slip-up, or one tiny discrepancy in the details he remembered, and his testimony could be discredited. And the possibility that the creep who did it could walk away, fired Tim's determination to stay levelheaded and as emotionally disengaged as possible.

As a result, Tim didn't leave any messages on Trisha's answering machine for two days. She would just have to understand he was busy. And he might as well set a precedent of conduct, if they were going to have a long-term relationship.

He stopped at the office just long enough to pick up his books, after having transported a take-out lunch from the Sidewalk Café to the veterinary clinic where Clarence was spending his every waking moment with Waldo.

"Trisha was just here and left you something," Patty said.

Brent let out a long, low cat-whistle from his chair, which he'd repaired. He and Patty were on good terms once again, having mended their relationship after a whole day of cease-fire agreement.

"Too bad you missed her. She waited upstairs a while, but then she had to leave," Patty added.

Tim glanced up at the balcony overlooking the office and pictured Trisha as he had seen her Saturday night. He blushed.

"She said to tell you to look in your refrigerator for dinner tonight," Patty continued.

"She waited upstairs?" Tim felt a little uncomfortable at the thought of Trisha in his apartment without his knowing about it. Possessiveness was a characteristic of being raised as an only child, and he wasn't used to sharing.

"I didn't think you'd mind," Patty said.

Tim nodded.

"You'd better go check and see what she put on ice for you, Lover Boy." Brent winked and smiled a self-satisfied smile.

"I don't have time right now," Tim said gathering his books. Taking lunch to Clarence had set his hectic schedule back by precious minutes.

"Mind if I check it out?" Brent asked.

"Mind your own business," Patty said as she made use of her largest stuffed animal toy. The Beanie Babies collection had reappeared on her desk overnight. It hurtled through the air and landed in Brent's lap.

All of which gave Tim time to explore his newfound feelings about sharing. "Sure. Go ahead," he said trying to sound nonchalant.

"The kid is my business," Brent directed at Patty as he jumped up to accept Tim's offer. He mounted the stairs, adding, "He's my best man, isn't he?" From the balcony railing, he sent the toy tumbling down to the middle of Patty's desk.

Moments later, Brent shouted, "I like what you've done to the place."

Tim was ready to leave, but he hung back.

Brent returned to the balcony, leaned over and called, "Hey, Kid! I'd invite myself to dinner, but she obviously wants to be the only one on your mind tonight."

The suspense was killing him, but Tim left for his class as Brent came downstairs. It was evening when he eagerly ventured upstairs to see what Trisha had provided for his dining pleasure. She was certainly making amends for any misunderstanding in their relationship.

The table was set for two with elegant lacy place mats and his good china. But taped to the back of one chair were her photograph and a note, which he unfolded and read:

> Tim,
>
> I wish I could be with you tonight. I miss you terribly when we're apart.
>
> > Love,
> > Trisha

Was this the prerequisite pliable heart necessary for a relationship to work? Tim wondered. Or was it just emotion?

He looked in the refrigerator and removed the casserole with instructions for reheating it in the microwave. He dished it up and sat down in his chair. It was delicious, and as he looked at her beautiful face in the photo, he realized he longed for Trisha to actually be there with him.

She was right. Birds were chirping a summer serenade in the tree outside the window, and he spent the meal watching them from the table. He washed the dishes and went downstairs to study.

Saturday would mark the last day of his contract with the travel agency to find Bernadette Higgins. He was disappointed in himself for not being able to locate her. But now that he knew her dark secret, it was just as well. The million dollar grand prize would go to a more deserving recipient.

Bernadette Higgins was the lowest of lowlifes. Not only had she murdered for money, she had used Mary Harris' physical weakness to make her death appear an unfortunate allergic reaction. And then she'd vanished before Mary's body was cold in the grave. It made Tim wonder if she would've entertained thoughts of murder if she had known about winning the contest.

The murder method was ingenious, that much he'd give her. But there were things about the whole sordid scheme that didn't make sense. For one thing, there hadn't been a big score. All the planning and scheming had resulted in only two small withdrawals after Mary's death. Unless...could it be...she didn't know she was sitting on a fortune? Was the motive something other than money? Tim stared at the bulletin board until it blurred before his eyes.

He picked up the telephone receiver and punched in the numbers. He listened to the recording of Trisha's soft delicious voice and waited for the beeps to leave a message. "Seeing your face across the table made my dinner even more enjoyable, but the conversation was a little one-sided. Are you free for dinner any day this week, or do I have to wait until Saturday to be with you again?" He hesitated and hung up.

Tim ran a few extra laps at the high school field track Wednesday morning. After he showered and dressed, he joined Brent and Patty downstairs in the office. He made the final corrections on his research paper and printed out the copy for his instructor.

Then he tried to study while Brent and Patty discussed the need to reserve tuxedoes for the wedding.

"Isn't that one of the jobs my best man is supposed to relieve me of?"

"No," Patty said irritably. "You're supposed to care enough about how you look on our wedding day to pick them out yourself."

"What's to pick out? They're black monkey suits." Brent tipped back in his chair and a light seemed to switch on in his head. "Okay," he conceded. "But do we have to do it today?"

Patty smiled. "Yes, the sooner you pick them out, the better chance you have of getting exactly what you want."

"You mean, the better YOUR chances are," Brent muttered.

"What?"

"Nothing, Darling." Brent sighed.

Tim left to pick up lunch and run errands for Clarence.

Clarence and Waldo were back home, but acceptance of a homebound lifestyle was difficult. The elderly man had seemingly grown old and feeble before Tim's eyes during Waldo's recovery. And the convalescence was destined to be long and tedious.

"You need to get out once in a while," Tim suggested.

The Pekingese lifted his head from his front paws and blinked.

"We both need to get out in the fresh air," Clarence said.

Tim hadn't mentioned it, but he did notice the heavy dog odor when he entered the apartment. And it was getting to be more than he could handle, especially while eating.

"As a matter of fact," Clarence said, "I've been brainstorming an idea that your Brent Weaver might be able to assist me with." He got up from the table and went into his office.

Tim threw away the food containers and cleaned the table while Clarence busily gathered his plans on paper. Tim rubbed Waldo behind the ears before he sat down again.

Clarence returned. "Detective Weaver is good at building things. Do you think he could construct something like this?" he asked as he spread the paper before Tim on the table.

"I could ask him," Tim said. But he suddenly had a better idea. "Why don't you take your idea and explain it to him yourself?"

Clarence hesitated and looked at Waldo. "You mean, now?"

"I have an hour before I have to go to my class," Tim said looking at his watch. "I'll stay here with Waldo until you get back."

Clarence still hesitated.

"Go ahead," he urged. "Trust me. This is just the kind of diversion Brent needs to take his mind off his wedding jitters. And Waldo will be just fine with me."

Clarence, moving with more pep than he had in days, rolled up the paper and headed toward the door with it. He turned and pointed at Waldo. "This is for you, pal." And he quickly left out the door.

Waldo wanted to go with him and was uneasy at the sudden departure of his faithful caretaker. But Tim talked to him, and soon he grew calm and closed his big brown eyes. Together they waited until Clarence returned.

"Brent Weaver has the heart of a saint," Clarence declared. "He said he'll try to build it."

Tim gathered his books. "I don't think there's any danger that Brent will be nominated for sainthood." As he went out the door he turned and added, "Pray for me to get through these next two weeks and pass final exams."

"You'll make it with flying colors," Clarence said happily, "just like you always do. A bright young man like you shouldn't have any worries."

Clarence just wasn't aware of the pressures he was facing, Tim thought as he drove away.

Chapter 30: Say Maybe

"I was beginning to think I'd have to eat alone in my car," Trisha said.

Tim was pleasantly surprised to see her sitting in her Lincoln in the parking lot when he came home.

"Sorry," he said unlocking the door. "Class went late." He helped her carry in the meal she'd prepared. "And I wasn't expecting you," he added.

"I got your message," she said. He let her lead the way upstairs. "I added a new account this week. So my free time is a little scarce."

"That's good for your business, isn't it?" Tim asked as he set the table. Not good for their relationship, he realized.

"When it gets to be more than I can handle by myself, I'll have to decide if I want to pick and choose my best accounts or hire a helper." The microwave beeped, and she removed the casserole and set it in the middle of the table. "I've been so busy this week...I decided to take a break and come eat with you tonight." Trisha looked tired as Tim watched her in her loose-fitting bib overalls and cotton T-shirt.

"I'm glad you did," he said. He pulled out her chair, and she sat down with a sigh. "But you're spoiling me." He sat down across the little table from her. "I won't want to eat store-bought prepared food anymore."

"Does that mean you want me to fix your supper every night?" She sounded like it was a job she could enjoy.

"Are you offering?" Tim asked.

She smiled coyly as she poured the iced tea. "It would take some juggling, but I could arrange to take my break every night at this time."

"Then I wouldn't have to leave messages on your answering machine." He smiled and contemplated Trisha's willingness to make a commitment. He'd have to rethink his own long-term plans. He wanted to quit the P.I. business, but he needed a steady job if he was going to make a commitment to their relationship. "Right now, I have a job that doesn't allow me the same kind of freedom you have. My hours are totally unpredictable, and I can't always get away for meals. Sometimes a missing person investigation requires me to travel and be away for more than a day or two."

"I can adjust," she decided.

They ate a while in silence, and Tim had more to digest than just his food.

"Don't get me wrong," Tim said trying to lighten the mood. "It takes more than good food to win my heart. What else can you do besides cook and clean?"

"I'm a good mother," she offered.

Tim choked on the food he was swallowing and took a big gulp of iced tea. "You keep trying to break a speed record with our relationship."

Trisha ate quietly and glanced at her watch to keep track of the time.

"I'm not in a position to consider anything more serious than dating," Tim explained. "I haven't even thought about marriage or children." He gave a nervous chuckle.

"Why not?" she asked without smiling.

"I'm...I'm just not ready for it. It's too much responsibility."

"Sometimes it just happens," she said, "whether you're ready for the responsibility or not."

"We have to juggle our schedules just to get an evening together. It would require a major overhaul to find enough time to develop the kind of relationship that could lead to marriage."

Trisha avoided making eye contact with him as she finished eating and glanced at her watch again.

Tim took her hand in his and held it. "Let's work on it slowly," he suggested. "Okay?"

"Is there someone else in your life?" Trisha asked point-blank.

"No." Tim stood up and pulled Trisha to her feet and drew her close. The curves of her body seemed to fit perfectly within his tight embrace with her cheek resting on his shoulder. "You're the only one for me." Then he added jokingly, "Unless you count Bernadette."

"Bernadette?" Trisha pulled out of his arms and stared at him.

"My missing person case," he explained. "I've been very preoccupied with finding her, but my contract runs out in six days. Then it's up to homicide."

"Homicide?"

"Yeah, I already turned the case over to the police."

Trisha began clearing the dishes from the table.

"Sorry." Tim began helping her. "I promise I won't mention it again. I know it upsets you."

She didn't look at him.

"Is there someone else in your life?" He asked the question in fun.

She hesitated at the kitchen sink before turning to face him. "Yes."

"Oh," he said staring into her brown eyes.

"He's eight months old, and he's my baby."

"Oh," Tim repeated, caught off guard. He nodded and pretended not to be surprised by the information.

"His name is Justin."

"Nice name," Tim said recovering somewhat. He knew he should be full of questions, but he was too shocked to think of any.

"His father is...no longer with us."

That answered one of the questions that did come into his mind. "Why didn't you mention your...family obligations before?" Tim asked. Although he did recall her saying something about her family.

"Would you have wanted to take me to dinner and a movie, if you had known?"

"You should've said..." Tim began boldly. And ended weakly, "probably not."

Trisha nodded and lowered her head as if she were used to the kind of unwitting rejection he was giving her.

The silence was numbing. And Tim knew he was spoiling a perfect opportunity to turn the situation around by reassuring and comforting her in his arms.

"It makes a difference, doesn't it?" she asked.

He didn't feel like playing noble. She had sprung quite a surprise on him. "I just need some time to think about it."

She gathered her things and turned to leave. "I guess I won't be seeing you Saturday."

"I...I didn't say that." Tim followed her down the stairs. "Just give me some time to think. I need to get used to the idea. I have to adjust."

At the door, he took her by the hand. She turned, and he gave her a quick kiss...then another, which lasted longer. "I'll work through it," he finally said to reassure her. He stood in the doorway, pinching his knuckles, and watched her drive away.

Trisha's impetuous nature frustrated him, yet she had qualities he admired. She was hardworking and strong, almost to the point of overpowering everyone else around her. When he kissed her, she didn't melt, the response from the opposite sex he'd grown to expect. Instead, she seemingly gathered all her inner strength and met him with force. He liked that. It excited him, and as he thought about it, he decided everything else was worth it. He could accept her past. After all, she'd have to accept all his strange quirks and phobias. And his past was nothing to sneeze at. All things considered, he was willing to make an attempt at a deeper relationship with her.

At his desk, Tim attempted to concentrate on reading his class assignments. But just thinking about the end of the summer session at college made him feel like celebrating. Saturday marked the final day of his missing person contracts. It meant his contingency fee would've diminished to a big goose egg, but it also meant he could begin thinking about a new career that had nothing to do with private investigation. He wished he'd never even heard the name Bernadette Higgins. But then, he realized, he never would've met Trisha. The case had been a mixed blessing.

He picked up the receiver on his telephone and pressed the automatic redial. He listened to Trisha's recorded response followed by the beeps. "Let's make Saturday a celebration," he said. "I want to celebrate the end of summer classes, and the end of a lot of other burdens in my life. And," he added, "I want to celebrate the beginning of a new relationship between you and me. Let's begin a relationship of being open and honest with each other. No more hidden secrets. What do you say?" He paused. "And just to prove I mean it, here's my first secret." He hesitated. "I'm nineteen." He hung up feeling as if he'd leaped off the Empire State Building without a safety net below.

Thursday morning Tim awoke with a feeling of anticipation. He ran laps at the high school, came home, and showered and dressed. Brent and Patty arrived, while he was working at his desk, bringing with them their latest disagreement about the wedding plans.

"Why do I have to wear a tuxedo?" Brent exclaimed.

"What were you planning to wear?" Patty asked angrily with her hands on her hips. "That stupid green T-shirt?"

Brent looked down at his chest. "Well, yeah," he said splaying the bold slogan written all over the front of his shirt: **when Irish eyes are smiling (they're up to something)**. "Is the kid going to wear a tuxedo, too?" he asked drawing Tim into the fray.

"Yes," Patty answered. "And he'll be the most handsome man there."

"You mean," Brent said, "other than the groom."

"No, I don't," she replied stubbornly.

"I'm going to be miserable the rest of my life. Why does it have to begin on the very first day with a tuxedo?"

"Is that what you think..."

"Ahhh," Tim sighed dreamily. "Love is in the air."

Brent suddenly looked concerned. "I told you he's got the hots really bad. Next thing you know, he'll be pulled down the aisle by a nose ring, too...in a tuxedo."

"Not any time soon," Tim said thoughtfully.

"There you go, Kid!" Brent flexed his biceps. "Stay strong! Keep fighting! You can make it!"

"It's a battle you're destined to lose eventually," Patty said smugly. She turned her attention to her keyboard.

Tim returned to his textbook.

"I thought she liked green," Brent muttered, examining his T-shirt.

When Tim showed up with lunch at his apartment, Clarence was in high spirits. It was a transformation back to his former self that had begun the day before after his talk with Brent about the project. And the mood was contagious, causing a marked improvement in Waldo's outlook as well.

Afterwards, Tim attended classes. Then he dropped by the local library to check out some books and videos. His newest research topic raised the eyebrows of the young assistant librarian, who checked them out for him. He hurried home and saw that Trisha was not waiting in the parking lot. He was anxious to find out if she had paid a visit or left a message while he was out.

The table was set and the meal was waiting in the refrigerator. Tim read the note while he microwaved the casserole.

> Dearest Tim Darling,
>   Unfortunately, I will have only a few free hours on Saturday afternoon. But I know the perfect way to celebrate. See you at noon!
>   Love,
>   Trisha
>
>
> P.S. I knew that! Tell me a secret I don't already know!

Tim ate quickly and returned to his desk downstairs. He opened the first book entitled, *Child Development: A Month by Month Profile.* He had eight months of catching up to do.

Chapter 31: What Will I Do

Tim's celebrating mood was short-lived. The Mark Lander murder trial was unexpectedly moved up as a result of out-of-court settlements in cases scheduled ahead of it. And Friday afternoon Tim was called upon to give a deposition of what he knew of the events leading up to the young boy's death.

It was after seven in the evening when Brent and Tim returned to the IRISH EYES office where Patty was waiting. Exhausted, Tim was glad that part of it was behind him, and the actual trial would soon be over. Another event to celebrate tomorrow with Trisha.

"Are you sure you won't come along, Kid?" Brent had been trying to talk Tim into a late night tradition that he and Patty had every Friday night. "You don't know what a good time is until you've been to the Horseshoe on a Friday night. The 'Thank God It's Friday Night' bash has been going on for a hundred years. It's dependable. You can always count on the Horseshoe."

"Isn't that the tavern they used to call the Lucky Horseshoe," Tim asked, "until it burned to the ground a couple of years ago during the traditional Friday night fish fry?"

"Just a minor setback," Brent scoffed. "We all got out alive. What can be more lucky than that?"

"You were there?" Tim asked, "during the fire?"

"We were there," Patty answered. "All that grease and whiskey went up so fast, they claim it scorched the bottoms of jets flying into Le Guardia Airport."

Tim laughed. "I prefer the quiet and safety of my apartment."

"I don't blame you," Patty said. "Trisha visited a while this afternoon."

"What did she say?" Tim tried not to sound too anxious.

"She was, of course, disappointed that you weren't here," Patty said with a grin. "But she spent some time upstairs, and when she left, she said you'd be surprised."

"I want to see what the surprise is," Brent said changing direction at the door. "Staying here does sound better than the Horseshoe."

Patty grabbed his arm and gave him a shove out the door. "You leave Tim have his private life." She winked at Tim and closed the door behind them.

When they were gone, Tim bounded up the stairs. Nothing out of the ordinary greeted him in the kitchen. In fact, her photo was gone, and she hadn't left him a note this time with the meal in the refrigerator.

He mircrowaved the casserole she'd brought and, once again, ate in solitude listening to the birds in the big maple tree outside the kitchen window. The meal was delicious and nurtured a glimmering hope that he would never have to go back to eating the frozen store-bought meals he so recently fared on. And he was getting used to drinking iced tea in place of his usual glass of milk at every meal. While he washed his few dishes, Tim noticed the small changes that had taken place, little by little, in his apartment. The dishcloth was not his, Trisha had brought it with the first meal she'd prepared for him. A matching dishtowel and potholders had joined the country pink and blue dishcloth over a period of days. His loathing for refrigerator magnets had gone by the wayside the first time she adorned his with one in the shape of a heart and flowers. The inside of his refrigerator had changed over to her brand of butter and her taste in condiments. And in the cabinet, his small collection of spice bottles had grown to include much more than garlic powder and ground cinnamon.

Tim opened the double doors in the hall behind which his clothes washer and dryer were kept. On top of the washer was a basket of folded clean clothes. His freshly starched and pressed shirts and pants were hanging above the dryer. Trisha had done his laundry. And as he looked around, he became aware that she had also cleaned his apartment.

Her domestic invasion of his bachelor privacy made him feel a little uncomfortable. He cherished certain facets of his life, which he didn't feel prepared to share with her just yet. Revealing a secret here and there, now and then, was his idea of building a relationship. Her idea seemed to be a full-scale, non-hostile takeover of his personal life. He began to wonder if her relationship with her mother was such that he should fear she was planning to move in with him.

His assessment of the damage carried him into the bathroom where, he prayed, she wouldn't dare leave behind the ultimate evidence of a female live-in. He cringed and quickly opened the medicine cabinet, then heaved a sigh of relief at finding no PMS medications. The cabinet under the vanity, where he kept the toilet tissue, likewise, revealed no feminine intrusion into his private life. All was well, he decided. He'd been worried over nothing. And he'd speak to her about the things that made him uncomfortable. He could adjust, if her visits were less invasive.

Tim headed into his bedroom to relax. He opened the door and reached to turn on the lamp. It wasn't in its usual place. Tim squinted and peered around in the dim light from the hall until he found the lamp and turned it on. He caught his breath. Trisha had told Patty he'd be surprised, but nothing could prepare him for the transformation his bedroom had undergone.

Actually, the change hadn't entailed as much as his first impression led him to believe. The whole fairyland effect was accomplished almost entirely by the ceiling-to-floor shimmering white bed curtains. A closer inspection revealed the pearlescent beads and sequins, which caught and reflected the light and seemed to hang suspended in midair around all four sides of the double bed. They were, in actuality, attached to the translucent white curtains, which started out thickly gathered on a gold ring suspended from the ceiling over the middle of the bed. From there the material spread luxuriantly across the ceiling to points above the four corners of the bed, where it continued to spread and cascade downward into rich soft piles on the brown carpet.

The bed was covered with a crocheted white bedspread, and the pillows stuffed in matching shams, all of which were bordered with a long gathered edging of the same pattern. It was a pattern that spoke of countless hours of work by expert hands. And Tim had a vague inkling whose hands they were.

On one of the pillows lay Trisha's photograph, now in a frame. An aromatherapy ring filled the room with the scent of cinnamon, released by the heat of the lamp.

She had gone too far, Tim decided. This called for the gloves-off treatment. He needed to put her in her place, which wouldn't include his bedroom anymore. Before undressing for bed, he closed the blinds on the window, adorned with curtains of the same crocheted white pattern. His nightstand and dresser also had matching doilies. The whole handcrafted ensemble would cost a fortune to buy.

Tim pulled down the bedspread and bared his pillow before lying down. He took Trisha's framed picture from the other pillow and set it on the nightstand next to him. And as he tried to sleep, he began to realize the value of the priceless treasure Trisha had given him and what it meant. Not only was the monetary value beyond measure, but the fact that her friend and business partner, Mary Harris, had wrought it by hand made it a treasure that could never be equaled.

He couldn't stay upset with Trisha. She obviously had a problem with keeping her emotions in perspective. Having carried and given birth to a baby, without the support of a man in her life, certainly explained a lot. She was trying to show him love the only way she knew how. First, by giving herself; now, by giving material possessions. If he continually rejected her, he'd lose her love. And he didn't want to do that.

Chapter 32: Hurtin' You Don't Come Easy

Being with Trisha for lunch on Saturday made it impossible to be with Clarence and Waldo at the same time. But they were in good hands, as Brent had decided to spend the day with Clarence working on his project.

Tim was waiting outside when Trisha drove into the parking lot. "Thanks to you, I'm running late," she said when he opened her car door.

"Sorry," he said bewildered. He helped her carry the things she'd brought.

"I just spent the whole morning at the police station," she said angrily. "Now I have to make up that time somehow."

"Should've paid your parking tickets," he teased.

"It's all because of your raising questions about the cause of Mary's death." She led the way upstairs in a huff. "They wanted to know everything I knew about her. And they kept asking the same questions over and over."

"That's just routine questioning," he explained. "That's the way cops do things."

She began preparing the meal and Tim quickly set the table. "She's as big a pain in the butt dead as she was alive."

"Murder tends to do that to people," he said hoping Trisha would drop the subject and change into a celebrating mood.

"Just the same," she said. "I can't stay long. One of my best clients is a Saturday job. So now I have to leave after lunch and catch up before my next job."

Tim began massaging the tense muscles in her shoulders. "Maybe I could go with you," he offered, "and help out today."

Her shoulders relaxed and she turned around to face him. "Working with a trainee takes longer," she said, "but I did want to spend more time with you today."

"Maybe I could help out on other days, too, when I have time." With his hands still on her shoulders, he pulled Trisha close and kissed her.

"We'll see how quick you learn." She wrapped her long arms around him and responded with a passionate kiss that left Tim feeling weak in the knees. And she only stopped when something boiled over on the stove. She grabbed a potholder and removed the pan, while Tim turned off the burner. "Time to celebrate!" she said.

She removed the salads from the refrigerator and set the bowls atop their plates. Then, after Tim pulled out her chair and seated her, she poured the iced tea. He sat down and they started eating.

"Besides being a single mom," he began, "what other secrets have you been keeping from me?"

"I have a secret ambition to rule the world." She smiled, but seemed almost serious.

"A Napoleon complex," he said laughing. "I have no doubt, you will clean up."

They laughed and ate.

"What kind of salad dressing is this?"

"Do you like it?"

Tim nodded. "It has an interesting flavor."

"It's my own special recipe." She smiled. "Just for you."

Her words reminded him of last night. "That surprise you left me yesterday..."

"Did you like it?"

He coughed and looked down at his salad. "I love it." He looked up and met her eyes. "I know you meant it to be special, which it is," he quickly added. "But I don't think we've reached a point of no return in our relationship. I just want you to know that if it doesn't work out between us, you may have it back. It's too special."

Tim ate a dinner roll to quell the hot sensation in his throat. He reached for his glass of iced tea.

Trisha placed her hand on his before he lifted the glass. "I want to propose a toast," she said lifting her glass.

Tim lifted his.

"Here's to freedom from life's burdens." Their glasses came together above the middle of the table with a soft clink. She stopped him before he brought it to his lips. "Now remember," she said, "you have to drink the whole glass down, or the toast is meaningless."

Tim looked at the large twelve-ounce glass in his hand and frowned. "As long as you don't say anything, if I rush to the bathroom to spring a leak."

She smiled and watched him chug it down.

"Now for the food," she said ceremoniously lifting the lid from the hot dish containing meat and sauce.

The steam clouded his vision, and he felt unexplainably anxious to get something solid in his stomach. Trisha spooned large portions onto his plate, and he began eating. She refilled his glass with more iced tea.

"When do I get to meet him?" Tim asked. His voice seemed quiet and distant in his own ears.

"Who?"

"Justin." He focused on her eyes. "Your baby."

"Soon," she said looking down at her plate where she was going through the motions of moving her fork. "Very soon, I think."

"Does he talk yet?" Tim blinked and shook himself, trying to recover from the weak and wobbly sensation his head was experiencing.

"Yes, but not to anyone but me." She cocked her head and seemed to be studying her food. "Maybe he'll talk to you."

"Can he... walk?" Tim was having difficulty concentrating.

"He wants to."

"If he's anything like his mother..." The fork slipped out of his hand and dropped on his plate with a loud clatter. "Ooops," he slurred and wiped his mouth clumsily with his hand. He knew he should be concerned that his body was experiencing a sudden freedom of movement he had no control over. But his mind wasn't registering the true nature of his situation.

"It's your turn to tell a secret," Trisha said. "And this time make it something I don't already know."

Tim was having difficulty holding his head up to look at her, and he could barely hear her over the roar of the ocean waves in his ears. "I'm...mmm..."

"A virgin. C'mon! I know that one too."

"...not feeling very well!" He lost track of the conversation for a while.

"I said..." He was losing track of Trisha as well. Her face kept melting into distorted lines. "...the secret to celebrating is lots of eating and drinking."

"Drinking?" He looked around the table and finally found his glass of tea. The food made him thirsty. As he reached for it, he tipped it over and the iced tea spilled and soaked into the beautiful crocheted place mats.

"Damn!" he said disappointed in himself. His close examination of the mishap turned into resting his head in the middle of it.

"Don't worry." He heard Trisha reassuring him. "I'll clean up the mess." He felt her hands lifting his head. But before he could stop it at the normal upright position, the momentum caused his head to drop onto the back of his chair. And he couldn't pick it up again.

"Did you know," he slurred and giggled convulsively, "I have cobwebs on my ceiling?" He tried to point them out, but his hands were too heavy dangling on either side of the chair.

"Did you know you can't hold your iced tea?" Trisha said giving him a hard shove to keep him from falling out of his chair.

"What? Did I wet my pants?" He was unable to look at anything but the ceiling. And his Adam's apple was beginning to hurt from talking in a strained position.

"Not yet," Trisha answered. "But I think we'd better go take care of it." She bent down and put his arm around her shoulders. His hand flopped unfeeling against her chest. She moved his head against her neck, giving him a close-up view of the inside of her ear. "On the count of three," she said. "Try to stand. One...two...three." She grunted and rose slowly.

"Pretty," he said trying to kiss her ear.

Trisha started walking, and Tim stumbled and dragged his feet. "It won't be as much fun now that you're drunk," she said.

"Drunk?" he muttered in her ear. He was vaguely aware of stopping in the bathroom where she helped him use the toilet in a sitting position. She woke him up, and they continued into the bedroom. He flopped down like a rag doll on his bed.

She began undressing him. And he slipped into a stupor where he knew she was doing things to him, but he was unable to stop her. "You know," he heard her say, "I don't think you'll be much help to me at work today, after all. Too much celebrating! You'd better sleep it off."

Chapter 33: I Am...I Said

Tim wasn't aware of anything afterwards, until hours later—many hours later, when the pain gnawed him back to consciousness. And as he lay on his bed in the dark, recalling, his uneasy feeling changed to anger. He was angry with Trisha. She had gotten him drunk and so easily seduced him he felt humiliated. He hadn't been consenting, and even worse, he couldn't even remember how it happened. He just knew it had happened. His fascination with the beautiful Trisha was over. Everything was over, and she was no longer welcome in his life.

He tried to move, but his body was as uncooperative as before. The only difference was that all activity now produced pain. With much effort, he managed to sit up, which set off a pounding sensation in his ears that kept time with the throbbing sensation in his extremities. He sat until the pulsing of his heartbeat seemed to lessen. Then he moved his feet over the side of the bed where they dropped to the carpet like heavy weights. He realized standing would be no easy task, so he moved the flimsy bed curtains out of his way. After several attempts he stood up stark naked.

Being modest prompted him to spend the extra time and effort required to find his clothes. He put on his pants, but time was running out as the contents of his stomach applied pressure to his throat and made him hurry to the bathroom. He hadn't been sick very many times in his life, but this was the most miserable he'd ever felt. The thought of dying to put an end to this present misery was actually comforting. And his stomach continued to revolt long after it was empty.

Why anyone would ever drink to get himself like this, on purpose, was beyond his comprehension. If this was what a hangover was like, the price was too great. And he hadn't even enjoyed it, he realized, feeling nothing but disgust at what little he could remember.

He flushed the toilet and tried to think back. While he'd drunk his entire glass of iced tea, Trisha's glass had remained full even after lifting it to her lips. The salad had made him thirsty with hot spices, and the meat and sauce had been salty. He remembered seeing her refill his glass several times, but not her own. And now that he thought about it, she hadn't eaten anything either. Why had she done this to him? What possible motive could she have to want to hurt him?

His heart was pounding and he was sweating profusely, so he pulled the towel down from the holder to dry himself. He felt chilled, having not bothered with his shirt, so he wrapped the towel around his shoulders. He left the bathroom groping the wall with one hand and holding the small trashcan, ready near his face, with the other.

He painstakingly made his way to the kitchen and turned on the light switch. All signs of their earlier revelry were gone. The dishes were washed and put away, and the mess was cleaned up. Even the trash was emptied. It was as if the celebration had never taken place.

The towel was now soaked with his sweat, and the cold air from the refrigerator made him tremble as he checked and saw that there were no leftovers either. The pitcher of iced tea was gone. And he wondered at Trisha's foresight to remove any evidence of her having been there and what she had done to him.

He staggered from the kitchen and advanced to the living room, locking his knees with each step so he wouldn't fall down. This was one time, when he wished he'd taken the emergency precaution of installing a private telephone in his apartment. He'd have to make it downstairs to the office in order to call anyone. But whom would he call? And what would he say?

Brent would come running, all right, but not to help him. Brent would come to gloat and laugh his butt off, if he ever got wind of the fact that "the kid" was suffering from a hangover, suffering in the worst way. Even Patty would have a hard time sympathizing with his very unmanly behavior as a result of drinking spiked iced tea. And she would laugh off his outrage at being the victim of Trisha's enticements. Under normal circumstances, Clarence would be his first choice. Clarence would come and be his friend, no questions asked. But Clarence couldn't leave Waldo now, and he wouldn't ask him to.

Tim stared at his watch and had difficulty reading the time. No one would want to hold his hand at two in the morning anyway. But the pain in his stomach grew

worse, approaching the point of being unbearable.
He'd never had a hangover before, but he was getting a
terrifying sense that something more serious was
wrong with him. He decided to get to the telephone.
When he reached the top of the stairs and peered
down, the telephone looked far away. A feeling of
despair overwhelmed him with a renewed fear of
heights. He struggled not to cry. That would only make
his descent more difficult. And he was having difficulty
just lifting his feet.

He set the trashcan down and held onto the railing.
He'd never had to hold onto it before. Each stair step
was etched into his memory by the care with which he
and Brent had built them. But now they seemed to
veer in different directions as his eyes played tricks on
him. He made an error in judgement that sent him
dropping faster than he could recover from.

Fortunately, he was near the bottom, and he
landed mercifully on his rear instead of shattering his
bones as he imagined he would during the split-
second fall. But it sent shock waves through his body
that registered a reading of ten on the pain scale. Now
he was beyond crying as he sat on the floor moaning
and reeling for a long while.

Finally, he opened his sore eyes and waited for his
blurred double vision to return to a synchronized
picture of one of everything. He didn't trust himself to
stand again. He was too weak. But he had to reach the
telephone. He made slow progress toward his desk by
scooting on the seat of his pants. When the effort
became too great, he fell over sideways and attempted
to crawl. At times, he wasn't sure where he was going,
because he couldn't see. Something was definitely
wrong and he knew he needed to hurry. But he had to

stop and catch his breath. Every movement seemed to squeeze the breath out of his body.

He lifted his head and struggled for more air. The images on the bulletin board shifted around as his eyes moved across it. He tried to focus, and the sight that caught his fuzzy view sent his head spinning as his heart raced even faster.

His cross-eyed perspective revealed Bernadette's secret hiding place. With the photo of Bernadette Higgins merged atop the photo of Mary Harris, he saw where she was—where she had been all along. Bernadette Higgins was Mary Harris in disguise. They were one and the same. He had found her at last. The puzzle was complete.

But...she was dead. There was more to the puzzle. Bernadette couldn't have killed Mary. Which meant someone else had. He hadn't considered other suspects, so sure was he that Bernadette had disappeared as the culmination of her evil scheme.

Panic gripped Tim's soul as he grasped the full meaning of what he'd just figured out. The pain in his lower back and stomach felt as if he were being torn in two. His body contorted on the floor, but his mind refused to release him into unconsciousness.

He heard someone at the door. He opened his mouth to yell for help, but no sounds came out, as much as he tried. He heard the key in the lock and then the door opened and closed. He felt a rush of relief flow through his limp muscles. At any moment, Brent and Patty would turn and see him in trouble on the floor. He heard footsteps. Help was on the way, he told himself. But why weren't they hurrying? He pushed his head up off the floor and saw Trisha looking down at him, smiling.

"Help me!" he whispered frantically.

She knelt down beside him and placed his head on her knees. She tenderly stroked his hair and leaned down to kiss his forehead.

In futility, he attempted to convey to her how desperately he needed help. But she was blind to his agony.

"I decided you shouldn't be alone through this," she said softly. "I'll stay with you until it's over. It won't be long now."

He wanted to scream, he felt so repulsed that she was fondling his chest, while watching him heave for every breath.

The light glinted off something shiny on her wrist and his eyes caught it. He remembered it from dinner. When she had kept track of the time. She hadn't had a watch before, he recalled. She had always looked at his when she wanted to know the time.

He closed his eyes and squeezed out tears from the excruciating pain. He felt Trisha's fingers, but they weren't a comfort to him now.

"You were such a good boy," she said, "drinking all your tea and eating all your food. You didn't even taste the methanol, did you?" She continued. "That's because it tastes sweet." She laughed. "You didn't even realize you were getting drunk until you were completely soused."

An abrupt recollection sent chills up his spine, followed closely by a pain that ended like a hammer on his skull. He cried out and writhed on the floor. The shiny watch was the one Patty had bought and prepared as bait for the postal drop box surveillance. Wearing the watch could only mean one thing. It meant Trisha was cashing in on Mary's embezzlement scheme. It also meant Trisha had poisoned Mary Harris aka Bernadette Higgins. Tim stared up into her face horrified.

"The only problem with methanol is that it has some nasty side-effects. But don't worry, I'll be with you. The pain will last only a couple of hours, at most, and then you'll—"

Tim gathered every ounce of strength remaining in his body and shoved himself off her lap. He rolled toward the desk and ended with his arms stretched over his head and tears of agony streaming down his cheeks. The will to live was stronger than any fears he had. He pulled himself forward on his stomach and grabbed and missed the telephone cord hanging down the side of his desk. A second try nabbed it, and the telephone crashed to the floor with a loud dull clang of the ringing mechanism. He clutched the receiver in both hands and laid it against his ear. No dial tone.

Trisha smiled at him. "You really ought to invest in a cordless, so you can keep it with you. Would've been easier."

He let the receiver fall to the floor, and he let his head drop, ignoring the pain. He had to keep thinking.

"You keep spoiling everything. I knew you'd try the phone, so I cut the line outside." She crawled to him on her hands and knees and brushed the tears from his eyes with her fingers.

He cringed from her touch.

"No one would've ever known, if you hadn't found the hand lotion," she said. "I tried to find it the next night while cleaning, but it was gone. And still, no one would've known, if you hadn't let Patty use it. It would've stayed undiscovered forever, if it hadn't been for you."

The distorted logic of a murderer was unreliable, Tim realized, but appealing to Trisha's emotions was his only chance. He summoned his strength to speak. "If that's what you're upset with me about, I'm sorry." His voice came out in a hoarse wheeze, but he continued. "I won't tell anyone. I promise."

He wasn't reaching her. Her eyes were staring off in the distance unseeing. "It's too late," she said.

"Look at me!" he pleaded.

She stared down at him unmoved.

"You said you loved me." The pain was spreading through his hips and growing intense.

"It's too late...for you."

The statement unnerved him and he gave in to uncontrollable sobbing.

"Don't cry."

She began swaying, which made him dizzy, so he looked away. Brent's desk was a few feet away. The middle drawer was where he kept the cellular phone... whenever he wasn't using it on surveillance, or forgot to put it there. "Why were you upset with Mary?" Tim asked to keep her occupied.

"Mary deserved to die," she pronounced matter-of-factly.

Tim slowly inched his arms and legs into position so he could begin wriggling across the floor. His movement was painful and tedious, trying not to draw Trisha's attention to what he was doing.

"She was a stingy old broad. She was loaded, but all she wanted was more money. When I found out what she was doing, that was when we came to our business agreement. All I wanted was a little piece of the action."

Blackmail, Tim thought. He was making slow progress toward Brent's desk while trying to keep an eye on Trisha. She knew about Mary's embezzlement scheme, but she didn't know about her split personality.

"Then I got pregnant. Mary said she'd give me money for an abortion, but not for the birth."

Mary had seen a chance to turn the tables on Trisha, Tim reasoned, and to remove her blackmailing stranglehold. He looked up, but he couldn't make out whether Trisha was watching him as she talked. The pain lessened and his breathing came easier as he lay perfectly still. He prepared himself to make a lunge for Brent's desk.

"She was a murderer!"

Tim reached the desk as Trisha looked at him to confirm her judgement of Mary. She got up and stood over him watching as he swooned from the exertion.

"Shhhh," she said and knelt down beside him. She began running her hand through his sweat-soaked hair. "Don't struggle. You'll just make it hurt more."

She was right. The pain immobilized him and there was nothing he could do but try to lie as still as possible.

"You have to admit," Trisha's sweet voice droned on, "I outsmarted her. Mary had only enough time to figure it out before she died. I used her mortal weakness, her allergic reaction to formaldehyde."

With all his determination, Tim reached out and yanked one of the desk drawers open. The pain was blinding, but his hand fell on the bulletproof vest and grappled for Brent's Smith & Wesson underneath. This was one survival situation his shooting range instructor hadn't prepared him for—blood running from his mouth and a pain in his stomach so severe he was sure he wouldn't survive, even if he managed to shoot-to-kill her.

"Are you thinking bad thoughts toward me?" Trisha asked as she easily grabbed the handgun away from his fingers. "We can't let you think that, can we Justin?" She flung the gun on the floor all the way across the room.

Tim collapsed in utter torment as a spasm went through his entire body.

"I gave you even more time to figure it out," Trisha went on. "But you're only just now figuring it out, aren't you?"

He tried to press his hand on the pain gripping his stomach, but his hand caught on his pants pocket. With torturous effort, he shoved his hand all the way into his pocket and felt the pager.

"Your mortal weakness is alcohol. I put methanol, methyl alcohol, in your iced tea." She smiled down in his face. "I outsmarted you, too."

Tim began desperately pressing all the buttons on his pager. His fingers were numb and reluctant to cooperate. It wouldn't do any good anyway, but it was the only thing he could think of to do. Supposedly, all the IRISH EYES pagers were on the same exclusive wavelength, and his last-ditch effort was to cause something to go haywire.

"By the time you slept off our little celebration, your body was metabolizing the methanol and transporting it to every part of your body through your blood stream. Your ignorance convinced you it was just a hangover, until it was too late."

"Help me," Tim sobbed, pleading for his fading life. "Please, God, help me!"

"You and I were good together," she said holding him close against herself and rocking gently.

He tensed and groaned as another spasm of pain gripped his muscles. He allowed her to give him the last comfort he'd ever feel. "Why?" he gasped.

"Nobody wants you, Justin," she said in a singsong voice as she rocked him. "Nobody wants you."

What seemed a long time passed as he fought to stay conscious, alternately gripped by pain and then panic as he felt himself slipping away. He couldn't open his eyes, but he became aware of faraway sounds. The sounds grew closer, and Trisha stood up. There were voices, and he tried to sort them out.

He made out Brent's voice, shouting profanities that were sure to make Trisha very angry. Brent had a knack for saying the wrong things to people.

Tim felt unreasonably calm and relaxed, despite his physical condition. And he decided he'd finally died and gone to heaven. But when Brent shook him back to awareness, the pain flooded back and he decided he'd died and gone to the wrong place instead.

He heard a desk drawer slide open and Brent's take-charge voice. "I need a police unit and an ambulance...on the double..."

So the cell phone had been there all along, Tim thought.

"Hang on, Kid!" Brent's presence loomed over him and his voice was music in his ears.

"Trish..." Tim uttered without opening his eyes. He needed to warn Brent that she knew where his gun was.

"She's down for the count," Brent assured him. "What'd she get you with, Kid?"

He wasn't sure Brent could hear him when he whispered, "Methanol," just as the pain intensified and he drew his legs up convulsively into a fetal position.

"Oh God!" Brent said. Seconds later, he felt the warmth of being cradled in Brent's arms. "Here. Drink this."

Tim jerked as the burning liquid touched his lips.

"You gotta try," Brent urged forcing him to be still. "It's the only thing that'll help until the ambulance arrives. I had a dog once drink some antifreeze. Trust me. This'll help!"

Tim let it fill his mouth and overflow. Then he swallowed and gagged. A coughing spell racked his body with pain.

"More," Brent demanded showing no mercy.

Tim tried to refuse, but it was no use. At the end of another gagging and coughing session, he opened his eyes painfully to look at Brent's blurred face. "Am I... dying?" he gasped.

"Not if I can help it." Brent hugged him closer and continued pouring the Irish whiskey down his throat until Tim passed out, and he could do no more.

Chapter 34: Remember Me

Brent's voice was the first thing he heard again two days later in the hospital. "Well, you did it again, Kid."

Tim quickly reached up and felt the bandages. His eyes no longer hurt, but he couldn't see. "Did what again?" he asked miserably. His memory came rushing back with a painful force that made his weak body tremble.

"Stared death in the face and won."

He didn't feel like he'd won. He moved slowly and felt parts of his body to make sure he was all there. An aching sensation assured him in his other parts. And he wasn't so sure that being alive and in one piece was a sign of winning.

"Next time, though," Brent continued, "you better let me pick the female companionship you hang around with."

He heard Brent yell, "ouch," after being hit with something.

"Patty?" Tim said and smiled in the direction where he thought he sensed her presence.

"I'm right here, Dearie," she said and took his hand. "You don't have to worry about a thing."

After a moment, he asked, "Trisha?" He wanted details, not a comforting pat on the hand.

"She's where she belongs, Kid."

Tim heard Brent pull a couple of chairs close to his bed. Brent sat down. Patty continued to hold his hand as she sat down.

"She'll get the kind of help she needs," Brent continued.

Tim knew he should pity her, but it might take some time before he could feel anything but hatred toward Trisha. "What about her baby, Justin? Will her mother get custody of him?"

"Trisha talks about Justin a lot," Patty said. "But there is no Justin. She had an abortion eight months ago. Apparently her denial keeps him alive in her mind. And she transfers her guilt to others."

"Mary Harris wasn't Trisha's first victim," Brent added. "Her previous boyfriend, the father of the baby, tried out her cooking also. Only he didn't live to talk about it."

"That explains the business card," Tim said.

"What business card, Dearie?" Patty asked.

"The one Dennis Lakey gave me in Mary Harris' stuff. It was for an abortion clinic. I thought it had been put with her stuff by mistake. But Mary was the one who recommended the abortion. Trisha said Mary was a murderer, because she offered to pay for her abortion, but wouldn't help out with the expenses of having the baby."

"Such a pity," Patty said. "What should've been a joy was turned to grief."

Tim automatically reached up to rub his eyes. They itched and the tape holding the bandage tight was uncomfortable.

"The nurse said that'll come off today."

"Then I can see," Tim said optimistically. His last memory was of not being able to see through a shadowy fog, even with his eyes held open.

Patty tightened her grip on his hand.

"Sure you can," Brent said.

But there was a long silence, during which Tim pictured Patty looking at Brent the way she always did when he said something not quite right. Which was most of the time!

"Oh, hell, Kid!" Brent finally broke down. "The truth is...they're not sure how you'll end up. Maybe permanent damage. Maybe partial vision. Maybe fully restored vision...eventually."

"Oh," Tim said weakly. "I guess..." his voice cracked, "...I'll need your help, after all." He made a feeble attempt to smile.

"Yeah, Kid." Brent bent over and hugged him. "You got it!"

Tim realized he had an IV in his hand when he put his arms around Brent and felt the tug from the drip tube. "Thanks," he said swallowing back his emotions. "Thanks for helping me when I needed you."

Brent sat back down.

"But how'd you know?" Tim added, "that I was in trouble...at two in the morning."

"I didn't," Brent admitted. "Patty did. I was sound asleep. She called from her folks. She was spending the weekend there, remember?"

Tim nodded, even though he didn't remember.

"All day," Patty joined in, "something kept bothering me. Even after I went to bed. I couldn't sleep. And then it hit me. I remembered something from the day before. Something about Trisha. She had been wearing a watch...the watch I'd picked out for the surveillance the day we went shopping."

"That's when Patty called me," Brent said. "And told me about it. I told her I'd look into it, first thing in the morning. But then I couldn't sleep. I remembered at the police station the day before, there'd been mention of Trisha being questioned again in connection with Mary's death in light of the unusual circumstances surrounding the death of a young man six months ago. I hadn't thought much of it, at the time.

"But then I decided to call you. The line was busy, but I couldn't sleep. So I decided to drive by. I saw the lights on and figured you were up late studying. I almost turned around and came home, when, all of a sudden for no apparent reason, I knew something was wrong. In my mind, when I slipped Trisha into the missing person puzzle you were working on, she fit. Then when I slipped you in place of the young man who died six months ago, I realized you were in serious trouble."

"You were right," Tim said. "You even warned me that the puzzle might not be the way I was picturing it."

"One thing's sure," Brent said. "Visiting you in the hospital, sure beats the heck out of visiting you in the morgue."

After Brent and Patty left, Tim had time to think about his situation, and to be thankful he was still alive. He also thought about how stupid he'd been. Stupid enough to trust a complete stranger and allow her entrance into the innermost parts of his life. Stupid enough to fall into the arms of a killer. It nearly cost him his life, and it might've cost him his sight. It would never happen again, he vowed. Never again would he let down his friends who really cared for him.

While Tim was busy kicking around his bruised and bleeding ego, one of his doctors, an eye specialist, came to assess the damage. After introducing himself, he adjusted Tim's bed to a semi-sitting position.

"Keep your eyes closed until I tell you to open them," he told Tim while he removed the bandages.

Tim nodded and said a quick silent prayer.

"And don't worry if you can't see anything immediately. I'm going to have the lights turned off."

Tim waited while he felt coolness on his exposed eyelids, and a glimmer of hope at what seemed to be a lessening of darkness to his eyes.

"Now," the doctor said, "very slowly open your eyes."

He opened them just a little, but had to close them. He tried again.

"Believe it or not, that's a good sign."

He finally managed to hold his eyes open. But what he saw didn't look good. All he saw was blurry blobs barely distinguishable from each other by shades of color.

"Tell me what you see."

Tim squinted and discerned the small blob in front of his face. "I think it's your hand."

The doctor covered his left eye. "How many fingers am I holding up?"

Tim studied for a moment. "Three," he said uncertainly.

The doctor covered his right eye. "Now how many?"

Tim squinted. "The naughty one." He was certain this time.

"That's good enough for now! I'll check on you again tomorrow. By then, you should be able to see the beautiful Nurse Atkins." His doctor with the strange bedside manner left the room.

Tim looked around still unable to see anything clearly. He had felt his physical attachment to tubes and monitors, but now he could almost see the vast array of life-support equipment. And it made his condition look even worse than he'd imagined. "When can I go home?" he asked a blurry blob moving near him—the beautiful Nurse Atkins, no doubt.

"I get to keep you a while, Handsome," she answered.

A nurse with a sense of humor, he thought. Even if he could see her, he wouldn't trust her.

"And today," Nurse Atkins continued, "I get to feed you the epitome of the cafeteria's culinary skill, chicken broth with crackers." She moved the bed table within his limited visual range and tucked a paper napkin around his neck.

He blinked.

"Open wide, so I don't spill."

"You taste it first," he insisted.

Her look revealed that she didn't think much of his uncooperative behavior. But she slurped a big spoonful while he watched. "There," she said changing spoons and preparing the next one for him. "If you manage to hold all this down, I have some nice yummy Jello for dessert."

To his amazement, it tasted good and soothed his empty stomach.

"Want to catch up on the news you missed?"

"Might as well," Tim agreed.

She pressed the button on the remote and the TV came on.

"Turn it off, please," Tim said changing his mind. Watching TV in bed triggered a feeling of panic, even though he couldn't see it.

Nurse Atkins turned it off and continued feeding him. "You have a private room with a telephone, and you can watch all the TV you want," she informed him. "Your friends said to make sure you get the very best."

"They're the very best," he said.

Over the next few days, Tim was gradually weaned from the machines, and the tubes were removed that aided his recovery. When he could see and walk, and perform all his normal bodily functions by himself, he was allowed to go home.

Running just one lap around the high school field track seemed an impossible goal, at first. He walked it the first day, but he determined to resume his normal activities as quickly as possible.

In the meantime, Brent had taken over the daily activity of providing lunch and companionship to Clarence Drib. In fact, the two had hit it off so well, Tim was surprised when his old friend called and asked to meet him for lunch at the Sidewalk Café. Tim arrived early and sat waiting in the shade of the table umbrella.

It was a sunny sweltering day, typical for the end of August. Tim left his sunglasses on, so no one would notice when he closed his eyes to rest them. Finally, in the distance, he caught sight of Clarence approaching. And at his side, Waldo, his faithful companion, was moving under his own power.

Tim stood up as they drew near, and Clarence
embraced him joyfully. "When I nearly lost my two best
friends, in such a short time, it was almost more than
I could bear." Clarence didn't worry about hiding his
tears.

Tim bent down and rubbed Waldo behind the ears.
The Pekingese responded with a short excited dance
on his front paws. His rear legs were confined in a two-
wheeled contraption that allowed him to use his front
legs to move. "So this is what you designed and Brent
built," Tim said as he examined Waldo's rear
attachment.

"Pretty nifty, don't you think?" Clarence said as
they sat down at their usual table. "It allows Waldo to
move and exercise all the parts of his body he can still
use. And, most importantly, it gave him back his will
to live."

Tim smiled and rubbed his eyes. "You're a blessed
dog to have a friend who won't give up on you."

"We're going to look into getting a patent. Maybe
call it the Doggie Wheelchair. Maybe Waldo and I
might travel a little and let vets and pet owners know
there is an alternative to just putting a pet out of its
misery when they suffer a debilitating injury or
illness."

"Sounds like a very worthy cause."

Their food arrived, and they ate.

"What about you?" Clarence asked. "Are you
recovering?"

"My liver is functioning almost normal," Tim
answered. "The black hole in the vision in my left eye
might improve a little, but it's permanent." He
shrugged and looked down at his plate.

"Take off your glasses and look at me," Clarence said. His voice was soft, but firm.

Tim responded to his request and squinted at Clarence.

"I mean YOU. What about YOU? Have you found YOUR cause yet?"

"I think," Tim said and closed his eyes, "I'm getting there."

"You will," Clarence said. "You will."

Epilogue: Solitary Man

"You sure you don't want to wait and have Brent help you do this?" Patty asked.

"No, I can do it myself," Tim answered. They were upstairs in his apartment. "I just want to make sure I get everything exactly like it was."

"Okay," Patty agreed solemnly.

They began in the kitchen. Tim moved the table and chairs back against the wall where they had originally been. Then he moved the microwave to the counter next to the doorway, so he could eat frozen dinners on the run as before.

"You need to slant it just a bit more," Patty said.

Tim sighed and made the adjustment.

"You said you wanted it EXACTLY like it was!"

"I know," Tim said. He also wanted to get the task done quickly, so he could get over the depression that was daunting his complete recovery. "I'm counting on you."

Together they switched the flatware and utensils back to the original drawers they had occupied, making sure to discard anything that had belonged to Trisha. The dishcloths, dishtowels, and potholders that had appeared with her home-cooked meals were tossed into the box also. They moved dishes in the cupboards and got rid of boxes and containers of foods and spices. The laundry area and bathroom required a few changes and removals also before Tim was satisfied, and Patty agreed that things were back to his bachelor bland decorum.

"Brent will be upset," Patty said with a worried expression, "if I let you tire yourself out too much."

"I'm not tired," Tim reassured her. "Besides, this is good for me." He was surprised at his own energy.

"Oh my," Patty exclaimed when she saw the bedroom. "She had quite the romantic notion..." Patty stopped abruptly. "Sorry, Dearie. I didn't mean to speak about..."

"There's nothing to speak about," Tim said looking around. He unplugged the TV and carried it out. Patty hurried to get rid of Trisha's picture and other personal items left behind, before Tim returned.

"This is so lovely," Patty said fingering the shimmering bed curtains. "It's a shame to have to... never mind," she added as she began carefully folding the bedspread.

"I promised to return it, if things...didn't work out between us," Tim said. He pulled a chair over and stood on it to remove the hooks in the ceiling that held the delicate arrangement. "But I could ask if she'd like to make it a wedding gift for you and Brent. Trisha won't be needing it where she's going." He moved the chair and undid the next hook. "Besides, I believe if Mary Harris had known you, she'd want you to have it."

"Does that mean you're planning to visit her, Dearie?" Patty worked at taking the crocheted curtains down.

"I'm thinking," Tim said, "it wouldn't hurt to see her."

They packed everything in a box. "I'll just set this in the closet," Tim said, "until I ask her about it." He looked around the bedroom and breathed a huge sigh of relief. He felt better. "I probably should pay her a visit real soon, and warn the warden not to eat her cooking."

The remark wasn't really funny, but Patty laughed. "I think that's a good idea," she said. "And another good idea would be meeting Brent on time, like I'm supposed to." She gathered her purse and Tim carried some of the boxes to put in her car. Patty had agreed to dispose of the items. "Are you sure you want to be alone tonight?" she asked. "You're always welcome to have dinner with us."

"I'm sure," Tim answered as he closed her door. "But I'll take a rain check. I just need to eat a frozen microwave dinner tonight, so I can feel normal again."

Patty reluctantly agreed. "Be sure to look at the mail on your desk. And congratulations on your first year," she called as she drove away.

"Thanks for everything," Tim called back to her.

He walked inside and locked the door. He stopped at his desk to gather the stack of mail that had accumulated during his absence. On top, was a newspaper opened to an article entitled, Million Dollar Winner Announced in Travel Agency Sweepstakes. He set it aside on his desk to be cut out later and included at the end of the Bernadette Higgins (Mary Harris) missing person case file.

He carried his mail upstairs and popped a dinner in the microwave. He poured a glass of milk and took it to the living room where he spread his mail and his meal on top of the coffee table in front of the sofa.

Before he sat down, Tim walked to the railing and looked down at the IRISH EYES office area. His fear of heights still bothered him, but he was determined to overcome all his phobias, in order to become the best missing persons investigator he could be.

The textbooks were gone from his desk, put away in preparation for the fall class session at the college. The bulletin board was a field of green once again. Gone were the photos and sketches, fingerprint cards, and lists from the missing person case that had been right up his alley, according to Brent. Patty's toy stuffed animals were all in a neat row across the back of her desk. And occupying the center of Brent's desk was a Bible, which Brent had taken up reading after his experience when he went to church with Patty. The Sunday morning of Tim's close encounter with death had led to Brent's close encounter with God.

Tim sat on the sofa and said a sincere prayer of thanks for his food, his friends, and another day to enjoy them all. Then as he ate, he opened and read his mail.

An important-looking envelope on top announced that he was a contest winner. But inside was a long letter listing the requirements and a bunch of games to qualify. He tossed it on the discard pile. Life was too short for playing no-win games.

Another envelope contained advertising for a life insurance policy. He set it aside for later, when someone else could read all the small print he was unable to see.

Next, he opened get well cards from friends and people he didn't even know at church.

Then at the bottom was an envelope containing his grade transcript from college. He thought he remembered doing well on the final exams, but he'd been so preoccupied, it was really hard to know for sure. He opened it with trepidation, and breathed a sigh when he saw the column of three A's. Combined with his previous grades he was maintaining a four-point grade average and a position on the dean's list. That was what Patty had meant when she congratulated him on his first year.

The last items in his stack of mail were his computer emails Patty had printed out while he was recouping in the hospital. They included: two congratulations from classmates on his excellent grades; a memo from Dr. Morgan reminding him to sign up for her pathology class next semester, along with congratulating him on his exhaustive research paper, Poison as a Means of Homicide; and a long letter from Rhonda.

He read Rhonda's letter last of all. She had a conversational style of writing that made it seem as if he were right there with her enjoying the adventures of babysitting miniature tyrants, shopping for the upcoming school year's wardrobe, and trying various hairstyles in an attempt to achieve a smart look for her junior year in high school. In the end she had opted to cut several inches off her hair, which made Tim groan when he read it. "It's too beautiful to cut," he recalled telling her last summer when she decided it was too hot.

Rhonda ended her letter with a reminder that it had been exactly one year since they had walked a church aisle together to accept Jesus as savior and Lord of their lives. Tim looked at the date, August 22. And he remembered the rainy day on a highway headed toward New York when he'd picked up a hitchhiker wearing a strange neon orange backpack. That hitchhiker, it turned out, was a little fifteen-year-old runaway named Rhonda. And their lives were destined never to be the same after that. THAT was the one-year anniversary Patty had congratulated him for!

Tim picked up the receiver of his newly installed telephone in the living room. He punched in some numbers and waited for an answer. "Just checking in," he said in response to Brent's brusque greeting.

"As well you should," Brent replied. "That's what friends are for."

"See you tomorrow," Tim said and hung up.

He relaxed a few minutes and contemplated whether to be lazy one more day or to answer his letters.

He trudged downstairs, switched on the computer, and sat down in his chair. He began typing and before long the monitor screen was filled with words. They were the words he hadn't dared speak to anyone, not even his best friends, describing the awful hurt he had suffered at the hands of someone he thought he loved and the fears he now faced. The words and the tears both seemed to flow endlessly.

It was a very long letter, but it made up for the whole year of not writing her a single word. He ended by telling Rhonda how he really felt about her.

He moved the cursor to the top of the screen to tell the computer what to do with the letter. He typed in his email password and moved the cursor to the send position. The letter had served its purpose as a catharsis, and he moved the cursor to the delete position and clicked. The computer screen flashed, "Are you sure you want to delete this message?" Tim clicked again, and the letter disappeared. He had no right to do it! It was wrong to burden a little sixteen-year-old girl with his problems.

S.D.G.

If you enjoyed this book, or any other book from Koenisha Publications authors, let us know. Visit our web site or drop us a line at:

Koenisha Publications
3196 – 53ʳᵈ Street
Hamilton, MI 49419
Phone or Fax: 616-751-4100
Email: koenisha@macatawa.org
Web site: www.koenisha.com

Do you belong to a reading group, teach a class, etc? Download free study guides from our web site, or send $3.00 for mailing costs to the address above.

Read the latest news from authors Sharolett Koenig and Flavia Crowner in their newsletter, "Partners in Crime," at our web site or send $3.00.

Koenisha Publications authors are available for speaking engagements and book signings. Send for arrangements and schedule or visit our web site.

Purchase additional copies of this book or others in the Tim MacCulfsky mystery series from your local bookstore, visit our web site, or send $19.95 for each book plus $3.00 for mailing costs.

Send for a free book catalog of titles from
Koenisha Publications.